Big Little Spies

Krista Davis

BERKLEY PRIME CRIME
New York

BERKLEY PRIME CRIME
Published by Berkley
An imprint of Penguin Random House LLC
penguinrandomhouse.com

Copyright © 2021 by Krista Davis

ISBN: 9780451491701

First Edition: March 2021

Printed in the United States of America
1   3   5   7   9   10   8   6   4   2

To the veterinarians.
For the late nights and the cold mornings,
for your gentle hands and brave determination.
You are our heroes.

*Thorns may hurt you, men desert you,
sunlight turn to fog;
But you're never friendless ever, if you have
a dog.*

—Douglas Malloch

WAGTAIL RESIDENTS

Holly Miller—co-owner of the Sugar Maple Inn
   Trixie, her Jack Russell terrier
   Twinkletoes, her long-haired calico cat
Liesel Miller (Oma)—co-owner of the Sugar
   Maple Inn
   Gingersnap, her golden retriever
Rose Richardson—Liesel's best friend
Holmes Richardson—Rose's grandson and
   Holly's beau
Judge Grant Barlow—Theona's widower
Dovie Dickerson—Judge Barlow's housekeeper
Aunt Birdie Dupuy—Holly's aunt
Sergeant Dave Quinlan (Officer Dave)

VISITOR TO WAGTAIL

Seth Bertenshaw—Pet Detective

THE WAG LADIES

Brenda McDade
   Fagan, her Scottish terrier
Joanne Williams
   Hershey, her Somali cat
Louisa Twomey
   Loki, her husky
Oriana Renouf
   Garbo, her saluki
Addilyn (Addi) Lieras
   Inky, her long-haired black cat

One

🐾 🐾 🐾 🐾

The trouble with whispering is that it draws the attention of everyone within earshot. I was enjoying the summer sunshine, a tall frosty glass of iced tea, and a shrimp salad when I heard Oriana Renouf whisper to Brenda McDade, "You don't think she would actually hurt him?"

There was no one else on the terrace except for three dogs. My Jack Russell terrier, Trixie, sat with Brenda's Scottish terrier, Fagan, and Oriana's saluki, Garbo, at the top of the stairs that led to the lawn. They had undoubtedly heard the unusual question, but gave no sign of it.

Brenda and Oriana were part of a group of five friends that included Louisa Twomey, Joanne Williams, and Addi Lieras. Around the town of Wagtail, the women had been dubbed the WAG Ladies, after WAG, Wagtail Animal Guardians, the rescue where they volunteered their time.

They didn't reside in Wagtail, but they had taken the town by storm. Theona Barlow, a longtime resident, had set up a satellite branch of Wagtail Animal Guardians in Raleigh, North Carolina, about a five-hour drive from Wagtail, on the theory that more animals would be adopted there by the city's burgeoning population. Not everyone had the time to travel to Wagtail, she'd reasoned. She had been right. And it was there, at the Raleigh branch of WAG, that the five very well-heeled city-slicker WAG Ladies donated their time.

They had recently arrived with ferocious intensity, turning our peaceful town on its ear. Wagtail, the place where people came to vacation with their beloved pets, was hosting the biggest, fanciest ball in its history. The gala's name, 'There's No Place Like Home,' evoked nostalgia and pulled at rescuers' heartstrings. People interested in adopting animals had sent in applications in advance, and we hoped to clear the Wagtail adoption center. The WAG Ladies had coaxed amazing donations out of people to benefit WAG rescue and adoption centers, and their affluent friends had been arriving for the ball, filling every hotel room and leasing most of the rental houses.

Oriana and Joanne had left their husbands at home while they undertook arrangements the week of the ball, but the gentlemen were expected to join them for the weekend and the big event.

I was surprised that they were friends at all, but the five women in their thirties and forties ran in the same social circles in Raleigh, North Carolina. Brenda looked the oldest, probably because her face was aged as though she had spent too much time in the sun. She wasn't unattractive but did nothing to enhance her appearance. Brenda's simplicity was accentuated by her friends Oriana and Joanne, who dressed exquisitely, even on vacation in the mountains. I didn't know their exact ages, but Addi and Joanne appeared to be the youngest. Louisa, a fair redhead, dressed conser-

vatively. She was ladylike in style and leaned toward traditional clothes.

I had first met Addi when we were children spending
summers in Wagtail with our grandmothers. I didn't know
the others, but I had fun memories of Addi. She had always
been game for an adventure, often stumbling over her own
feet, but laughing anyway. Even then, she had been an artist, rendering sketches that I couldn't have managed as an
adult. She was gifted and had since made a name for herself
in the art world with gallery showings and an international
following. I still had one of her pieces, drawn when we
were about nine. The remarkably detailed pen-and-ink
drawing depicted the Sugar Maple Inn. I had framed it and
hung it in my living room.

The five of them were having a grand time staying at the
Sugar Maple Inn. They often left the doors to their rooms
open, as if they were in a college dorm, and wandered the
hallways from room to room with glasses of wine in hand.
Laughter echoed through the inn, and none of the other
guests seemed to mind. Some of them even joined the fun.

The Sugar Maple Inn lent itself to the sort of freedom
that one might not find in a regular hotel. Their dogs and
cats wandered about freely, enjoying one another's company
as they raced along the halls and sought treats from guests.
Not everyone acted that way at the Sugar Maple Inn, but this
particular group appeared delighted to kick up their heels a
bit. At least they gave the impression of being very happy.
But maybe it was just because they were away from their
homes, their lives, and their troubles, in a safe place where
they could let down their hair.

I was minding my own business, eating a late lunch on
the terrace of the Sugar Maple Inn. I had every right to be
there. After all, my grandmother and I owned the inn. It
wasn't as though I was hiding or scooching closer to eaves-

drop on a conversation, so I didn't feel one bit guilty for hearing their exchange.

The WAG Ladies were the kind of women I had known so well when I had been a fundraiser in Washington, DC. Smart multitaskers completely at home with themselves and the world as they saw it.

Impeccably stylish Oriana was an interesting contrast to Brenda, who generally looked as though she was planning to work in the garden. Oriana's black hair was perfectly coiffed in a short style that framed a beautiful petite face, while Brenda wore a canvas hat that seemed more appropriate for the outback and had most certainly seen better days.

Brenda, an earthy type who favored dusty colors and vintage clothes, didn't bother whispering like Oriana had. "In my experience, people do one of three things. Some take to their beds and cry for a ridiculous amount of time, and then they spend the rest of their lives feeling helpless and inadequate because of something they really should have gotten over. The second group tells all. They find their blathering cathartic, but family and friends are usually driven to drink because it's so annoying and excruciatingly repetitive. And then they wonder why they're not invited to anything anymore. The third type is the one we have to worry about. Those are the people who suffer in silence. They're stoic and keep it inside. They carry on quite well and often prosper. But deep in their hearts, they have not forgotten that which caused them great pain, and when the time is right, they strike."

"Well, now you've scared me. Thanks, Brenda," Oriana grumbled. "I suppose there's not much we can do about it." She looked at her watch. "Joanne will be wondering where we are by now."

Brenda cackled. "She has been somewhat insufferable on this trip, hasn't she? I wonder what's bugging her. I would ask who died and left her in charge, but I know the answer to that," Brenda quipped.

"You're right." Oriana collected her purse and stood up. "I should have realized that. If Theona had been here, everything would have been different. Isn't it interesting how one person can change the dynamics in a group of people?" She turned and called, "Garbo!"

They walked past me on their way into the inn. Either they had already forgotten the nature of their discussion or I blended with the inn and was simply part of the scenery. Perhaps both.

Theona Barlow's death six months earlier had cast a pall over Wagtail. The There's No Place Like Home Gala and the WAG Ladies had been her babies, and now the WAG Ladies were left to pick up the pieces. My grandmother, whom I called Oma, German for *grandma*, was close friends with the Barlows. She was devastated by Theona's demise. Theona hadn't been particularly young, but her death had still come as a blow.

I finished my lunch, collected all the dirty dishes left on the terrace, and called Trixie. She followed me inside and waited at the door of the commercial kitchen, the only room where no animals were allowed. They were welcome everywhere in Wagtail except in commercial kitchens. I was told that local laws allowed them to be inside areas where food was served in a business but not where it was cooked. I scrubbed the dishes and loaded them into a dishwasher.

My sweet Trixie waited loyally outside the door. I had found her, or she had found me, at a gas station at the base of Wagtail Mountain. It had been pouring rain, and the sweet little girl was ragged, hungry, and sopping wet. She had jumped into my boyfriend's car, making a mess. At the time, I didn't think I could keep her, but I knew I couldn't leave her there, eating what she could find in the trash.

As things turned out, she became my little darling. Her rough yellowish fur had changed to a silky white, accented by black ears and a black spot on her rump that went halfway up her tail. Her eyes reminded me of a seal's, and anyone who studied them for a few minutes would realize that Trixie was smart. Too smart. Her only shortcoming was a nose for trouble. Not just ordinary dog mischief like snatching cookies or chewing shoes. My Trixie's nose led her to corpses, specifically victims of murder. That curious quirk had saddled the two of us with a reputation in Wagtail, although, if pressed, most residents would have to admit their own snoopiness when it came to crime, especially murder.

It was approaching that odd time of day between lunch and afternoon tea when the inn was relatively quiet. People were out and about, enjoying the balmy weather. The inn phone rang, and I walked over to the lobby desk to answer it. "Sugar Maple Inn."

"Hello? Holly?"

I recognized the sweet voice of my grandmother's best friend, Rose Richardson, who also happened to be the grandmother of my boyfriend, Holmes Richardson. "Hi, Rose."

"Honey, would it be possible for you to drop by Judge Barlow's house in the next half hour or so? We would very much like to speak with you."

It sounded like she was whispering.

"Yes, of course."

"Wonderful. Oh, and, honey, let's not mention this to Liesel or Holmes." The line went dead.

Two

❀ ❀ ❀ ❀ ❀

I hung up the phone, worried about Rose's odd call. As luck would have it, my grandmother happened to be walking across the empty lobby, straight toward me, carrying a small basket.

I held my breath, hoping she didn't need my immediate assistance with a project.

"Liebling," she said, "would you mind taking our auction donation to the WAG Ladies at the hotel? I do not want it to get lost." I hardly noticed Oma's German accent anymore. She wished she could lose it, but most people found it charming.

"No problem. I was just on my way out."

"Thank you." She checked her watch. "Have you heard from Holmes today? I thought Rose would come for tea, but she canceled."

I nearly choked. It wasn't like Rose to keep secrets from Oma. I told her the truth, sort of. "I haven't spoken to Holmes today."

"I hope nothing is wrong." She walked up to the second floor of the inn and turned right toward her quarters.

I took the basket and headed out the door before she could return to ask more questions.

My parents had sent me to stay with Oma every summer when I was a child. I had worked at the inn along with my cousin (and Rose's grandson) Holmes. But Oma made sure we had plenty of time for playing and wandering around Wagtail. They had been lovely summers of swimming in the lake, frolicking in the woods, and drinking afternoon tea with Oma from her delicate china.

Oma had prepared an apartment for me even before *I'd* known I would come back to Wagtail to live. She had been convinced that I would return to help her run the inn as she aged.

My apartment was lovely, with French doors that opened to a terrace overlooking Dogwood Lake. On the other side, my bedroom overlooked a plaza in front of the inn and, beyond that, the town of Wagtail. The Sugar Maple Inn anchored one end of town, and the Wagtail Springs Hotel anchored the other end. In between was a large park, known as "the green." On each side of the green, stores and restaurants lined the sidewalks. In the distance, I could see mountains curving gently against the sky.

Two hundred years ago, Wagtail had been a popular destination because of its underground springs. People had come to partake of the waters and to escape the brutal summer heat at lower elevations. Many wealthy families had built large homes to accommodate extended families. But as taking the waters lost popularity, Wagtail withered. Oma and other residents redefined the town by making it the premier destination for people who wanted to travel and vacation with their pets. Cats and dogs were welcome almost everywhere. Restaurants offered special menus for them, and there were animal masseuses, groomers, acupuncturists, and veterinary specialists. The stores sold everything a cat or dog could possibly want, from bowls and beds to clothing and toys. Much to everyone's surprise, Wagtail was booming.

Trixie and I were walking through the green when a stunning husky raced toward us, his blue leash flying in the air behind him.

"Loki, come! Loki, come! Loooookiiii!" A considerable distance behind him, Louisa Twomey loped along, wailing. Her copper hair and ivory skin made her easily recognizable, even from a distance. She carried her shoes in her hands.

Clutching the basket firmly, I rushed toward one of the enclosed dog runs. Trixie sprang along beside me and eagerly entered the double-gated dog run. I quickly closed the outer gate and opened the inner one to let her in.

As I did so, a man whom I judged to be in his early thirties opened the outer gate and stood on the outside with his arms extended as though he meant to steer the husky through the gate.

His plan worked perfectly. Loki swerved and zoomed into the enclosure with the man right behind him. I slammed the outer gate shut, and the man grabbed the husky's leash. "Gotcha, buddy," he said kindly to the dog. He patted the husky, who acted as if he knew the man who looked up at me. "Thanks for your help. This guy might have jumped the fence after a minute or two in here. Huskies are notorious jumpers."

Louisa caught up and let herself in, breathing heavily. "Loki," she choked, "what am I going to do with you?" She hugged Loki, and her eyes widened. "Seth! What are you doing here?"

"Louisa! I knew this dog looked familiar," he said. "But I thought he was—" He broke off his sentence and appeared to feel awkward.

She looked up at me. "Sorry, Holly, I didn't mean to ignore you. Without your help I would still be running in my bare feet."

"No problem, Louisa. I've had to chase Trixie more than once."

She shifted her gaze back to Seth. "You're quite right. Loki was Tom's dog." She glanced at me and explained, "My deceased husband. I love Loki to bits, but we're still learning to get along without Tom."

I winced. "I'm sorry, Louisa."

She slid on her shoes and squared her shoulders. "Thank you. I don't know if either one of us will ever recover from losing Tom. Everything has changed." She took a deep breath. "But Loki and I will manage, won't we, boy? We're just on our way to a training class."

She sounded cheery and brave, but I wondered how much of that was a front.

"Would you look at the time! I'm going to be late. Joanne will have a cow, but I have to drop off Loki at his class first. I hope he'll behave. He was there yesterday. They have running and tugging games to help dogs burn off some energy, but apparently Loki wanted to keep going when the other dogs were worn out!"

"Where are you staying, Louisa?" asked Seth. "Maybe we can grab some lunch while we're here?"

Louisa had a tight grip on Loki's leash and opened the outer gate. "That would be great." Her lips seemed tight, as though she was saying what was expected but not what she wanted. "I'm at the Sugar Maple Inn. Holly can tell you all about it." She hurried away, but I heard her saying, "Now, Loki, you have to behave or you'll get Mommy into trouble."

Seth handed me a business card. "Seth Bertenshaw, pet detective." He pulled a photograph out of a well-worn soft-sided brown leather briefcase on a shoulder strap. "I'm looking for this big fellow, Fritz." He held out a photograph of a German shepherd.

He was black and tan with a charcoal nose and intelligent black-rimmed eyes. "Judge Barlow's dog," I said. I was well aware that he had gone missing. It was my job to post official announcements on the Wagtail Facebook page, and Oma had asked me to add the lost-dog announcement about Fritz.

"Great! You know him. That should make my job easier. Have you seen him around?" asked Seth.

"Not recently."

His excitement diminished. "Let me know if you spot him. What was the name of the inn where Louisa is staying?"

"The Sugar Maple Inn. You can't miss it. Just head in that direction. I don't think we have any vacancies, but Zelda, our desk clerk, might know of a rental."

He thanked me and started in that direction but quickly veered off to the west.

Trixie and I headed in the other direction. Judge Barlow was a familiar figure in Wagtail, most often seen walking with a crookneck cane covered in medallions from the places where he had hiked. I had never seen him without his loyal dog, Fritz, by his side.

The judge lived in a massive three-story home. The first floor had been painted white. A Southern-style porch sprawled along two-thirds of the front, and a picture window dominated the other third. The second story was dark wood, nicely accented with white windows. A couple of the windows had old-fashioned diamond-shaped grilles in them, giving the house a slightly Hansel and Gretel feel. The top floor was probably just an attic, but French doors with a balcony overlooked the street.

I walked up to the house and rang the doorbell.

Rose answered the door. Her warm hazel eyes squinted with worry, accentuating her crow's feet. Rose looked a decade younger than her midseventies. She wore her blond hair short and maintained a trim figure.

I reached out for a hug, but she quickly held a finger up against her lips, indicating that I shouldn't speak. She embraced me and then beckoned me inside. Trixie shot in before me.

The foyer was an incredible hall featuring possibly the best woodwork I had ever seen. Heavily carved arches led in different directions. In the middle stood a round table with a tall vase filled with white gladioli, vibrant blue delphiniums, and giant fuchsia zinnias. I set my basket by the door so I wouldn't forget it when I left.

I wondered if other people were in the house and that was why I wasn't supposed to speak. I listened, thinking they might be gathered elsewhere, but the house was eerily silent.

Rose crooked her forefinger at me. Trixie and I followed her through a huge kitchen that had no cabinets above counter height. She pulled a pitcher from the refrigerator and poured tea over ice cubes in tall glasses that waited on a tray. She added two bone-shaped dog cookies.

We still hadn't spoken.

Rose motioned for me to follow her and led me into a remarkable conservatory that nearly burst with plants. It was like walking into a jungle. Vines grew up trellises along the walls until they met on the ceiling. Potted plants were outgrowing their pots. Blooms in every variation of pink broke the overwhelming green.

Rose closed the door.

Three

❀ ❀ ❀ ❀

Judge Grant Barlow sat in the middle of the remarkable greenhouse at a wrought-iron table, his cane leaning against his chair. He was portly with well-trimmed white hair and an ivory mustache that overwhelmed his upper lip. Faded blue eyes watched me so carefully that I felt I was being judged. A crease under his lower lip bent downward on both sides, imparting a dour expression, as though he was disappointed with everyone. I reminded myself that he had lost his wife recently. In spite of his age, he exuded an intimidating fierceness that had probably been honed in the courtroom. The judge was no pushover.

I offered my open hand to him. "Holly Miller."

"Liesel Miller's granddaughter," he muttered. "Liesel is a very fine and intelligent woman. I have the utmost respect for her. One can only hope that her granddaughter shares her intellect. Regrettably, I know from experience that is not always the case. Most of my own progeny and their offspring fail to tie their shoes successfully. After three decades of listening to idiotic excuses from daft criminals who didn't have the good sense to get their stories straight, I'm afraid I have exceedingly low expectations for the human race in general."

I could understand why he might expect the worst from people after a lifetime of hearing lies, but I had a feeling his cranky nature might come to him naturally.

Rose smiled at me cheerily, as though he had said something pleasantly upbeat. She gestured toward a wrought-iron chair outfitted with green and pink cushions. "Don't mind him. He's not half as grumpy as he seems."

I sat down. "This is an amazing room."

"The judge takes his meals here, weather permitting. In the winter we used to eat by the fire."

I hoped she didn't notice my little intake of breath. *We?* They were a couple?

She continued speaking without hesitation. "I hope we'll be able to do that again. There's something so cozy about a fire. Come here, little Trixie. I have a treat for you!"

Trixie waggled her hind end and received a dog biscuit.

"Is this about Fritz?" I asked.

"Oh! We are heartsick." She looked at the judge. "How could Dovie have let that happen? I suspect she accidentally left a door or gate open and Fritz simply strolled out."

Judge Barlow appeared pained. He glanced at the floor by his chair as though he hoped his beloved dog would suddenly appear and it would turn out it had all been a nightmare.

Rose hastily added, "Dovie has called in a pet detective."

I was about to say that I had met Seth when the judge said sternly, "Such nonsense! Ordinarily, I would have undertaken a thorough search for Fritz myself, but I'm no longer as agile and able as I once was. I can walk the streets of Wagtail, but I'm afraid my days wandering through the woods and hiking mountains have passed me by."

"He came highly recommended," said Rose. "He was here earlier. I thought he seemed quite competent. There have been sightings of Fritz. We think he's still somewhere on Wagtail Mountain."

"I hope he can find Fritz." I tried to smile encouragingly.

Rose sighed, and her shoulders actually dropped a bit as if she was carrying the burdens of the world. "If you're wondering why we're speaking in here, it's because there are bugs everywhere."

I glanced around the room. She had to mean the wiretap sort. But that seemed unlikely. Just to be certain, I asked, "Do you mean insects or listening devices?" The creepy-crawly kind wouldn't be terribly surprising given the number of plants.

"Insects never hurt anyone, dear. Well, not much anyway," said Rose, handing Trixie another cookie.

"She means listening devices," growled the judge. "Rose and I made sure this room was quite safe, but the house is large. We are still in the process of ensuring the privacy of the other rooms. We began by testing the rooms we use the most."

I wondered if they were suffering from delusions. Could they have talked each other into thinking someone was spying on them? I tried to sound like I believed them. "How did you test the rooms?"

"It all began in the kitchen," said Rose. She handed me a sheet of paper that contained notes in her precise handwriting. "We kept track. You see here where it says 'kitchen—rain'? Well, the weather report wasn't calling for rain at all. But it had been so cloudy, and the wind was blowing from the southwest like it does when rain is imminent. We talked about how we thought the weather forecast was wrong and that it would probably rain and we should make sure all the windows were closed. The next morning when I got up, someone had opened the kitchen window."

"You're certain it was closed?" I asked.

"Absolutely. I did it myself," the judge grumbled.

Rose smiled at me.

"I know what you're thinking," said the judge, "because Rose and I thought the same thing. Dovie Dickerson is my housekeeper. She must have opened the window. What a funny coincidence. But Dovie claims she did no such thing. Then Rose and I grew suspicious. And we set up an innocent test."

"The judge always eats eggs for breakfast. Two sunny-side-up eggs fried in olive oil with a little sea salt, a piece of buttered toast, and a bowl of fruit on the side," said Rose. "So, one morning in his bedroom, I asked him if he would like something different, like oatmeal. And he said, 'Yes, please. I would enjoy a steaming bowl of oatmeal.'" The two of them laughed.

"He was being sarcastic," she said. "Grant loathes oatmeal. But later that day, I found a box of oatmeal on the kitchen counter. Brand-new and never opened. Now I know *I* didn't buy it and forget about it. Dovie is well aware of Grant's aversion to oatmeal, so she never buys it. Yet there it was."

"We recognized that these two events had to be attributed to Dovie," the judge explained. "My granddaughter Addi is in town, but other than that, no one is here except for Dovie."

"But then something else happened. This time we were conversing in the living room." Rose wasn't smiling anymore. "It was about flowers for Theona's grave. She has been gone for over six months now." Rose gestured around the room. "As you can see, she was a great lover of color, especially pink."

"I ordered a spray of pink roses for her grave." The judge was grim. "But when I visited her grave yesterday—"

"They were white." Rose placed her hand over his. "But they were very beautiful."

"Someone had swapped my pink roses for white ones." The judge's nostrils flared in anger.

"Who placed them on the grave?" I asked. "Maybe the florist misunderstood or got mixed up."

"They were very confused," said Rose, seemingly trying to comfort the judge. "They told Grant that they had personally placed pink roses on her grave."

"Last night, during dinner out here, I made a big fuss about not being able to find my favorite walking stick," said the judge.

"He did an excellent job. Grant, you really could have been an actor," said Rose, eliciting a smile from him. "I hid the walking stick in the foyer where anyone would have seen it upon entering the house."

"When you tried your trick in here, nothing happened?" I asked.

"Exactly. Grant also asked me if I had bought a lottery ticket. We were sitting right here, just like we are now. I love playing a lively game of bingo at the church now and then, but in my opinion, you might as well throw your dollar in the trash bin as play the lottery."

"And no lottery ticket turned up?"

"That's right. We came to realize that whatever is being used to bug the house doesn't work out here."

I felt terrible for them. I didn't want to belittle their worries, but I was having trouble believing them. As sweetly as I could, I asked, "Rose, who would want to listen?"

"Well, that's the question, isn't it? Why on earth would anyone be interested in what goes on in this house?" asked the judge.

"Have you told Officer Dave?" Our local police officer, Dave Quinlan, had been promoted to sergeant but was still affectionately called "Officer Dave."

"Yes, of course," Rose responded.

The judge scowled. "He thought it very odd and had a good look around but couldn't find a thing. He wasn't helpful at all."

"I don't understand," I said. "Why have you called me?"

Rose leaned toward me. "I don't dare say this to anyone else," she whispered. "I think someone did these things on purpose to frighten Grant."

Four

* * * * *

My Oma, who was the same age as Rose, some-times told me things that seemed unlikely. In every in-stance she had been proven correct. Oma was very sharp.

But was Rose? What about the judge? I glanced at the judge, who eyed me.

"I'm not quite clear." I couldn't bring myself to tell them the white roses could have been an innocent mistake or that Dovie, someone who had every right to be in the house, had opened the kitchen window. They knew that anyway. "While the issue with the roses was understandably upset-ting, how would that or the oatmeal frighten you?"

"By driving him out of his mind!" Rose said with un-warranted conviction.

I looked to the judge, who remained stoic. "Do you think this person is responsible for Fritz being lost?"

"I have considered that, of course. But it appears to be the result of Dovie's carelessness." He tapped his forefinger on the crook of his cane. "On the surface, these events would seem like unimportant pranks. Perhaps you have noted two things about them. They are getting worse in terms of maliciousness. And, most troubling of all, someone is listening to us."

"Pardon me for being blunt," I said, "but what would they have to gain?" I thought it unlikely that someone who brought him oatmeal was inclined to kill the judge, but he had a point about someone listening. That alone was distressing if it was true. No one wanted to be spied upon. "Sir, in your career, you must have sent people to prison. Is there anyone who stands out in your mind? Someone who would want to take revenge on you?"

The judge nodded. "Indeed. A few people. Most of them are still in the prison system. However, one stands out, a Wallace McDade."

McDade? One of the WAG Ladies was a McDade. "Wallace is out of prison?" I asked.

"Yes. I checked his status immediately. I didn't send him to prison. But Wallace has it in him to torment. He was born gripping the proverbial silver spoon in his hand. He came from a fine upstanding family. Good people, the McDades. His parents and grandparents made a fortune through diligence and hard work. But Wallace is an odious human, seemingly indifferent to the pain and suffering he causes others."

"Can you share the nature of his crime?" I asked.

"Certainly. I'm not telling you anything you wouldn't find in public records. In his youth, Wallace killed my daughter in a drunk-driving incident. Alas, he hardly served any time due to a new program designed to rehabilitate youthful offenders. Later on, Wallace was convicted of attempted murder."

Rose drew a sharp breath. "Oh my word! I remember Bobbie! Why didn't you tell me? That was such a terrible tragedy. I never knew that he attempted to murder someone else."

"His father. It was fate and a little dumb luck that saved his father's life. His sister, an avid gardener, happened to hear the scuffle and ran into the house still clutching a wickedly sharp three-tine cultivator she had been using in the garden. She slammed it on Wallace's neck from behind, nearly hitting his spinal cord. He wasn't paralyzed, but it seems he did feel his *own* pain. When the police arrived, they found him in a garden shed, bleeding profusely. They tell me the father tore down the garden shed and built a new one because no one could bear to go inside it anymore."

I wondered if the sister in question was Brenda McDade, our guest at the inn. "And you believe that Wallace is sufficiently deranged to harass you and wish you harm?"

"Holly, I encountered a goodly number of miscreants and thugs during my career. Many physically intimidating and vicious. But Wallace terrified me more than any of them. He was intelligent, affable, and courteous. People consider him pleasant and will not see the evil lying behind his facade until it is too late. He is educated and eloquent. A monster who cleans up well."

"You're sure he was released from prison?" asked Rose, who looked around anxiously, as if she thought she might see him peering through the glass.

"He was given the maximum time that the law allowed for his attempt to murder his father, ten years. A ruling that generated a considerable amount of opposition by those who saw his refined appearance and did not understand the truth about him. Interestingly, not a single member of his family objected to the sentence. I always suspected they preferred to have him safely locked away from decent people. He was a rather young man at the time. I pray that he has changed, though I think it unlikely."

"Have you seen him around town?" I asked.

"No. I am pleased to say that I never set eyes on him again after he was hustled out of court in handcuffs."

"Presumably, he may look somewhat different now," I mused aloud. "Forgive me for asking, but who benefits from your death?"

"I have provided for Dovie, of course. She has been with us for a long time. I don't know how I would have managed without her during Theona's illness. And there is a special trust for Fritz as well. Beyond that, everything goes to my granddaughter Addi."

"Addi? Is she still notoriously late for everything?" I asked.

"You must know her!" exclaimed the judge.

"We played together when we were children."

"She's staying at the inn, isn't she?" asked Rose.

Her grandfather added, "Addi has no concept of time. She's just like Theona was. Always stopping to move a turtle out of the road or driving forty miles out of her way to pick up someone's favorite pie. She's a dear."

I was getting into precariously emotional territory, but I forged ahead. "I was under the impression that you had a number of children and grandchildren." Surely that was enough to point out to him that any one of the others might be upset if they knew they would receive nothing from his estate.

"Bobbie, the daughter I mentioned, predeceased us, as did one of our sons. That leaves Addi's mother and one son. Addi's mother has no need of money and has no interest in Wagtail. As far as I know, my son is still living." The judge sounded completely unemotional.

"You cut him out of your will?" I asked.

He raised his eyebrows. "I would not have said *that*. Your question presumes he was once *in* the will."

Ouch. I assumed I had hit a sore spot and moved on. I was as blunt as the judge had been. "At this point, you haven't really told me anything that suggests someone intends to harm you. Perhaps one of them was trying to frighten you, Judge Barlow?"

I supposed it could be murder if someone intentionally induced enough distress to cause a heart attack, but oatmeal and roses didn't seem to rise to that level. It sounded to me like someone was trying to help them. The means was certainly creepy, but I wondered if that person had good intentions.

And wouldn't murder by gaslighting be difficult to prove? Especially when the only witness was a frightened elderly lady? I needed to talk with Officer Dave. He was a reasonable guy. If nothing else, maybe he could provide some insight.

"We thought you might find the person who is doing this," said Rose. "You're so good at identifying killers."

I certainly hoped we weren't dealing with a murderer. "Who else has a key to the house?" I asked.

Judge Barlow snorted. "I have no idea. This house is at least eighty if not one hundred years old. I don't know exactly when it was built, but I do know that no one has changed the locks as long as I have lived here. For decades, no one in Wagtail locked their doors. I have a key, as does Dovie. I presume my wife had one as well."

That would mean a lot of people could have keys. "Is there anyone in particular whom you know for sure has a key?"

"Why are you asking about keys? Do you think someone will enter the house at night while we—" Rose coughed "—Grant is sleeping?"

I had suspected as much, but now that she had slipped a couple of times, it was clear that the two of them were an item. I tried to bite back my smile and allow Rose to maintain her dignity. "I'm pretty sure that it's possible to eavesdrop on someone from outside the house. But it's probably much easier to set up something inside the house. And if oatmeal was on the kitchen counter, someone must have entered the house."

Judge Barlow huffed. "That's what Officer Dave said, but he didn't do anything about it."

A horrible thought crossed my mind. "Do you leave a key outside somewhere in case you get locked out?"

"Yes," Rose gasped. "I see what you're getting at."

"Is it under a mat?" I asked, certain of the answer.

"Of course. I know some people keep them on the door frame over the door, but it's getting too hard for us to reach up that high. I get dizzy if I look up too long. Can't decorate the top of the Christmas tree anymore unless I'm on a tall ladder."

I shuddered at the thought. She really shouldn't be climbing ladders.

Rose drew her shoulders back and sat up straight. "What do you charge? I would like to hire you."

"Oh, Rose. You know I don't charge anything. Besides, I don't honestly know if there's much I can do without any evidence."

"That's disappointing! I can show you the container of oatmeal. It's in the kitchen cupboard."

"Let's start with this. Maybe Judge Barlow could pay for some new locks on the doors. I can send our handyman, Shadow, around to change them out for you. Rose knows him. You can trust Shadow. He's a decent guy."

"Since I don't have Fritz here to bark, that's probably a good idea, but it won't help me catch the perpetrator," growled the judge.

"Would you mind if I had a look around? Maybe fresh eyes will help spot the listening device."

Rose showed me to the stairs. "There are six bedrooms. When you come down, don't overlook the judge's library."

I was on my own. The house was huge. The bedrooms were lovingly decorated with drapes that matched chairs or bedspreads. I looked behind curtains and under beds, scanned desks and bookcases. In the master bedroom, I dared to lift paintings away from the wall ever so slightly. I found a wall safe under one, but nothing else. Dovie did a good job of cleaning. Surely she would have noticed anything that didn't belong.

Trixie trotted along, sniffing, but she didn't find anything of particular interest, either.

I returned downstairs and walked through a formal living room. I found the judge's library, a beautifully paneled room with a fireplace and three walls of books. It was clear that he spent time there. One leather chair was well worn. A favorite, I guessed. A massive desk was equipped with a computer, a printer, and all the paraphernalia that went along with them. I'd heard of listening devices disguised as pens and thumb drives. But how could a person tell the difference? Of all the rooms in the house, the library would have been my top choice for hiding something. With all those books, how would anyone ever notice a pen behind one?

Feeling terrible for them, I returned to the conservatory. Rose was one of my favorite people. The judge appeared composed, but he must have been troubled, or he wouldn't have agreed to speak with me. Even if someone had their best interests at heart, he or she had managed to frighten them. "I don't see anything that would be suspect. If anything at all happens, I want you to call me. Okay?"

They agreed, and Rose showed me to the front door, once again holding a finger across her lips. I picked up my basket and stepped outside. Bending over, I lifted the corner of the doormat. A dull silver key lay underneath it. I picked it up, handed it to Rose, and whispered, "Let's find a better place for this, shall we?"

Instead of saying goodbye, she took the key and walked me out to the sidewalk. "You *will* keep this under your hat?"

"If that's what you want."

"You don't have to look at me like that. Theona has been dead for more than six months." She watched my reaction. "Not long enough?"

"Rose, I'm sure everyone just wants for you and Judge Barlow to be happy."

She snorted. "Don't be so sure. Liesel and Holmes can be quite critical. And Dovie must suspect. She's always trying to get me to leave when I'm here. She doesn't know the extent of my relationship with Grant, of course, but she throws Theona's name in my face constantly."

"Is there any chance that Dovie is doing these things? Maybe she's jealous? She was hoping that with Theona out of the way, the judge would depend on her?"

"I've thought about that." Rose waved at Mae Swinesbury, the neighbor who was peering at us through her lace curtains. Mae disappeared instantly.

Five

❀ ❀ ❀ ❀

"It's a possibility that Dovie isn't happy. She hasn't actually said anything to me, but I do get the idea that she's miffed. I'd better get back inside. Were you able to get someone to cover for you tonight? I so want for you and Liesel to be at the WAG Lady dinner."

Rose had invited the WAG Ladies to her home for dinner to thank them for all their hard work. She'd included Oma and me, mostly because Oma was her best friend, but also because we were housing them during their stay in Wagtail. "I believe Mr. Huckle has agreed to watch the inn."

"Wonderful! Thank you for coming, sweetie. Leave the gate open for Fritz, will you?" Rose pecked me on the cheek and returned to the house.

I stood on the sidewalk and studied the gate. It connected to a fence that extended out of sight on both sides of the house. This was very likely the gate through which Fritz had escaped. Had Dovie left the front door open? It could happen, of course. But given the odd things that had occurred, I wondered if letting Fritz out was part of the plan. He had always seemed devoted to the judge. If I was right about that, then he probably would have hung around outside the house unless something lured him away.

Mae Swinesbury waved to me from her porch and hurried toward me. "Hi, sugar. How's your grandma?"

"She's well, thank you."

"I'm so worried about the judge. As strong as he seems to be, it was really Theona who was the stalwart one. She was so quiet and gentle, but he relied on her. I loved it when he was using fancy lawyerly words to make a point and Theona would ever so discreetly tell him to shut up. I don't know how he'll manage without her?" She ended her sentence on a higher note, as if she was asking a question. She gazed at me with raised eyebrows, but I wasn't that stupid. I knew she wanted information about Rose's presence.

"I just spoke with him. He seems to be doing fine." Quickly changing the subject, I asked, "Were you here the day Fritz ran away? I'm just wondering who let Fritz out. Most people around here would have known better."

Mae rolled her lips inward and looked down at her hands. "I tell you, I feel a bit guilty about that myself. I saw Fritz out on the sidewalk. I figured the judge was somewhere nearby. It never dawned on me that Fritz would wander off and wouldn't come back home. If I had known that, I would have dashed out there and nabbed him. He got out on the day Theona died, too. That was about the saddest thing I have ever seen. When they removed her body from the house, Fritz followed behind the gurney. He sat right over there and watched them load Theona into the hearse. When it drove away, I saw him trotting behind the hearse, like his own little procession honoring the woman who had rescued him from a dreadful life."

"That's so sad. Poor Fritz."

"It brought tears to my eyes. But he came home that day. I can't imagine why he hasn't returned this time."

"So it wasn't intentional," I said aloud. Trying hard to find out if she knew anything about the alleged eavesdropping, I asked, "Are any relatives taking care of the judge now?"

"Well, there's Addi. She's sweet as can be. But she doesn't live here. She's in town for that big gala, and I saw her at a restaurant, but I don't know if she can stay."

I still wasn't getting the kind of information I hoped for. "That's a very big house, and Dovie isn't young anymore. Surely she doesn't clean it all herself?"

"I believe she does. I don't mean to be a busybody, but Dovie has been with the Barlows for decades."

"Yes, of course." I smiled as sweetly as I could. "You understand, I don't want anyone taking advantage of the judge. Perhaps you could let me know if you see strangers or anyone who seems out of place hanging around the house?"

Mae blinked at me. "It wouldn't surprise me at all if Dovie had an interest in the judge, if you know what I mean. But I see what you're getting at. Wagtail is such a lovely place that it didn't occur to me someone might try to fleece him."

She paused and gazed at the house. "So many people were here when Theona was ill. Nurses and caregivers, not to mention when she died. People were in and out like there was a revolving door on the house. But it should all have calmed down now. That's always the worst part, isn't it? When everyone leaves and there's not a sound in the house. You're all by yourself with nothing but your thoughts. I suppose that's what they mean by a deafening silence."

I had the distinct feeling she was speaking from experience.

After a moment she patted my shoulder. "Don't you worry.

I'll keep an eye out for anyone suspicious and let you know. Wagtail will rally around the judge and keep him safe."

I thanked Mae and called Trixie. Figuring that Dave was somewhere around the green, we headed in that direction. Trixie sped ahead, pausing occasionally to sniff a particularly enticing spot.

Not too far from us, I caught sight of Seth talking with Oriana. I couldn't hear what they were saying, but she seemed angry and shouted after him when he walked away from her.

I found Dave outside of Café Chat. The café name was an intentional double entendre easily realized by anyone who took a moment to consider the café's logo over the door of two cat silhouettes, back to back, with their tails entwined.

Trixie reached him first and danced around his feet. He bent to pet her and looked up at me. "I knew you couldn't be far away."

Sergeant Dave Quinlan had been a sailor in the navy before returning home to Wagtail. He was now part of the police force located on Snowball Mountain, but Dave lived in Wagtail and was our primary law enforcement officer. He was in his early thirties, not much older than me.

I skipped the niceties and launched into my question. "What do you know about Judge Barlow?"

Dave straightened up and tilted his head at me. "Why are you asking about him?"

"You're not concerned about the strange goings-on at his home?" I asked.

Dave was a nice guy and I knew it. He would have leaped to their aid if he had thought it was necessary. So it surprised me when he said, "I didn't say *that*."

"You think someone is messing with him? Gaslighting him?" I asked.

"There's no evidence. In my experience so far, the judge

has always been honest and straightforward. I hope this isn't the first sign of his mind slipping. Losing Theona has been very hard on him. Dr. Engelknecht says it's unlikely that it brought on sudden confusion of this sort but that he could be sliding into dementia."

"He seemed fairly clearheaded to me."

He nodded. "Me, too. And he has stuck to his story. He doesn't waiver on it or embellish it. The hallmark of truth in my experience."

"Oh great. So you don't know what to think, either."

"I'm keeping tabs on him, but there's really nothing I can do." Dave shrugged. "He forgot he opened a window. Dovie probably bought oatmeal and didn't remember. I find things in my kitchen all the time that I forgot I bought. There's just nothing there, Holly."

"You could search for listening devices in the house," I suggested.

"I already did that. There are too many ways to listen in on people these days. I love modern technology, but it comes with a price. You don't have to be a computer genius to set up listening devices anymore. They come inside flash drives and wall plug-ins. You'd never know they were there. And those are the ones I've heard about. There are many more."

"I wasn't allowed to say a thing inside the house," I pointed out.

"Listen, Holly, my time is best spent finding Fritz and bringing him home. He'll watch out for the judge around the clock. Besides, while it is sufficiently creepy and most certainly illegal to listen to what's going on in that house, roses and oatmeal hardly sound sinister," he protested.

"I suppose you've met Seth, the pet detective?" I asked.

He looked at me with surprise. "No. I haven't. Did Dovie hire him?"

"Apparently so."

"She feels responsible for Fritz's escape. But I don't

know if he'll have much luck. No one has seen Fritz. By the
way, I've asked for additional police presence for the gala.
Wouldn't want anyone swiping our visitors' jewels. They
advertised that thing from here to Pasadena."

I smiled at his exaggeration.

"No joke, Holly," he persisted. "That's like waving a red
flag in the faces of thieves." He pointed his finger in a pan-
oramic way. "Out there, mingling with kindhearted people
who want to save dogs and cats, there are degenerates without a conscience who think what's yours should be theirs."

"You're awfully grim today," I observed.

"Just doing my job."

I left him to his thoughts of crime and walked over to
the Wagtail Springs Hotel to check on the WAG Ladies and
the There's No Place Like Home Gala preparations.

The old Wagtail Springs Hotel had been restored to its
former glory by a new owner, and the ballroom was simply
gorgeous, with large arches that melded together at the tops
into a curved ceiling.

Garbo, the saluki, and Fagan, the Scottish terrier, rested
on a stage, watching their people fuss. Trixie raced to join
them. All tails wagged on her arrival.

I walked over to Brenda and Oriana and held out the
basket from Oma that contained a bottle of wine, locally
baked cheese sticks and gingersnaps, as well as dog and cat
treats. "This is for a weeklong stay at the inn. Where should
I put it?"

Joanne Williams was across the room, but her head
snapped up as soon as I spoke. She strode toward me impe-
riously. Joanne struck me as a meticulous woman, which
probably accounted for her frustration with those who were
less organized. I had yet to see her without a clipboard in
her hand or nearby. Although Wagtail was on the casual
side, Joanne wore a fitted sky blue dress with three-quarter-
length sleeves. Multiple gold necklaces draped over her

dress. She wore her hair in a simple chignon at the nape of her neck, and her makeup was flawless. She was elegant in an office-setting way. I could imagine her striding along corridors while wary employees jumped back to work.

She reached out her hands. "I'll take that. We can't have it getting lost, can we? Addi is responsible for the donations." She swept her arm wide, as if showing me the room. "As usual, Addi is late. I have no idea why we put her in charge of anything. You could line her arm with a dozen wristwatches, and she would still be the last to arrive. I really don't understand people like that. It drives me nuts. How can you get anything done if you're not on time? And Louisa has disappeared again! Well, I'll log this in and be sure it doesn't fall into *their* hands."

Joanne marched toward a table and set the basket on it.

"Don't mind her. She's only happy when she has something to complain about," Brenda McDade grumbled in a gruff way.

An unexpected streak of caramel brown ran between the tables, and a small cat jumped up on one. He wore a handsome green collar that couldn't compete with the glowing green of his eyes.

"Hershey!" Joanne smiled and watched him fondly as he dropped a stuffed cartoon mouse on the table. It had a comical expression and tiny feet that jutted out, giving it a look of eternal surprise. Hershey promptly gave it a whack. It flew to the floor, and Hershey looked down at it, his fluffy tail waving. He pounced, picked up the fabric mouse, rolled over, and zoomed to the other side of the room.

Brenda laughed. "He follows Joanne around like a dog. I'm told that's typical of Somali cats."

I studied Brenda with fresh eyes, wondering whether Wallace McDade was her brother. Had she saved her father's life and testified against her brother? How did a person cope with something like that?

She had removed her hat, revealing fluffy honey blond hair. It stuck out at odd angles as if she might have cut it herself.

Oriana gazed at her with huge brown eyes and said softly, "Give her a break, Brenda. Joanne means well."

"How can you manage a huge company and be so overly sensitive? Or does your husband do all the dirty work?" Brenda stalked off, calling to Joanne, "Are those supposed to be the silent auction tables? The setup is all wrong."

I wasn't sure if Oriana was struggling to maintain her composure or if she was always so serene. At least outwardly. For all I knew, she was seething underneath.

"We really ought to give Joanne a task to complete," she said. "That way she'll be too busy to interfere with the rest of us."

"That sounds like an excellent idea," I said, glad it wasn't my problem.

Without sounding snide, Oriana said, "*That* is how one runs a big company. One defers to a person's strengths. Brenda was right about one thing. Joanne is happiest when she's busy. She has a need to be on top of things." She walked toward Joanne.

I watched as Oriana deftly distracted Joanne and moved her focus to place cards while Brenda pushed the silent auction tables where she wanted them.

Across the room, Loki the husky bounded in and headed straight for the stage. Louisa followed him, pale and devoid of energy. Her face showed the strain she had been under no matter how cheery she pretended to be.

"How nice of you to show up," called Joanne. She picked up her clipboard and bustled toward Louisa, her head held high and rigid.

Louisa wilted at the sight of her. Fortunately, Oriana and Brenda rushed to Louisa's side.

"What kept you?" asked Joanne. "Oriana and Brenda have been here for hours."

Louisa opened her mouth to respond, but Joanne held up her hand like a stop sign. "Never mind. I don't want to hear another sad song and dance, no matter how creative. Now you promised to take care of table settings." Joanne swung around and gestured toward the tables. "They appear naked to me. I hope this isn't what you had planned for tomorrow. And just let me say that I have no intention of working through the night to fulfill your responsibilities."

Louisa's face flushed. But I had to give her credit. In spite of her discomfort at Joanne's chiding, she maintained her dignity.

At that moment, the ballroom doors opened and a hotel employee brought in a luggage cart packed with boxes.

I would have been tempted to shoot a nasty glance at Joanne, but Louisa simply smiled, turned on her heel, and thanked the man, handing him a tip. He unloaded the boxes and left. Louisa withdrew a box cutter and a frighteningly large pair of scissors from her purse and proceeded to open them.

From the first box, she withdrew snow white tablecloths. Oriana, Brenda, and I took several and spread them on the tables. As we worked, Louisa came around to each table, added round votive holders of a golden hue, and placed a candle in each.

Joanne stood by and watched until she noticed the candles. "No, no, no! Do you really want dogs and cats overturning candles, Louisa? I think not!"

Louisa kept working. Her voice didn't reveal even a tinge of aggravation. "They're battery operated, Joanne. No pups or kitties will get hurt."

Oriana picked one up and turned it on. The flame flicked just like a genuine candle. "Unbelievable. They look real. They even feel like candles."

"They're dipped in wax," explained Louisa.

I wasn't part of their group, but since Addi hadn't shown

up yet, I stuck around and helped. With everyone except Joanne pitching in, the tables looked great in less than an hour.

Joanne still busied herself with the place cards. "No flowers?"

By that time, I wanted to smack her. Did nothing ever please this woman?

"They're being delivered tomorrow so they'll be at their freshest. They're very pretty." Louisa, her complexion now burning crimson, faced Joanne head-on. "Roses, snapdragons, and baby's breath, all nontoxic to cats and dogs."

Joanne blurted, "Then where is Addi? We should start unloading the donations for the auction."

I took that opportunity to slip away. I gave Trixie my hand signal to come. She jumped off the stage and ran toward me. The two of us stepped outside, drawing only the attention of the other dogs.

As we left the hotel, Addi rushed up the stairs and promptly fell face-forward.

I stopped to help her up. She gladly took my hands to stand, then lifted her long gauzy dress to examine her legs. Blood oozed from scrapes.

"Let's go inside," I said. "Maybe they have a first-aid kit and you can clean up your knees."

"No need." She sighed and sat down on the stairs. Her dress had torn in the fall.

Trixie immediately sniffed her and demanded to be petted.

"Hello, Trixie." Addi rubbed her ears and, for a moment, seemed to forget about her mishap.

Nonplussed, Addi pulled a small unmarked bottle and tissues from her oversized Vera Bradley bag. It was a lovely pattern of blue swirls.

She fingered the skirt of her dress. "Rats! Oriana says I shouldn't bother wearing cotton silk. I'm too hard on my clothes." She poured liquid on a tissue and cleaned up her knees. "I don't know if I would be happy wearing rugged canvas clothes like Brenda, though. Not that I have anything against them, but they're stiff and heavy. I love cotton silk because it's so light and delicate."

She brushed long chestnut hair off her forehead and stashed the bottle away in her bag.

"Not to be nosy, but what did you put on your legs?" I asked.

"It's just hydrogen peroxide. I carry it with me because I'm always tripping over my own feet. My shrink says it's not my fault, that it's some kind of genetic thing. I'm not sure that's true"—she smiled at me—"but I'll take it as an excuse."

"Your friends are inside in the ballroom," I said.

"Thanks. I'm sure Joanne is complaining. That's her thing, you know. Joanne is never happy unless she's fretting. It can be quite disconcerting if you don't know her. But it's tolerable once you realize that's her happy place."

Sounded about right. "I met your grandfather, Judge Barlow, this morning."

Addi looked horrified. "Pops? I hope he was nice to you."

"He was fine."

"That's a relief. He can be kind of gruff. He's an old marshmallow inside, but that crusty exterior can be very annoying until you get to know him better."

"Addi? Is that you?" called someone who sounded just like Joanne. "What in the world are you doing sitting around out here when there's so much to be done?"

Addi's eyes widened. "I hope she didn't hear what I said about her," she whispered.

"I was just on my way in." Addi cringed and glanced at me with big eyes.

"My fault, Joanne," I said. "I needed to speak to Addi."

Addi shot me a grateful look.

In a tolerant but undeniably seething tone, Joanne demanded, "Where have you been?"

"Oh, Joanne. Please. You know perfectly well that I've been helping out my grandfather. Are you really going to berate me for that?" Addi smiled, picked up her bag, and strolled past Joanne, her head held high.

Joanne looked at me, her eyebrows raised. "I didn't even know my grandfathers. Did you know yours?"

"Only one of them."

Joanne glanced at her watch. "I'm off to pick up a gift we ordered for Rose. She's been such a help, stepping in and organizing things on this end. I don't know how we would have managed without her."

She bustled off, and I continued on my way. Oma's husband had died before I was born. The story went that he had won the Sugar Maple Inn in a poker game. I found that hard to believe, but whether it was true or not, I gathered he was quite a character.

Restaurants and bars were beginning to get busy. That meant afternoon tea would be over and things would be quieting down at the inn again. I stopped and stared at the show window of Best Friends, which carried dog and cat accessories. I thought I had found just the things for Trixie and Twinkletoes to wear to their first black-tie gala, but the sun sparkled on the faux diamonds of a tiny tiara, and I couldn't resist it.

While Trixie ran to the counter where she knew she would be rewarded with a mini treat, I plucked the tiara out of the window display and checked the price. It definitely wouldn't break my budget. I carried it over to Marsha Deadmond, who rang it up for me.

As Trixie and I walked out the door, we nearly ran into Seth the pet detective.

"Perfect timing," he said with a grin. "I was just going to find that inn."

"I'll be happy to show you the way, but unless there was a cancellation, I don't think we have any rooms. I'm afraid you've arrived just before the There's No Place Like Home Gala and everyone has been booked for weeks."

Just to make chitchat while we walked, I asked, "How do you know Louisa?"

He drew a deep breath. "She's the girl who got away."

Six

❊ ❊ ❊ ❊ ❊

"I grew up with her husband, and then we went to the same college," Seth explained. "Tom was the good-looking bad boy who attracted women. I have never understood why. Some kind of primitive desire to tame him or something? I don't know. I met a lot of nice women through him. But I was the one left to make excuses for him when he went out with someone else. The bearer of bad tidings, you might say. He and Louisa broke up and got back together on a regular basis. But you can't go after your friend's girl, even if he is a womanizing blockhead."

"Did you know she would be here?"

"I had no idea." He seemed to have trouble containing a grin. "Maybe fate brought us together again."

We walked across the plaza and up the front steps of the inn. The original building had once been a grand home to a large family. Oma had built several additions, including a cat wing and the new reception wing. The original house was built with mountain stone. A front porch filled with rocking chairs ran across it from end to end.

We entered the main lobby, and I steered Seth to the right through the hallway to reception, where Zelda York was manning the desk.

The first thing I noticed was my long-haired calico cat, Twinkletoes, sitting among stuffed animals on a shelf on the glass wall of the Sugar Maple Inn gift shop. Her green eyes seemed to glow in the light. A dark chocolate spot and a butterscotch spot on the top of her head looked like she had raised colorful sunglasses to her forehead. I hoped no one would grab her, mistaking her for a toy. She watched our every move like a stealthy spy.

At the sight of Seth, Zelda uttered a soft sigh. Oma's golden retriever, Gingersnap, who was the canine ambassador of the inn, strode straight to him with a wagging tail.

I took a better look at him. Medium height with fluffy dark hair, he looked like the guy next door. He had intense brown eyes and an engaging smile. He wore his mustache short, and second-day stubble gave him a trendy appearance.

When he smiled at us, Zelda actually whimpered. He wasn't handsome in a movie-star way. There was something appealingly cute about him, though I was fairly certain he would hate knowing that women thought of him as *cute*.

Gingersnap sniffed his jeans with interest, indicating her approval by wagging her tail. Not that we had ever turned anyone away based on her assessment.

"This is Seth. I told him we were booked—"

"It's your lucky day," Zelda blurted. "We had a cancellation an hour ago." She peered over the counter. "Are you traveling with a cat or dog?"

"Not this time." Seth handed her his business card and brought out the picture of Fritz again.

Zelda recognized him immediately.

"It looks like he's smiling in the picture," I observed.

"He probably is," said Seth. "I'm told he's too smart for his own good."

"I'm sure someone around here must have seen him," said Zelda. "Did Judge Barlow hire you?" she asked.

"Dovie Dickerson phoned me. She was frantic, which is often the case when I'm called in. I gather she feels responsible for letting Fritz get away."

"Of course." Zelda nodded at him. "She's been Dr. Barlow's housekeeper for as long as I can remember. She's nearly as old as he is. I can't imagine her taking care of anyone."

"Apparently someone left the gate open and Fritz took off," offered Seth.

"He's completely devoted to Dr. Barlow. I'm surprised that he ran away," said Zelda. "His wife, Theona, adopted Fritz from WAG. You should stop by and talk to Paige McDonagh. She's in charge of WAG. It's possible that someone has called her about Fritz."

Seth nodded. "I'll be meeting with her right after I check in. There was something about Dovie's phone call that worried me. Everyone who calls me is upset and frantic because they've lost a pet. But Dovie went beyond that. Is there any chance that someone took the dog on purpose to upset them?"

Zelda, who had blond hair down to her waist, big eyes, and no luck with men at all, turned her gaze toward me in horror.

I knew why. It wasn't long ago that someone had taken dogs. They had all been recovered and were quite fine, but the memories were too fresh.

"You don't suppose . . ." she said.

"Don't even go there, Zelda," I said. "The only dog who is missing is Fritz. I'm sure Seth will find him."

Zelda handed me the key to Seth's room. As I walked toward the stairs to show him the way, I noticed that Twinkletoes had flattened herself the way cats do when they don't want to be seen. Her eyes were big and round, and both her ears had flattened to her head. At first I thought she was avoiding being seen by Seth. But she was ignoring him. Her eyes were fixated on something or someone in the hallway just outside the registration area.

Seth traveled light. He hauled a backpack up the stairs as he followed Trixie and me. I unlocked the door to Hike and held it for him to enter.

Seth paused at the door. "Hike? Is that a suggestion to take a hike?"

"All the rooms are named after dog and cat activities," I explained.

"Maybe that's appropriate since Fritz has taken a hike," he said as he entered the room.

French doors opened to a balcony overlooking Dogwood Lake. A red-and-white-plaid armchair by the stone fireplace matched the coverlet on the bed as well as the curtains.

Seth raised his eyebrows and nodded in approval. "Nice."

"We serve breakfast, lunch, and tea, but not dinner. There's a menu on the desk for limited room service. Please let me know if there's anything you need."

I handed him the key and let myself out. Curious about who might have been lurking in the hallway, I tiptoed to the balcony that overlooked the registration desk.

"The truth about Addi is she's too nice," said Joanne. "She would stop to assist the devil himself. You can't help but like her for that no matter how much it might inconvenience the rest of us. But it makes me completely crazy."

Trixie took that moment to bound down the stairs. I hurried after her. She ignored Joanne and ran behind the check-in counter to Zelda.

Joanne was staying in the cat wing with her Somali cat, Hershey. Taking a cue from Oriana, I changed Joanne's focus. "How does Hershey like your room?"

"He loves it! Putting a tree inside the screened porch was brilliant. He lounges on the top branch like a lion and gazes out over the world. I can barely get him to come inside at night."

"I'm so glad." When the cat addition was built, a screened porch was added to each room for vacationing kitties. They were outfitted with chairs for humans and floor-to-ceiling trees for cats to climb. We also hung bird-feeders in a clearing outside to keep the cats entertained.

"Now you ladies are coming to the gala, aren't you?" Joanne asked. "I have some extra tickets for VIPs." She handed two to Zelda and four to me. "Please make sure your grandmother attends. It's so important for locals to know she's supporting our efforts. Now I must get back to the ballroom. Things just don't get done when I'm not there." She walked toward the door, her head and clipboard held high.

When the automatic doors had closed behind Joanne, Zelda asked, "Why does she make me feel like I dribbled coffee on my blouse and my lipstick has wandered to the left?"

"It's not just you," I assured her. "I guess it's because she always looks so flawless."

"She does seem to have everything under control and perfectly in place all the time. I couldn't do that no matter how hard I tried." Zelda ran her hands through her hair and brushed cat fur off her sleeve.

I looked down at my own sleeveless button-down shirt and jean skirt. It wouldn't hurt me to step it up a bit. At least I hadn't spilled any coffee on myself. Not today, anyway.

Zelda answered the inn phone when it rang and quickly passed it to me. "It's Diane from Golden Paws."

Golden Paws was the highest-end shop in town. If you were after an expensive gift, like jewelry or a sterling trinket, that's where you would find it. "Hi, Diane."

I knew there was trouble right away. She spoke in a hushed voice. "One of the WAG Ladies came in earlier to pick up a gift for Rose. But when she paid for it, her credit card was declined. I put it through a second time, but it still didn't work. She tried two other cards, but they wouldn't go through, either. She came back with cash, though I have no idea where that came from. I wouldn't have called except for the fact that she's a WAG Lady and most of them are loaded. You might want to tell Liesel. Merchants need to be cautious."

I thanked her and hung up the phone. That was curious. Of course, sometimes something went awry with a credit card, but not usually with three of them. Oma worked at the desk in our office. I closed the door behind me so no one would overhear, and I told her about the phone call from Diane.

She lifted her eyebrows. "It would be highly improper to alert merchants. Now that she knows there is a problem, I do not expect her to try again. Her room here is gratis, of course. We are donating the use of the rooms. We will keep this between ourselves, for now. Yes?"

I readily agreed. Still, it was strange that several credit cards would go bad at the same time. But Oma was wise. Whatever the problem, Joanne would probably take care of it. We didn't need to go spreading rumors about her.

Mr. Huckle arrived to babysit the inn at exactly six thirty. We had a relatively well-behaved and amicable group in-house, so I didn't expect problems to arise. Not to mention that most of them would be out to dinner for the bulk of the time he was there.

I hurried up the back stairs from the reception lobby to get dressed. Addi sat on the top step.

"Are you okay? Is there something I can do for you?" I asked.

In a very soft voice, she said, "No. I'm good. I'm just . . . waiting for someone. See you at the dinner!"

Trixie and I rushed along the hallway and took the grand staircase up to our third-floor apartment.

I slid into a sleeveless turquoise dress with a full skirt that fell below my knees. Casual but sufficiently citified for the guests. Trixie and Twinkletoes wore round floral bows on their collars in a matching turquoise. We picked up Oma and Gingersnap at the registration entrance. Oma wore a long skirt with a cream top and a light green jacket that had creamy hydrangeas imprinted on the fabric. Gingersnap, the golden retriever, wore a lion's mane. Her photo in which she was dressed as the cowardly lion from *The Wizard of Oz* had been all over the promotional material for the There's No Place Like Home Gala. She swished her beautiful tail and pranced through the registration lobby as if she knew she was wearing something special. I pulled a golf cart around, and we all piled in for the ride to the party.

The WAG Ladies arrived when we did, all dressed impeccably, except for Brenda, who wore ill-fitting pedal pushers with a vintage sleeveless shirt that was too large for her. It didn't matter, of course. In an odd way, it made me like her even more. It took guts to be yourself, especially when you hung out with polished friends who all looked like they came straight from a spa.

They admired the rose arbor at the entrance to Rose's property. Loki dashed through the yard, sniffing every corner. Brenda, the avid gardener, took special interest in the roses, examining them from root to bloom.

We walked around the corner of the house into Rose's backyard. An English cottage garden surrounded a perfect green lawn, where she had set a beautifully rustic farmhouse table for us. Beyond the lawn was a dense grove of trees, mostly evergreens. We helped ourselves to a choice of iced lemonade, iced tea, or salty dog cocktails and goodies from a cheese board that overflowed with cheeses, crudités, grapes, crackers, nuts, and sliced salami.

Rose was like a second grandmother to me. She was

well loved in the community and usually the first one to lend a hand in time of need. Her eyes sparkled with joy.

Holmes had inherited those eyes. I gazed around for him, but quickly realized the dinner was for ladies only.

The scents from Rose's grill were heavenly. I helped her serve the pups and kitties first so they wouldn't beg while we ate. Rose had prepared a pasta, beef, and zucchini dinner for the dogs and catfish for the cats.

As soon as they were finished, I helped Rose serve grilled summer corn, prawns, and a juicy beef tenderloin to her two-legged guests. We all sat down to eat, and for just a few minutes, everything was quiet, save for the sound of utensils clanking. We passed around bread and pasta salad made with avocados, and the WAG Ladies shared stories of remarkable adoptions that they'd thought might never happen.

Thankfully, the dogs lounged after their dinner. There were a few hisses from the cats, but it appeared to me that Inky and Hershey were so thrilled to be at a party that they soon forgot about the dogs and roamed the gorgeous lawn peacefully.

The sun was beginning to set, and charming lights above the table turned on. I was clearing the dishes for dessert when I noticed Trixie's nose twitching.

In moments, we smelled someone else's dinner cooking.

"Salmon," declared Oriana.

Brenda shook her head. "That's oak wood burning."

"Can you cook with oak?" asked Addi.

"That smells more like mesquite to me," said Rose.

But the black plume that rose against the deepening blue twilight sky suggested otherwise. Trying not to worry anyone, I slipped away to the front of the house. Trixie and some of her dog friends followed me. We weren't the only ones who had noticed the smell. Along the street people were coming out of their houses to check it out.

The smoke appeared to be coming from a house five doors down. I ran toward it. Trixie, Twinkletoes, Gingersnap, and the WAG Ladies' dogs and cats raced ahead of me, much faster than I could possibly run. Fortunately, the light of the moon shone nicely on Wagtail, and the sooty smoke was readily apparent as it twisted upward. I had no trouble locating it.

A crowd had clustered in front of a white cottage. No doubt about it, there was a fire. I called 911 just in case no one else had bothered and was told a fire truck had already been dispatched.

Behind me I could hear people speculating.

"A grill fire? It's easy for them to spark up when there's too much grease."

"When's the last time you gave our grills a good scrubbing, honey?" asked a woman.

"Can't be a grill fire, there's too much smoke. Must be the kitchen. Dovie isn't that young anymore, you know. I wonder if this is the end for her living alone."

Dovie? Was this her cottage?

The wail of the fire truck screamed close by. Parked golf carts lined the road. I assumed our local firefighters had arrived in them.

The WAG Ladies crowded around me, watching in horror. Oma and Rose walked more slowly and lagged behind.

People had come out of their homes in all imaginable attire. They watched from the street and from their porches. Some were wrapped in robes and holding blankets over their pajamas.

Holmes Richardson, Rose's grandson and my childhood crush and current flame, grabbed my arms. A volunteer firefighter, he was dressed in his flame-resistant gear like other locals who rushed around. "Stay back, Holly."

"Is the house on fire?" I asked. I could hear a woman screaming and wailing.

"So far it's just a shed behind Dovie's house. Stay out here. There's nothing you can do."

I remained on the sidewalk and watched him charge toward the fire. He wasn't gone long. He kindly walked a blond woman toward me. I recognized her from seeing her around town, but I had never met her.

Holmes thrust her at me with a curt "Take care of Dovie" and loped back to the fire.

So this was Dovie Dickerson, Judge Barlow's housekeeper. I didn't know what to make of her. Under the streetlight, I could see that Dovie's face was thickly made up with powder and she had used a very heavy hand on her eye makeup, complete with false eyelashes that extended nearly to her eyebrows. Her hair was the orangey yellow color of hair dye.

Maybe I was simply used to my Oma, who thought pinching her cheeks and adding a dash of lipstick was adequate. I knew other women, though, who slept in makeup. Many of them grew up in the South, where a proper lady never left her house without full hair and makeup. I suspected Dovie might fall into that category. But she reminded me of movie stars who had aged and tried so hard to look as beautiful as they once had that the result was somewhat comedic and heartbreaking.

"I don't think we've ever met, but I've seen you around town. I'm Holly Miller."

To my surprise, Dovie inhaled deeply and examined me with cold eyes as though I was a foe.

"Yes," she said. "I've heard of you and your little dog."

Good heavens. She made it sound like Trixie and I were Toto and Dorothy, and she was the Wicked Witch of the West. I forced myself to overlook that. After all, she was stressed because of the fire.

"Are you okay?" I asked gently.

She looked frightened. "My house. Do you think it will spread to my house?"

Poor Dovie. I wanted to be honest, but it wouldn't be fair to mislead her. "Let's hope not. What happened?"

"I don't really know. I had dozed off watching TV. I woke up and thought I heard someone in the back of my house. When I went out to my screened porch in the back, my little shed was on fire."

"Shed?" I repeated. Holmes had said that, too. My heart beat harder. "Like where you keep gasoline for your lawnmower?"

She stared at me, her eyes wide. "It could explode."

Holmes was back there! And Dave. And probably half the men in town. I gazed up and down the street in panic. Every one of Rose's dinner guests had come to watch, wisely staying well away under a streetlight, but I didn't see Holmes or Dave.

"It's old," said Dovie. "I haven't mowed in years. Young Bradley from next door mows for me for some pocket money, but he uses his own lawnmower. Doesn't gasoline evaporate or go bad or something?"

My dad had cautioned me against using old gasoline, but I wasn't sure why. It was probably still very flammable!

Sirens drew our attention. Additional firetrucks arrived, most likely from Snowball, the next mountain over.

"Stay here," I said to Dovie, and ran toward the driver of the nearest fire truck. "There's an old can of gas in there."

"You sure?"

"That's what the owner tells me."

He took off at a trot, and I hurried back to Dovie.

With my arm around her, I gently coaxed her along the sidewalk, away from her house and toward Rose's. But where were Trixie and Twinkletoes? I gazed up and down the street. Dogs and cats roamed, including Loki, but I didn't see my two. Surely it was too hot and noisy where the firemen were. They wouldn't be back there, I reasoned.

And then it happened. A blast reverberated behind us.

Seven

❉ ❉ ❉ ❉ ❉

I turned around and watched a shower of glowing embers fall to the ground. A cheer went up among the firefighters, which confused me. Was it a good thing for the shed to explode? I was terrified. All I wanted was to find Holmes, Trixie, Twinkletoes, and Dave. I needed to know they were all right.

But Dovie clasped my arm with a vise grip. Her eye makeup oozed down her face in black tears, leaving behind sooty trails.

I gazed around for help with Dovie. People had backed away from the falling cinders. I didn't see Oma, Rose, or the WAG Ladies in the immediate vicinity.

"You should probably sit down," I said. "Do you recognize anyone? A neighbor perhaps?"

"Is my house on fire now?"

"I can't tell for sure, but from here it looks like it's okay."

She weighed heavily on my arm, and I realized that her knees were buckling and she had begun to sink to the sidewalk. I gazed around and spied my aunt Birdie. She would undoubtedly fuss at me for yelling at her, but I had no choice. I couldn't drag Dovie over to her.

"Aunt Birdie," I yelled.

She pretended not to hear, but I knew she had. Biting back the temptation to shout something mean at her, I yelled, "Aunt Birdie! I could use a hand here!"

No fewer than six people hurried over to us. One brought a folding lawn chair so Dovie could sit properly. Another brought Dovie a glass of something that smelled suspiciously like bourbon. Dovie didn't mind. She gulped it like she hadn't seen liquid in a week.

Once Dovie was surrounded by friends and neighbors, Aunt Birdie deigned to stroll over. "Did you need me, dear?"

She was so aggravating. Still, I had to admit that Birdie, who was probably close to Dovie and Oma age-wise, was the most strikingly dressed woman on the street. She wore white silk pajamas with a Nehru collar and fine embroidery. The top looked like a well-tailored daywear jacket that she could easily have worn to lunch with friends. If she had any.

I forced a smile. "Everyone has been so kind to help Dovie."

"It certainly appears that Dovie needs some help. Maybe it's time for her to look at Green Meadows."

Dovie wasn't completely out of it. She snapped back, "You have some nerve, you old crone. Nothing like kicking a woman when her shed is on fire."

"Good riddance to it. It was nothing but an eyesore and needed to be torn down anyway."

I couldn't believe Aunt Birdie. There was a huge fire in Dovie's backyard, and this was how Birdie treated her? I turned to the woman who had brought the bourbon. "Could you keep an eye on Dovie?"

She shot a disgruntled look at Aunt Birdie. "Of course,

Holly. Unlike other people, I am pleased to help in time of need."

I spied Oma and Rose standing with some of the WAG Ladies. Rose shouted to me, "Have you seen Holmes?"

"Not since the blast."

I shot off toward Dovie's house at a trot, desperately scanning for Twinkletoes and Trixie. I peered at groups of dogs and cats that played along the street, not troubled by the fire. But neither Trixie nor Twinkletoes was part of the fun.

A group of firefighters clustered near one of the trucks. I was relieved to make out one of the grimy faces as Dave's. He smiled when he saw me.

"Are you okay?" I asked.

"I'm fine. It was a crazy little fire. Good thing they warned us to get out before the explosion."

"Little fire?"

"All things considered, it could have been far worse."

"Did it damage the house?"

"Naw. Could have killed someone who was standing close by when that gas can exploded, but we all got out in time."

"Even Holmes? Where is he?"

He clapped my back. "Especially Holmes. Now that he's back in Wagtail, we're not letting him get hurt. I don't know where he is this minute, but he's fine."

I knew that his friends were as glad to have him back as I was. They would look out for him. "Did you see Trixie or Twinkletoes back there?"

He stared at me in shock. "They're not stupid. They wouldn't have wanted to be close to all that heat and chaos. They must be around somewhere."

I knew what he said was true. Animals would run from flames. It was instinctive. But why couldn't I find them? Had they gone home looking for me?

When I returned to Dovie, her neighbors had circled around her discussing whether she should sleep in her cottage that night. Aunt Birdie had disappeared. I assumed she had gone home since various neighbors were offering their guest rooms for the night and Aunt Birdie certainly wouldn't have gone out of her way to accommodate someone else. It wasn't in her.

Fagan stood by Brenda, Rose, and Addi. I looked at him more closely. What was that around his mouth? I walked closer. Something white clung to his whiskers and fur.

"Brenda? What did Fagan get into?" I hoped it wasn't anything dangerous.

She picked him up and moved under a streetlight. "It's sticky. Really sticky like glue or something. Oh no! Where's the closest vet? I'd better have his stomach pumped! Fagan! What did you do? Stop that. He's licking his whiskers! How do I stop him?"

Rose walked over and bent close to look at Fagan. She touched the white substance on his fur and when she pulled her fingers away, we saw streaks of red on the white goop.

Brenda screamed, "He's bleeding!"

Rose calmly said, "Now wait just a minute. She plucked more of it off his fur. "I believe this little stinker got into my Very Berry Meringue Pie."

"Are you sure?" asked Brenda. She gazed at Rose's fingers. "Is that a raspberry?"

"That's what it looks like to me. The sugar isn't good for him, but at least it's not poison," Rose said in obvious relief.

Brenda set him on the ground. "Come on, Fagan. Let's go wash your face."

"Oh dear!" said Rose. "It's all over your shirt. I'm sure the meringue will wash out, but the berries might stain the fabric."

Brenda wiped at her shirt, which only succeeded in

making it worse. "I'll see what happens if I wet it." She and Fagan walked back toward Rose's house.

I didn't see Garbo or the cats. Maybe that was a good sign. Maybe they had sensibly fled from the flames and were playing somewhere with Trixie and Twinkletoes.

I spotted Holmes helping someone with a fire hose. Even from a distance I could see that his face was covered with soot. In spite of Dave's assurances, I was relieved to see him with my own eyes. I stood quietly and scanned the neighborhood.

Still troubled, I pulled out my phone and dialed Mr. Huckle at the inn. "It's Holly. I guess you heard about the fire. Looks like it's mostly out. Have you seen Twinkletoes or Trixie?"

I could hear him opening the front door. "I'm afraid I have not seen them, Miss Holly. They're not on the front porch waiting to get in."

"Would you please call me if they come home? I'm worried about them." I thanked him and hung up. Walking away from the fire, I traced our steps back to Rose's house. With fewer people and less commotion, I could hear a dog barking not too far away.

As overjoyed as I should have been to hear Trixie's bark, my heart sank. I knew that sound all too well. Trixie had many barks. Happy, frisky, playful, and the one I hated to hear. It was mournful, yet frantic, like she was calling for help or sending a message. It was the bark that meant someone had been murdered.

Eight

❁ ❁ ❁ ❁

I followed the sound of Trixie's bark. Activity on the street diminished as I walked. The streetlights and a few porch lights, along with the moon, were enough to show me the way. I paused once in a while to listen for Trixie's barks to be sure I was heading in the correct direction. Brenda and Fagan passed me on the other side of the street, returning to the scene of the fire. In seconds, I was back at Rose's house.

I walked through the arbor and around to the side of the yard. Someone had turned out the party lights that had glowed in strands above the dining table. Just before a cloud washed across the moon, I spotted Twinkletoes and Trixie at the edge of the garden—with a wolf.

We didn't have wolves in Wagtail, I reasoned. But that didn't stop my heart from pounding. The creature I had seen could devour them. It was far too big to be a coyote.

I stopped in my tracks, paralyzed with fear. For them as much as for me. "Trixie! Twinkletoes!" I called softly.

The cloud moved on, and I was able to see them better among the bushes and trees that lined the backyard, providing privacy from the house that backed up to Rose's. The wolf sat up and looked toward me. He didn't seem particularly interested in Trixie or Twinkletoes. But when Trixie began to bark again, he joined in, and Loki romped toward them.

My hands shook as I turned on the light on my phone and aimed it at the wolf. He was too far away for me to get a good look. I called Dave. He had to be worn out after fighting the fire, but he was our only police officer. If I called 911, they would patch me through to him or have him call me back. "I know you have your hands full, but I think there's a wolf behind Rose's house."

I heard him sigh.

"Why are *you* behind her house?"

"She was having a dinner party for the WAG Ladies. Everyone left to watch the fire. Trixie led me here."

"I hear Trixie barking. Is there a corpse?"

"If there is, I haven't seen it yet. I thought it prudent to call you so someone would know about it when I'm attacked by the wolf. And it might be a good idea to stop the WAG Ladies, Oma, and Rose from coming back for the moment."

"Be there as soon as I can." The line went dead.

I could still make out Trixie and Twinkletoes sniffing something in the dark. Either the wolf was gone or his fur had merged with the colors of night. I edged closer very slowly. Did Rose lock her doors before she left? I hoped she had left them open so I could seek refuge there now if necessary. Could I reach the back door before the wolf could get to me? Probably not. Didn't they say not to run from wild animals because they think you're prey if you run?

I asked Siri to turn on the light on my phone, but I was still too far away to see if the wolf had left. I glanced around for a weapon. I realized there was no weapon besides possibly a gun that would help me fend off a wolf, but I felt better

anyway when I picked up a folding chair. It wouldn't incapacitate a wolf, but it might deter it some. Maybe.

I continued toward Trixie and Twinkletoes. If it was really
a wolf, wouldn't it have attacked them already? As far as I
could tell, neither of them appeared to be afraid of him. It
seemed to me that they would have run away from him by now.

I could hear female voices behind me. I didn't dare take
my eyes off the wolf. I yelled, "Stay back! Better yet, go
inside the house." Sucking in a deep breath, I aimed the
light on my phone at the faint white cloud of Trixie's fur.
Just to her left, I could see the wolf.

He looked straight at me, and I felt a complete fool. It
was Fritz, the missing German shepherd. No question
about it. But with his long fur, he sure looked like a wolf in
the dark.

Feeling much relieved, I walked toward the bushes. Fritz
wagged his tail like he was happy to see me. But at his feet
lay a human body.

Fritz appeared to be guarding the person, who was
curled in a fetal position. Trixie was busy sniffing his shoes,
and Twinkletoes was pawing at his abdomen. "Hello?" I
called. There was no response. I wanted to check on the
person. Maybe he or she was still alive. But I wasn't sure
how Fritz would react.

In a soft, high voice I said, "Well, Fritz, do you know that
everyone has been searching for you? Where have you been?"

I offered my hand to Fritz to sniff. He wagged his tail
and leaned against me, almost as though he was glad I had
arrived. I took it as a sign of approval. Maybe he could smell
my scent on Trixie and Twinkletoes and had deduced that I
was okay. I stroked his large head while peering at the body.

I aimed my phone light at the lifeless person on the
ground. Dark hair fell over his forehead. He had a mustache
and needed a shave. It was Seth.

Twinkletoes mewed and pawed at his stomach.

I squatted next to Fritz. In a sweet tone, so I wouldn't alarm Fritz, I called, "Seth! Seth!"

Moving slowly, I held my hand out toward Seth. It didn't appear to disturb Fritz in the least. I moved closer to Seth and stretched my fingers to reach his neck. I couldn't feel a pulse, but his skin wasn't cold.

"Holly?" Holmes's voice cut through the quiet night.

"Back here." I replied, noting that Fritz showed no agitation whatsoever.

A strong light beamed at us. "Is that Fritz?" It was Dave's voice.

"Yes. He looked like a wolf in the dark. I found the corpse, Dave. It's Seth. Fritz hasn't left his side, but he seems okay with me here."

I watched as Dave and Holmes moved toward us slowly.

"I don't know if he found Seth or if Seth found him. Rose has overhead lights, maybe even spotlights. It would help if they were turned on. Have all the ambulances left?" I was having so many thoughts at once I felt like I was blabbering incoherently, jumping from one subject to the next.

Suddenly the lights turned on. We were still far enough back in the yard to be in semidarkness, but I could see Seth clearly enough. Dave must have been on the phone because I heard him asking for an ambulance to return.

Dave walked over to Fritz and calmly said, "We're glad to see you back in Wagtail, champ." He gently stroked Fritz's back, which made his tail swish back and forth.

"He seems okay," he murmured, moving toward Seth.

Holmes scratched behind Fritz's ears.

Dave knelt next to me and checked for a pulse, much as I had.

"He's still kind of warm. Is he alive?" I asked.

Dave aimed his flashlight at Seth's head and scanned it along his body. "No pulse. No sign of injury. No blood."

But then something moved. I screamed and jumped to my feet. "Something is under him," I breathed.

Dave stood up and aimed the light at Seth's abdomen. Twinkletoes, who clearly thought she was superior to Dave, gently tapped her paw on the spot that had twitched.

"It could be a snake," Holmes cautioned. My heart pounding, I hustled around Seth's body, bent, and quickly swept Twinkletoes into my arms.

She yowled in protest and squirmed, but I held her tight. "Not a chance, little one. I'm not having some snake bite you."

Dave cautiously walked around Seth's body.

"See anything?" I asked.

He shone his strong light at the area in question. "It's moving, but—" he squatted and his tone changed "—it's a kitten!" Dave scooped up a tiny kitten that couldn't have been more than a couple of weeks old.

Fritz immediately sniffed the kitten and wagged his tail.

I set Twinkletoes on the ground. "I'm confused. Do you think Seth found the kitten and then died?"

"Possibly. Shove over. I'm going to start CPR."

At that moment, an ambulance pulled up. I couldn't see the vehicle, but flashing lights strobed in the night on the other side of the house. In less than a minute, three emergency medical technicians calmly walked past Rose and her guests to join us and assess the situation.

But their presence alarmed Fritz. He took one look, turned, and ran through the bushes.

"Oh no. Not again," I groaned. "Why didn't I bring a leash?"

Twinkletoes inspected the kitten and began to groom it like it belonged to her.

"I thought he would stay," I said to no one in particular. They were more concerned about Seth, which was fully understandable. "I'll go after him."

I found I was trembling when I stumbled through the

grass to Rose and Oma. "Do you have a rope or an old leash in case I can catch Fritz?"

"What happened?" asked Oma. "Who is that?"

Oh no. I didn't want to be the one to break the bad news. But I didn't have much choice. I had to tell them. "It's Seth."

"Is he hurt?" Oriana pressed a hand just below her throat. Her chest heaved with each breath. "Was he at the fire?"

"They're trying to revive him. He's not responsive."

Addi wilted, but I caught her. She clung to me, whispering, "It can't be."

Brenda and Joanne appeared stoic, but they exchanged a look, and I suspected that Seth had not been a stranger to them.

Louisa and Oriana appeared to be in shock.

"How?" asked Oriana.

"What happened?" blurted Louisa.

Addi bit her lower lip and tears ran down her face.

If I had been a cop, I would have made note of the guilty look on Louisa's face.

"We don't really know. He was—" Someone nudged me from behind. I turned to see Dave and guessed that he had seen their reactions and didn't want me to divulge much information. Not that I had much to share. "—just lying there when I found him. This is Sergeant Dave Quinlan."

"Did any of you ladies know Seth?" he asked.

The awkward silence that followed went on much too long. Joanne was the one who finally spoke on their behalf. "Just to be clear, Sergeant, we all knew Seth. But we didn't know him well. Obviously, since we were involved in rescuing animals and he was in the business of finding lost animals, our paths were bound to cross occasionally."

"Dave?" asked Addi, letting go of me. "Dave Quinlan? It's Addi." She placed her hand on her chest. "Addi Lieras, don't you remember? Gosh, I haven't seen you since we were probably twelve years old."

Dave grinned. "No kidding. I heard you were here visiting the judge."

I stepped to the side to make room for Dave. He might have been speaking to Addi, but I could see how carefully he was observing all of them.

"Maybe we can find some time to catch up, Addi. I hope you might be able to tell us where to find his family or next of kin."

Brenda mashed her lips together. Joanne was finally at a loss for words. Oriana was, for the first time since I had met her, losing her composure. She looked positively ill and nervously twisted her diamond-encrusted wedding band.

Brenda spoke up. "The last I knew, his parents lived in Cary. Larry and Barbara, I think. I don't have an address or a number for them, though they used to live on Mourning Dove Lane. He was a friend of my brother's when we were growing up."

"Thank you very much. Did any of the rest of you ladies know him?" asked Dave.

Oriana said softly, "He worked for our company while he started his pet detective agency. Do you think he'll be all right?"

"What company is that?"

"My husband and I own Treats and Toys, the pet supply company."

"Rose," I whispered. "A rope for Fritz?"

Rose fetched a rope from her house and handed it to me. "It's better than nothing, I guess."

I had wasted precious time, and the search for Fritz would now probably be for naught. Nevertheless, I had to try to find him. I fervently hoped that snakes slept at night. I left Dave with the WAG Ladies and stepped around the area where Seth lay to go in the direction Fritz had taken. I overheard an EMT say, "Doc will probably call it."

So Seth was definitely dead. It couldn't have happened long before I found him. I staggered back a little bit in shock. I'd hoped they could bring him around. He'd been loping along in Wagtail only hours earlier, not showing any sign of illness or even fatigue.

I struggled to shift my focus. "Fritz! Fritz, come!" I called him in a tone that I hoped would sound encouraging to him.

I asked Siri to turn on the light on my phone again, wondering how long it would last. And then I heard what I thought was Fritz barking and turned in that direction. I waited for more sounds from him. Unfortunately, dogs all over Wagtail were barking.

The moonlight illuminated Trixie's white fur up ahead. I squeezed through bushes and past trees in spite of sharp twigs grabbing at me.

Trixie suddenly zoomed around me.

"Slow down!" I hurried after her, hoping she knew where Fritz was and that I wouldn't trip over something in my haste. She was leading me through dense trees that ran behind backyards. My sandals weren't the best thing to wear in the woods. I panted and did my best to catch up, but the truth was that I was slowing with each step.

I came to an abrupt stop at the road that marked the western boundary of Wagtail. The local church and graveyard weren't too far down the road. But across from me was nothing but dark woods. Only then did it occur to me that Seth might have been in that exact location earlier in the evening. Had he ventured into those woods in pursuit of Fritz?

Trixie barked, and I caught a flash of her white fur. I crossed the silent street and entered the forest, moving much more slowly. I found Trixie standing next to Fritz. He sat like he had by Seth while Trixie was busy sniffing and wagging her tail like a little flag. I fervently hoped it wasn't another dead person.

Nine

❀ ❀ ❀ ❀

I slowed to a creep as I approached them. The last thing I wanted to do was fall over a body. I kept my flashlight trained on the forest floor. And then I saw what Fritz was protecting—a mama cat and her kitten nestled in a hollowed-out tree that had fallen. The other kitten must have come from this litter.

The mom cat looked up at me like she was exhausted. I didn't have anything to carry them in, so I turned up the front hem of my dress, thankful that it was full and loose instead of tight-fitting, and gently lifted the mom into the little pouch I had formed. She was limp, clearly not well. I added her baby and poked around to be sure I hadn't over-looked any kittens.

Praying that I wouldn't trip and spill my precious cargo, I pulled the rope through a ring on Fritz's collar and started back. Fritz and Trixie led the way. But this time they didn't try to dart into the trees that ran behind the houses.

I continued on the street that was now almost empty, and

only then, under the bright light of a streetlamp, did I realize that Fritz bore a lipstick mark on the top of his head. Someone had kissed him. Someone who wore a rosy red shade of lipstick.

I was enormously relieved to reach Rose's house. The crowd of onlookers had moved there, but I wedged my way to the backyard and found Oma and Rose, who sat at the table where we had dined.

"I thought Fritz was guarding Seth, but now I think he was taking care of these babies. The mom doesn't look well."

Holmes peered into my makeshift kitty hammock. "The crime scene workers are almost through. I could drive you to the animal hospital."

It was a very kind offer, especially since he had been fighting the fire and probably wanted nothing more than to go home and shower.

Holmes and I watched as the EMTs lifted Seth's body onto a gurney and rolled it to the ambulance. Dave shooed neighbors out of Rose's yard and roped off the entire area with crime scene tape.

"I'm off to Doc Engelknecht's," Dave said to Holmes and me. "The EMT said it looked like a heart attack. Probably very sudden and quick."

"But he was young and in pretty good shape," I said.

"Apparently it's not uncommon to find undiagnosed heart issues, even in athletes," Dave said glumly.

He lowered his voice and said, "Liesel says he was staying at the inn. Make sure no one cleans or touches that room."

I gazed at him quizzically.

"Just in case," said Dave. "Trixie hasn't been wrong yet."

At the sound of her name, she placed her front paws on Dave's knee and wagged her tail.

He rubbed her ears. "You are too smart, kiddo. But if

you're right, and I'm beginning to think you may be, I'll buy you a steak dinner."

She pawed at his knees and wiggled her rear.

"You think Seth was murdered?" asked Holmes.

"I don't know." Dave shook his head. "I didn't see any obvious injuries. Then again, it's not the best light out here, so it's likely I missed something. Liesel said Rose can stay with her tonight. She's inside packing an overnight bag. I'll be back at the crack of dawn to see if we can find anything in the grass."

Oma drove Rose and Gingersnap back to the inn, and Holmes took the kittens, Trixie, Twinkletoes, Fritz, and me to the veterinary hospital.

People were waiting for us outside when we arrived. "Must be a slow night," I said.

"Rose called to let us know you were coming." The veterinarian and two veterinary assistants escorted us inside. As a veterinary technician lifted each kitten out of my skirt, Trixie, Fritz, and Twinkletoes were eager to see them, sniffing each one.

An assistant wrinkled her nose and gazed at Holmes's grimy face. "Were the kittens in the fire?"

We assured her they were in the woods.

When they took the mother cat out of my skirt, the veterinarian frowned. "Poor baby," she cooed. "She doesn't look good, but don't worry, we'll take care of this little family."

I believed her. In spite of the late hour, people swarmed toward the kittens and fussed over them while the veterinarian cuddled the mom and disappeared into the back.

Twinkletoes was reluctant to leave her new friends. I had to pry her away from the babies and carry her out to the golf cart.

"Your turn, Fritz," I said. I was never sure whether I should wake someone to bring home a dog or cat who had been missing. But I would have wanted to know Trixie or

Twinkletoes had been found healthy and fine as soon as possible.

Fritz readily jumped into the golf cart, and we drove through the silent streets of Wagtail to Judge Barlow's house. Not a single light was on. Not even the light by the front door.

I took the rope off Fritz. He readily jumped out and ran through the open gate. Fritz didn't go to the front door, though. He dodged to the left, and I wished I had kept a leash on him. Maybe he would come when the judge opened the door.

I banged the knocker and waited. Lights turned on inside the house.

Judge Barlow opened the door wrapped in a plush gray bathrobe. He seemed surprised to see us, but before Holmes or I had a chance to say anything, Fritz woofed joyously.

"Fritz!" cried the judge. "Come here, boy. Come on!"

Fritz ran to the judge, and I sighed with relief.

Judge Barlow bent over and stroked his beloved dog. "Where did you find him?"

"In Rose's backyard."

"He was that close to home? Fritz, you scamp. What were you doing there?"

Fritz wasn't telling. But his tail gave away his joy at being home again. And then he ran back to where he had been, on the left side of the house.

"What's he doing?" asked the judge.

Trixie and Twinkletoes followed him and were most interested in something.

Holmes and I exchanged a look. Now what?

"Do you have any spotlights you could turn on?" I asked.

The judge took one step back and flipped a switch. The exterior of the house flooded with light. He looked on as Holmes and I approached Fritz.

"Whatcha got there, Fritz?" I asked.

And then we heard the cries. The tiny mews of kittens. He had cleverly stashed two kittens in a nook under the porch. Holmes knelt and handed one kitten to me, and then another.

"Have you got your phone?" asked Holmes. "I don't want to overlook one."

I asked Siri to turn on the flashlight and handed it to Holmes. "All clear. I don't see any more."

"Back to the vet, I guess." I returned to the judge.

"Kittens? Aren't you a smart boy, Fritz?" He bent to pat him. "Thank you for bringing him home, Holly. I was afraid he'd been hurt." He stared at Holmes. "What happened to you?"

"There was a fire at Dovie's. The shed in the back was burning."

Happiness drained from the judge's face. "Is she all right?"

Holmes nodded. "A little shaken, as you might imagine, but she'll be fine. We're all very lucky it didn't spread to the house."

"Thanks to Holmes and the other Wagtail firefighters who rushed in to put it out," I added.

The judge placed a trembling hand over his mouth and looked me in the eyes. "How did it start?"

"We don't know yet," said Holmes.

I wondered if we should tell him about Seth. I didn't see the point in upsetting him even more at this hour, but maybe he should know. After all, it might have been Seth who'd found Fritz. I tried to start gently. "Fritz was protecting some kittens in the woods."

"What? More kittens?" The judge ruffled the fur behind his ears.

"He must have carried one over to Rose's house. We're not quite sure what happened, but these two look an awful lot like the other ones. I think he was bringing them home to you. Judge Barlow," I said gently. "Fritz was with Seth."

The judge's eyebrows rose. He gazed around. "Where is he? Why didn't *he* bring Fritz home?"

"I'm so sorry to have to tell you this, but Seth is dead."

"What?"

"He was found lying on the ground behind Rose's house. Fritz was sitting next to him. We'll know more after the autopsy. Dave thinks he may have had some kind of heart condition."

The judge looked down at Fritz. He swallowed hard and turned a worried gaze on me. "I'm shocked. He was a young man. In his early forties, I believe. He had no business dying yet." He ruffled the fur behind Fritz's ears before looking up at us. "Is Rose okay?"

"I think so. You know what a trooper she is," Holmes said.

"I've missed you, Fritz. Thank you for bringing him home, Holly."

"I was glad to do it. No more running off now, Fritz." His tail swished against the floor. I turned to leave and heard the judge speaking to Fritz about kittens as he closed the door.

One small issue taken care of. I was glad Fritz was home where he belonged. But there was a new and bigger problem in its place. Where had Fritz been? With the kittens? And why had he appeared in Rose's backyard with Seth? There was no leash attached to his collar. Wouldn't Seth have put some kind of harness on him to make sure he didn't run off again?

I knew perfectly well why the judge had given me that look. He thought the fire at Dovie's might have something to do with the peculiar things that were happening to him. But he didn't dare say so because Holmes was present, and he was keeping his relationship with Rose, Holmes's grandmother, a secret. And there was another mystery. Wouldn't most people be happy for them? Why did they insist on keeping their relationship secret?

Holmes drove Trixie, Twinkletoes, the newly discovered kittens, and me back to the vet. They were as astonished as Holmes and me when we explained what had happened.

It was past midnight when we returned to the inn. Holmes went home, eager to get out of his sooty clothes. In spite of the horror of Seth's death, I was exhausted and headed straight up to bed with Trixie and Twinkletoes. I changed into my nightshirt, but as tired as I was, my nerves were on edge and I couldn't sleep. Twinkletoes had curled up on my bed and didn't budge. But when I threw on the soft white Sugar Maple Inn bathrobe Oma had had embroidered with my name, Trixie followed me into the kitchen, probably hoping for a treat, which she received immediately. I made myself a mug of weak black tea with a lot of milk in it and wandered out on my back balcony. It was larger than a normal balcony, with room for chaise lounges and a small table that was well suited for breakfast. I rarely used it, though, because I preferred to eat breakfast in the dining area with Oma or Dave, who often dropped by.

The moon cast a wide swath of light on the lake where the water undulated gently. A few lights were visible on houses across the lake. I turned around and looked at the windows of the inn. All of them were dark on the east side. A good sign, I thought. The troubles of Wagtail weren't impacting the guests.

But on the west side, a light glowed behind curtains that appeared to be drawn across the French doors.

As I turned away, I remembered that I had promised to secure Seth's room. There wasn't really much I could do except put out the *Do Not Disturb* sign and make sure the door was locked. Not many guests left their doors unlocked, but it happened.

I looked back at the French doors where the light glowed

softly. Was that Seth's room? I counted windows and French doors. It was!

I tightened the sash on my bathrobe, slipped on running shoes, and grabbed my phone. On the way down to the office, I called Casey, who was probably dozing in the private kitchen. Trixie and I rushed down the grand staircase to the second floor. I heard a door close quietly somewhere. I looked up and down the hallway but couldn't tell exactly where it had been.

Casey sounded sleepy when he answered the call.

"Meet me at Hike right now. I'm stopping by the office to get the keys."

There was no sign of Casey on the main floor when I turned toward the reception lobby. I ran through the hallway. Trixie thought it was fun and sped ahead of me.

I unlocked the office as fast as I could and grabbed the master key ring. To save time, I left the office door unlocked and sprang up the back stairs to Seth's room.

Casey leaned against the wall with his eyes closed. He opened them when Trixie pawed him. "Oh . . . hey, Trixie! What are we doing?" he whispered.

"Did you see anyone come out of there?"

"No."

"How long have you been here?"

"I don't know. A few minutes? What's going on?"

I talked fast, though it didn't matter because anyone who was in the room couldn't get out now without being seen by us. "In case you haven't heard, Seth, who was staying in Hike, died a few hours ago. I couldn't sleep, so I was on my balcony, and I saw a light on in his room."

"Did he die in his room?" Casey wrinkled his nose.

"No. In Rose's backyard. At least that's where we found him."

Casey shrugged. "So he didn't turn it off before he left. My mom yells at me about that all the time."

"I thought you moved out."

"Things didn't go well with my girlfriend. She kept the apartment, and I'm back home."

I took a deep breath. He was right, of course, Seth had simply left a light on. No biggie.

I tried the handle. The door was locked. I inserted the key in the lock, twisted, and swung it open.

The room was bathed in moonlight, the curtains were open, and not a single light was on.

Ten

✿ ✿ ✿ ✿

Casey started into the room, but I held my arm out and blocked him. "Listen!" I hissed.

Trixie raised her nose and sniffed but pulled back as though she didn't like the smell.

"I don't hear anything," Casey whispered.

"He could be in the closet or the bathroom or standing behind a curtain."

"How do you know it's a guy?" he asked.

"It could be anybody. I'm going to turn on the overhead light, okay? He'll know that we're here. Play along with me."

I spoke in a loud voice. "Sergeant Quinlan said we should secure the room. Don't touch anything, but I want you to make an inventory of everything you see. Shoes, luggage, cash lying around. I don't want anyone blaming us if something has gone missing."

I flicked the light switch and the bedroom was bathed in soft light. I ventured inside very slowly, ready to bolt if need be.

While Casey checked the bathroom, I looked for shoes under the curtains. There weren't any. Casey emerged from the bathroom shaking his head. "All I see is a used towel and one of those razors that leaves a day's worth of stubble."

That sounded about right. So that left the closet and under the bed.

I pointed toward the closet and then held up my hand in a signal to stop. I needed a weapon. Something I could at least swing at an intruder if there was one. A tall brass lamp sat on the desk. I unplugged it, unscrewed the finial, whipped off the shade, and walked over to the closet door. I nodded to Casey, who swung the doors open. A lone leather jacket hung in the closet.

Casey nodded toward the bed. He casually walked over and dropped to his knees. "Well, that's it, Holly. Not a soul in here."

"The balcony."

Casey got to his feet and stiffened. Fear showed in his eyes. I handed him the lamp and strode over to the balcony. The doors were closed. The latch was locked. That was a relief. I twisted it and peered outside. "Unless it's Spider-Man, there's no one out there."

Casey set the lamp on the desk and joined me. We looked up and around, but no one was hanging on to the stone walls of the inn. Not even Trixie found any interesting scents. She trotted back into the room.

"It's only a one-story drop from here," Casey pointed out. "Guys do that on TV all the time. They land and take off running."

We went inside, and I locked the door behind us. "In the first place, they are professional stunt people, and in the second place, they make it look like it's high, but it's not, and they're usually jumping onto a mattress or something to cushion the fall."

"That's not true. There are people who could jump over a balcony, land on their feet, and keep going."

"Casey! That's ridiculous. You're too old to believe all those stunts are real. However, what is real is that I saw the curtains drawn and the lights on." I reassembled the lamp.

"Does it smell funny to you in here?" he asked. "It smells like—" he wiggled his nostrils, not unlike Trixie did "—hand sanitizer."

At that moment, I noticed room keys on the seat of the desk chair, and my blood ran cold.

Casey must have seen them about the same time. He reached for them, but I stopped him. "Fingerprints. They could have fingerprints on them."

"I doubt it. Whoever was in here wiped the place down with sanitizer."

"You're right. I bet that's exactly what happened. Someone didn't want anyone to know he or she was here. I wonder if he was looking for something."

"Or came back to retrieve something he left."

I shuddered. "Either Seth gave that person the key to his room, or his murderer took the key off of Seth and came back here to clean up or get something he didn't want anyone to find."

Casey stared at me. He swallowed hard. "Murderer?"

"Okay," I said, "we don't know that yet. It could be that he died from natural causes. But that key is suspicious."

"Maybe Seth left it in the chair. Or he couldn't find it. He was in a hurry and didn't want to bother anyone about another key, so he left. There's not a whole lot in here. The leather jacket is cool, but nothing else was worth a lot."

I smiled at him. "Very logical. But then who locked the door? Someone was in here only a few minutes ago. The light didn't turn itself off."

"Besides, how would a murderer get into the inn unnoticed?" He frowned, as if he was worried that he had let a killer enter.

"We ate dinner in Rose's backyard and didn't find Seth until the fire was under control. I think Seth had just been killed, so the murderer could have come back here then," I speculated.

"That's a relief. He didn't get by me. Mr. Huckle would have been in charge then."

I was about to spoil Casey's reprieve. "Except for one thing. If that were the case, why would he sit here for hours? No, I think there might be a different answer."

Casey blurted, "I did not let in any wild-eyed killers."

"I believe you. I don't think you did that, either. You did your job and allowed our guests to come into the inn. And you didn't see anyone leave around the time I phoned you, did you?"

Casey's face grew pale. "He's still in the building!"

"It's worse than that. Not only is that person still in the building, she's legitimately in one of our guest rooms. It's one of our guests, Casey."

Eleven

✿ ✿ ✿ ✿

I slipped the *Do Not Disturb* sign over the door handle and locked the door with the master key.

Casey scanned the hallway. "Now I'm not going to get any sleep at all."

I had to bite my tongue not to remind him that he was the night clerk and he wasn't supposed to sleep. Of course, Oma and I knew that he napped. As long as he got his work done, we didn't really mind. The reception entrance door was locked in the evening, forcing everyone to come and go from the lobby entrance, where we could keep an eye on latecomers and strangers who weren't staying at the inn. Besides, Casey was like family. He had worked for Oma before I returned to Wagtail. A couple of times we thought he would move on. He even had some great scholarship offers, but Wagtail was in his soul, like it was in Holmes's and mine. Oma and I feared that he might find a better job, or at least one that he could do in the daytime. We had

agreed we wouldn't stop him if something came along. We
wanted what was best for him.

I accompanied Casey to the main lobby. He settled at a
sofa in the Dogwood Room, which was open to the lobby
and grand staircase. He had an excellent view of anyone
arriving or leaving. Meanwhile, I let myself out the front
door. Since we were still awake, I thought Trixie might
need to go out.

Her nose to the sidewalk, she walked along to our dog
potty area. I waited for her, looking around. The night was
quiet. Stars sparkled and the moon still shone like a giant
light. Mountain nights could be chilly in the summer, but
tonight the air was gentle and summery. The scent of hon-
eysuckle wafted to me.

It was so calm and peaceful that I wondered if I had
overreacted. But if I were the person who had Seth's keys
and I didn't want anyone to know that, would I have wiped
the room down? Definitely not. If I had just stepped inside
and dropped the keys on the chair, there would have been
no need to worry about fingerprints. Of course, we were
assuming that the smell meant the room had been cleaned,
but we would know for sure tomorrow when Dave looked
for fingerprints.

We were walking back toward the inn entrance when
someone stepped out onto the front porch. The lights by the
door illuminated Louisa. Her copper hair gleamed under the
light. She glanced around quickly, as though afraid someone might be watching her. Apparently satisfied, she and
Loki hurried toward the green and into the cover of night.

I slept with the French doors open that night. When I
rose, I took a long, hot shower, and slipped on a black-and-
white summer dress that I thought was both charming and
professional. I braced myself for a busy day between the
gala and news of Seth's death hitting town. It didn't take
long for news to spread in Wagtail. Chances were good that

most of the residents were learning about it over breakfast this morning.

Trixie, Twinkletoes, and I walked down the grand staircase just as Fagan, Loki, and Garbo bounded through the front door, preceding the WAG Ladies, who chattered nonstop.

"Good morning," I said.

Addi gushed, "We are so in love with Fritz for rescuing the kittens. What an amazing story."

Louisa added, "We just took a shift bottle-feeding them."

"They are darling," Oriana added. "I'm seriously considering adopting one when they're ready!"

"How's the mama cat doing?" I asked.

Brenda bobbed her head. "She's weak, but the doctor assured us she would be fine. She'll need a home when her kittens are bigger. Seems she had developed tapeworms from fleas, which sounds horrible to me, but there's a treatment, and the vet thinks she should be okay."

"Wonderful! I was very concerned about her last night."

I spied Dave with Oma and Rose and headed for their table.

Shelley Dixon, our waitress, brought my hot tea before I even pulled out a chair. Trixie pranced at her feet. She knew who was in control of her breakfast. "Ham and eggs or a Florentine Havarti scramble?"

"I think I'll have the scrambled eggs this morning. Thanks, Shelley. Trixie might like it, too, if there's a dog version."

She smiled. "No problem. And tuna for Miss Twinkletoes." She hustled off.

Oma leaned toward me, her face grim and her voice low. "Seth did not die from a heart attack."

Dave kept his voice down, too. "The EMTs took him to Doc Engelknecht's last night. He found a spot on Seth's back that looked like a bite."

"A dog bite?" I asked. "Surely Fritz didn't harm him."

"No. It's very small, like a bug bite. A tiny puncture.

Engelknecht said it was so small he might have overlooked it except for the inflammation around it."

"Like a spider bite?" asked Rose.

"Possibly. We have two types of poisonous spiders in our area, and while a bite might look something like that, they don't usually kill anyone. Engelknecht says they'll make you sick, but according to him, one bite wouldn't normally incapacitate a person. Especially not a healthy adult."

"They are sending him to the medical examiner, yes?" asked Oma.

Dave glanced at his watch. "He should be there now. The doc said he thinks we'll have an answer soon. He asked for an expedited autopsy because of the strange nature of the arthropod bite."

"Arthropod?" asked Oma. "What is that?"

"A six-legged bug like an insect or spider. You know Doc. He likes to talk fancy. He's concerned that there's some kind of bug in the woods that might bite other people like hikers."

"I was in the woods last night when I collected the kittens." I nearly spilled my tea at the thought.

The three of them looked at me in horror. "How do you feel?" asked Rose.

A shiver ran through me. "Fine."

"Any bug bites?" asked Dave.

"I haven't noticed any, but now you're scaring me."

"If anything happens, if you feel woozy or tired or if you have an itch somewhere, I want you to call Doc immediately," said Dave.

Oma reached for my hand. "Do what Dave says, liebling. You promise?"

"I'm fine. Really, I am." I forced a smile in spite of the fact that I now had an urge to scratch the side of my neck. I picked up my tea mug and held it so I wouldn't be tempted.

Oma sipped her coffee. "I do not like this. I have lived

here for many, many years, and I do not remember anyone dying from a bug bite."

"I don't, either," added Rose. "We hike in the woods, and children have played in them for years without anything like this happening."

Shelley delivered our breakfast. As I ate, I noticed the WAG Ladies were unusually subdued at their table.

"Bee stings can kill," mused Oma. "Did it look like a bee sting?"

Dave shook his head. "Not to me."

"When we took Fritz home, we found two more kittens," I said.

Oma laughed, breaking the tension. "Your Trixie has a nose for dead bodies, and that big German shepherd sniffs out kittens."

"Do you think they're from the same litter?" asked Rose.

"We can't know for sure, but we think he may have been carrying them from the woods to his home."

"So Seth was probably tailing Fritz. A dog wouldn't think much of running through trees and brush behind people's houses," said Dave. "That may explain what Seth was doing behind your house, Rose."

"I had better get to the office," said Oma. "People will be calling and want more information when they hear about him."

"Could you wait just a moment?" I told them about seeing the light on in Seth's room. "What I can't figure out is how he locked the door."

"I'd better go up there and have a look," said Dave. "Just in case. It's possible that whatever the person wanted in Seth's room had nothing to do with his death, but it's definitely odd that someone was in there." He picked up his phone and asked for assistance with fingerprinting. "I just sent two people back to Snowball. We were up at first light combing Rose's yard."

"Can I go home?" asked Rose.

Dave gazed at her fondly. "Would you mind waiting until we get the initial autopsy findings?"

"Oh." There was no mistaking her disappointment. "If you think that's necessary. It's lovely to be here at the inn, but it puts me off my schedule. I hope I'll be able to go back and at least retrieve my gown for the gala."

"I'll make sure of it." Dave nodded.

"I do not like the sound of this. Someone had something to hide." Oma took a deep breath. "Holly, perhaps you can put out a notice to the Wagtail residents for me? That will cut down on the phone calls to find out what is going on." Oma rose from her chair. "Dave, you will phone me as soon as you know something. Yes?"

"You will be the first to know, Liesel. I promise."

As soon as Oma and Rose left, Dave said, "When you post on the Wagtail listserv, don't give any details. I don't know yet what happened or what might be important."

"I'll just say a visitor died last night. How's that?"

"Perfect."

Shelley brought refills of our tea and coffee. Sitting back, Dave sipped his and looked glum.

"Upset about Seth?" I asked.

"Informing the family is the worst part of my job. I hate it. There's no kind way to say that someone's loved one has died. You just have to come right out and tell them. And it's the worst over the phone. I can't see their reactions. They can't see my face. I'm just a stranger calling them with the worst news they've ever gotten."

"I don't envy you that job." I glanced toward the WAG Ladies. They were still there, enjoying their brunch. "The WAG Ladies all knew Seth. Do you suppose one of them was in his room last night?"

Dave observed them. "They're not being very cooperative. I questioned them last night while you were searching for kittens. To hear them tell it, they were tethered together the whole evening. Not apart for a moment." He shrugged. "Wouldn't hurt to say hi."

I knew perfectly well that he wasn't being polite. He wanted to see how they were acting. The two of us rose and strolled over to the table where the WAG Ladies sat.

When we approached, a stillness fell over them, and it was as though a jolt of electricity ran through the women seated at the table.

Louisa stiffened, her eyes meeting Oriana's. Brenda and Joanne made a point of looking down at their plates and moving crumbs around. Addi gazed at me apprehensively and rolled her lips inward like a child who had been caught misbehaving.

"Morning, ladies," said Dave, ever so politely. "Apparently someone was in Seth's room last night."

He stopped right there. I would have blurted out more, but when I glanced at him, I realized that he was letting them stew a little.

But they didn't respond. They were quiet as mice hiding from a cat. I couldn't help wondering if one of them would break under the pressure. Didn't they realize their silence was making them look bad? After all, at this point, they didn't have any reason to think Seth had been murdered. Or did they?

It was Brenda who finally looked up at Dave and asked, "Surely you don't think it was one of us who entered his room?"

"Was it?" Dave spoke softly, not in the least bit intimidating, although I suspected that his position as the investigating officer probably accomplished that.

Joanne looked up from her plate and held her head high. "Sergeant, none of us are in such dire financial straits that we would ransack the room of a dead man in search of riches. And from what I know of Seth, he probably didn't have anything worth stealing anyway."

"None of you noticed anyone hanging around or on the second floor who seemed out of place?"

Their silence was incriminating. They were friends. I got that. But if they had only acted more natural, they wouldn't have given the impression that they knew something. I made a mental note that clamming up was worse than some kind of phony innocent denial.

"If anything should come to you, I hope you'll let me know." Dave glanced in my direction. "Holly, I'll inform you when my fingerprinting experts arrive so you can let us into Seth's room."

He left me standing there with the WAG Ladies.

Oriana frowned. "I don't understand. Why are they fingerprinting Seth's room?"

I hesitated before saying, "Someone was in there last night, and we know it wasn't Seth."

Brenda squinted at me. "But he didn't die in his room. Why would anyone care? He was already dead by then, wasn't he?"

I tried to avoid getting in a tangle. "Well, that's the question, isn't it?"

I followed Dave's style and waited for one of them to speak.

To my surprise, Addi burst into tears, scooted back her chair, and ran from the table. Louisa jumped to her feet and ran after her.

"What was that about?" I asked.

The three remaining WAG Ladies shifted uncomfortably.

Joanne slapped her palms on the table. "Will you look at the time? We've got to get moving."

All of them made quick work of gathering their purses and beat a hasty exit.

Shelley came up behind me as I watched them scurry up the stairs. "They're up to something."

Twelve

❀ ❀ ❀ ❀

"Why do you say that?" I asked.

Shelley smiled. "Didn't you know? Waitresses are invisible. You wouldn't believe what I overhear."

"Like what?"

"Well, apparently they have agreed to tolerate Joanne's need to act like the boss because she called home to speak to her husband and thought she could hear a woman in the background. Being in charge will help take her mind off of that."

"They said that?"

Shelley nodded. "Joanne has been quite the topic of concern. And Brenda, too. They're wondering how to give her some clothes. I'm sure you've noticed how she dresses."

"It's not like she's wearing rags. She just doesn't have the same couture style as the others. I'm rather fond of khaki skorts and pants myself."

"That's not what *they* think. Oriana has actually brought some extra ball gowns with her that she thinks might fit

Brenda. But they don't know how to broach the topic without offending her. You can't just walk up to a friend and suggest that you have nicer clothes that she could borrow."

"I'm not sure that's fair to Brenda. She just has different taste."

"Her friends suspect she has run out of her inheritance. Brenda is what you might call a penny-pincher."

"What's that supposed to mean?"

"She leaves an embarrassing tip. You should see her friends trying to distract her while they add money behind her back."

"That's sad. Her brother went to prison for trying to kill her father years ago. He's out of prison now. Maybe that's the problem. She could be having trouble supporting him and trying to help him get back on his feet. Does she work?"

Shelley shrugged. "Want me to find out?"

"What? And lose your cloak of invisibility?"

"I have my methods." She winked at me and got back to work.

I scurried down the hallway to the reception lobby to retrieve keys from the office. I hurried up the back stairs with Trixie dashing ahead of me.

The housekeeper's cart was in the hallway.

I found her in Oriana's room, where Twinkletoes inspected a brown trunk that was not-so-subtly decorated with the famous Gucci logo in a slightly different shade of brown. A matching carry-on bag stood beside it with the same logo, but it was also decorated with a yellow butterfly and vivid flowers. The trunk stood open, as did the closet door. A selection of gorgeous evening gowns hung inside. "Twinkletoes! You're not supposed to be snooping."

She showed no shame. She bothered to stop her inspection to throw me a quick glance, then promptly went on her way checking out Oriana's belongings.

I stepped toward her and bent to pick her up, but the little rascal darted to the bathroom.

"Marina," I said to the housekeeper, "the gentleman in Hike died last night."

She gasped. "Is he still in there?"

"No. He didn't die here. But the police don't want us to touch his room until after they fingerprint and check it out."

"No problem. I am not interested in the dead man's room. How did he die?"

"We're not quite sure yet."

She nodded and made a cross over her chest before she continued cleaning.

"Holly?" I could hear Dave calling me.

"Right here," I said, stepping into the hallway, where he waited with two people whom I recognized from the Snowball police headquarters. "Hi."

"They're going to dust for prints."

I unlocked the door and followed the three of them inside. It looked just as it had the night before. Seth's bag rested on a chair. The coverlet on his bed was pulled back, which seemed illogical. He never made it back to the inn to sleep in it. He could have taken a nap, I supposed. He had changed clothes. A pair of trousers and a shirt hung over the arm of a chair.

"Anything change since you saw it last night?"

"I don't think so."

His phone rang, and he answered it with a curt "Quinlan."

Meanwhile, the other two got to work. One collected fibers, and the other began to dust for fingerprints.

Dave stood completely still while he listened to someone on the other end. He didn't say much, but thanked the person before hanging up. "You will be relieved to know that the irritated spot on Seth's back is not a bug bite."

I felt like I had been given a gift. "Thank goodness for that. What is it then?"

"It appears that it's from an injection."

"Where exactly is that spot?"

"Beneath his left shoulder blade."

"Who gives themselves injections in their backs?" Contorting, I reached my right hand behind my back. "I guess it's possible, but it would be difficult to give yourself a shot there. Are they certain?"

"I don't mean to gross you out, but they're used to cutting into that kind of thing." His mouth shifted uncomfortably. "Drug addicts who are in medicine or law enforcement are adept at hiding their injections. But if you slice into a suspicious spot, you find a small amount of coagulated blood that forms underneath the puncture. Unfortunately, the medical examiner sees that kind of thing more often than one would wish. In addition, Seth shows signs of an arrhythmic death."

I blinked at him. "You're saying he injected something in his back that made his heart beat irregularly and that's why he died?"

"People inject themselves in all kinds of places, but your point is well taken. I would agree that given the location of the injection, it was more likely administered by a second person. They're trying to figure out what was injected."

Why did I feel like we were going in circles? "So a doctor might have given him an injection for back pain and he had a bad reaction?"

"I seriously doubt that's where an injection for back pain would be administered. We'll know more from the toxicology report."

I had the distinct feeling he wasn't saying what he was really thinking. "But?"

Dave grimaced at me. "But I think someone came up behind Seth and injected something into him that killed him."

Okay. That was plenty clear and very scary. "You're saying any one of us could be walking along, minding his own business, and suddenly there's a little sting in his back and, whammo, he falls to the ground dead?"

"I wouldn't have put it quite so dramatically, but yes. That is what I suspect."

"That puts a new light on the saying, 'Watch your back.'"

Dave sighed. "Presumably, most of us haven't done anything to merit the ire of the person wielding the syringe."

"But we don't know, do we?"

"Not yet."

"Do you think the murderer set the fire at Dovie's to distract everyone?"

"It's a possibility. Something to consider. The timing is dead-on for that."

Dave looked over the shoulder of the woman bagging Seth's belongings.

"If you don't need me, I'll just make my rounds." Dave wasn't paying attention, so I called Trixie and left. I headed for the reception lobby, where I composed a simple message updating the residents of Wagtail.

It is with great sorrow that I inform you of the death of a visitor yesterday evening. At present I do not have information on the cause of death, but you will be notified if there is reason for concern.

Mayor Liesel Miller

I printed a copy and took it into the office, where Oma was conversing with Rose and Zelda. "Is this okay?"

She read it. "Perfect. I think you begin to sound like me. Short and to the point."

I returned to the computer and hit Send. Then I collected my clipboard and eyed the registration lobby.

It was my habit to make a morning tour of the inn, noting such things as burned-out lightbulbs, collecting items people had left behind, and making sure the common areas were clean. It was relatively calm that morning, as was the norm. Trixie scampered along, sniffing the floor as we walked through the halls. Not a thing was amiss until we reached the library.

It was a small, cozy room with a fireplace and a window seat. Located on the first floor, it connected the main lobby to the newer cat wing. Oma's and my reading tastes ran to mysteries, so the shelves were full of them, along with a selection of books in other genres and some fun children's books.

Fagan, Brenda's black Scottish terrier, lay stretched out on the window seat on top of a grubby navy T-shirt. He snarled at Trixie when she approached him to take a look. Trixie backed up, understanding his growly possessiveness, but still watched him, clearly curious about his treasure.

Loki bounded into the room and snatched the T-shirt away from Fagan. Trixie leaped at it and grabbed it in her mouth. Fagan joined her, and the two of them appeared to have teamed up against Loki. But Loki was having fun. He held on to the T-shirt, taking a step or two forward to let the smaller dogs think they were winning, but then he twisted abruptly, and Fagan lost his grip. Trixie didn't have the strength to wrest the prize away from Loki. He dragged her across the floor, but she held on with dogged determination and was soon joined again by her buddy Fagan.

I could hear Brenda upstairs, calling, "Fagan! Fagan!"

I walked over to the stairwell and shouted up to her, "He's in the library."

She joined me and immediately scolded him. "Fagan! What have you got there? Give it to Mommy." She held out her hand to him.

He pinned his ears back and made the guilty face of a dog caught in the act.

"Loki!" scolded Brenda. "Give!"

Reluctantly, he allowed her to take the T-shirt from him, and Trixie let loose, too.

"Ugh. It's filthy." She held it gingerly between her thumb and forefinger. It said *Walley World* under a picture of a moose. "Silly boy. Fagan does Earthdog, you know."

I didn't know, but I had heard the expression. "Is that some kind of game?"

"It's marvelous. It tests the natural hunting instincts of your dog." She leaned over toward Trixie. "I bet you'd be excellent at it." Speaking to me, she said, "You really should enroll Trixie. Terriers have such a strong ingrained ability to locate things, especially underground. That's what they were bred for, you know. Fagan probably dug this up somewhere."

I reached for the T-shirt. "I'll put it in the lost and found. Some kid probably forgot it."

"Thank you. I doubt anyone will come around for it, but you never know."

Now that he had nothing to protect, Fagan was quite friendly with Trixie, and the two of them had fun romping from the library into the lobby. But when Loki tried to join in, the two of them ran off by themselves as though they were ganging up against him.

We watched them like doting moms, but Joanne distracted us when she dashed down the stairs. As always, she was dressed in office attire, a chic navy dress with a gold belt. The long sleeves had been carefully folded back and shoved up. If she was flushed, I couldn't tell. Thick makeup concealed her true coloring. Her Somali, Hershey, walked eagerly on his leash, gazing around and not a bit afraid of the two dogs racing through the lobby.

Joanne marched up to us. "They tell me your grandmother is the mayor of Wagtail. I would like a few minutes of her time, please."

"Is it something I can help you with?"

"They told me I might have to go through you to get to her. That's clever business tiering. You take care of the little things, clearing her time for important items."

That was utter nonsense. But it suggested to me that whoever told Joanne that didn't think much of the urgent matter that drove her to seek an audience with Oma. It was all a bit humorous, given that Oma was probably in the inn office and readily available to speak to anyone who dropped by. "How can we help you?"

"I need to be sure that Seth's most untimely death isn't cause for canceling the gala. People have already arrived. It would be a catastrophe to cancel it."

Brenda listened calmly. I couldn't help noticing that while the two friends were involved with the same project, Joanne looked like she was ready to go on camera, and Brenda, without a stitch of makeup, wore a shabby olive green jacket that was frayed at the cuffs and khaki pedal pushers with a stain on the right knee.

"I haven't heard even a whisper of any intention to cancel," I assured Joanne.

"That's a relief. I overheard people discussing a cancellation. It would simply be a disaster."

"I suspect that many of the people coming from out of town don't have any idea that there was a death."

"See that it stays that way." Joanne glanced at her watch. "We're going to be late. There's so much to do." She strode toward the door and turned back to look at Brenda, who hadn't budged. "Well? Aren't you coming?"

"I'll be along soon." Brenda spoke politely but didn't seem ruffled in the least by Joanne's expectations.

Joanne looked like she'd been slapped. Her head held high, she stepped out onto the front porch and disappeared from view.

Brenda sighed. "Joanne hasn't been herself this trip. She's incredibly high-strung anyway. She's always efficient and work-oriented. She lives for the business she built. Eats, drinks, and breathes it. It's her life. Her baby."

"What kind of business is it?"

"It was very clever, really. She started out doing book-keeping and payroll services all by herself. She added employees as the business grew. Then she opened a human resources division. It's enormously successful. Suits her perfectly. I couldn't do it. You have to be very precise."

"What do you do?"

"I used to be a teacher."

"That must involve some degree of precision," I said.

She snorted. "It would drive Joanne out of her mind. When you teach, you have to roll with the punches. You never know what crazy thing some kid will do. Well, I'd better go check on Addi. She was quite distressed by Seth's demise."

"She knew him better than the rest of you?" I asked, trying to sound very casual.

"I suppose the two of us knew him better than most. He was a friend of my brother's. His parents will be devastated. They're nice people. He and my brother were apt to get into mischief, as boys will do. I am sorry to see him end this way. But, then, I've had so many losses in recent years that death seems to be the norm in my life now."

"That's very sad."

"Isn't it?" She appeared pensive. "I suppose now that he's deceased it won't matter anymore if I tell you privately that Addi was quite in love with Seth."

Thirteen

✿ ✿ ✿

I gasped. "I had no idea."

Brenda nodded. "Oh, the things we do for family. Her parents didn't approve of Seth. Addi pretended she wasn't dating him anymore, but she saw him on the sly. She broke it off about a year ago, but his death is hard for her."

"I can imagine. Poor Addi. I wish I had known. I might not have blurted the news about his death the way I did."

"You can't blame yourself. Not many people knew. Just her closest friends. She kept the relationship very quiet."

"I think I owe her an apology."

"Nonsense. One can't know everything. Especially not with the way people lie and keep secrets."

I gazed at her, taking in her pale blue eyes. "Is that wisdom you learned as a teacher?"

"That's wisdom I learned from life."

At that moment, just when I thought we were having an interesting conversation, Fritz bolted through the front door, followed by the judge, who had his stick with him but walked surprisingly well without actually using it.

"Judge Barlow!" I exclaimed. I was about to ask what I could do for him when I realized that his eyes were locked on Brenda, and she was fixated on him. "Judge Barlow, this is Brenda McDade. Brenda, Judge Barlow."

"I'd have recognized you anywhere. A bit older definitely, but you still have that same brave face," said the judge.

Brenda's laugh came out more like a bark. "*Brave* is an overused word where I am concerned. One does what one has to. There was no bravery involved in what I did."

"Don't sell yourself short, young lady. I've known men twice your size who stood by and watched as someone was attacked. How is your father?"

"He passed a few years ago. To be honest, I think he never quite recuperated from Wallace turning on him like that."

"It's understandable. To have one's own son attempt to take one's life is something no parent would ever overcome. It's bad enough to go through that with a stranger, but when it's your own child, well, that's horrific. I understand Wallace roams freely among us again?"

"I'm afraid so. I don't see him often, mostly when he wants money. I won't have him living at the house. But when your name is Wallace McDade and you're a convicted felon, for attempted murder no less, no one wants to rent you an apartment. So I bought him a little house out in the country where there are no neighbors close enough to complain. He can charge most of what he needs on a credit card that I pay, which also serves to give me a clue about what he's up to. I check it every day just to see where he is and what he's doing."

The judge looked at Fagan. "Is that your dog?"

"He is! He always lets me know when Wallace comes around."

The judge sniffed. "You should get him a fellow like Fritz as a friend."

Brenda bristled. "I dare say Fagan would come to my defense if necessary."

I didn't doubt that he would. But probably like the judge, I didn't think he could take a grown man down like a trained German shepherd would. Fritz had politely greeted Fagan and Trixie, but then he sat next to the judge, carefully watching everything that was going on in the lobby.

"I miss the years when he was locked up," said Brenda. "They were so freeing. I could sleep with all the windows open and the breeze wafting in. Now I'm always looking over my shoulder, closing and locking every possible entrance."

"You fear for your life?" asked the judge.

"I don't like to think about it in those terms. But he has proven his ability to disconnect from logic and integrity. I cannot trust him. I don't understand the way Wallace's mind works. It clearly goes places that I cannot begin to imagine."

"Is he under the care of a psychiatrist?"

"Allegedly. He needs to be in a facility, but no one can get him to go. That won't happen until he kills me. And then everyone will ask why he was allowed to be free."

Clearly dispirited, the judge nodded, as though resigned to Brenda's reality.

"I hope you'll be at the gala," said Brenda.

"The correct thing to say is that I wouldn't miss it. But I loathe being hit up for favors by all those phony types trying to figure out whose back to scratch to advance their own interests. A tiresome waste of time if you ask me."

I was a little taken aback by his response and held my breath, wondering how to cushion that blow.

But Brenda smiled at him. "I'll see you there, then."

The corner of his mouth turned up. As she walked away with Fagan by her side, the judge said, "I admire that young woman. She's quite remarkable." He watched her for a moment before turning to me. "I am concerned that the fire in Dovie's shed may be a message from the person tormenting me."

In the well of the grand staircase, anyone could listen in or overhear our conversation. I led him outside to the porch where we could speak privately. When he was settled in a rocking chair, I asked, "Were you and Rose speaking about Dovie's shed recently?"

"Yes. It has been an eyesore for many years. Your aunt Birdie started a squabble and upset Dovie by informing her that she would bring it up with Liesel. And since Birdie has a family connection to Liesel through you, she claimed she wouldn't even have to do it at a board meeting. She could go straight to the mayor."

Aunt Birdie was a pill. There was no way around it. I had seen her kinder side, so I knew she had a heart, but she could not help bossing people around. She thought she was an authority on everything and everyone. She was the first to point out anything she thought was a transgression on my part, like being born out of wedlock to her teenaged sister, which was utterly absurd, as I was the result, not the cause. But I had discovered that she had plenty of socially inappropriate infractions of her own. We'd had a few run-ins when I moved back to Wagtail. She didn't like that I stood up to her. But I wasn't about to cower and be her little servant. It was beyond me why she hadn't realized that people would like her more if she didn't try to rule the world and everyone in it.

"That almost sounds as if someone was trying to please Aunt Birdie. She has her nerve. And what Dovie may not know is that there's no love lost between Oma and Birdie. They tolerate each other, but if I wanted to accomplish something, Aunt Birdie is the last person I would send to Oma with a request."

"Small-town politics," he muttered.

It was actually family politics. Aunt Birdie, my mother's sister, had made no secret of the fact that she was jealous of my close relationship with Oma, my father's mother. But what he'd said worried me in a whole new way. "Are you suggesting that Aunt Birdie had something to do with the fire at Dovie's house?"

"I have no evidence of that."

I had dated a lawyer before moving to Wagtail, so I knew perfectly well how cautiously legal types selected their words. I understood exactly what he was saying. He meant she was his top suspect. But I saw a problem with that.

Aunt Birdie was quite adept with her computer. She wrote columns for antiques magazines and corresponded quite well with email. But there was a limit to her technical ability, as I could attest, having been called to her house several times to update her computer and fix her phone. "I seriously doubt that Birdie is knowledgeable enough to plant any kind of high-tech listening device in your house."

The judge's eyes opened wide. "She's a very intelligent woman."

"You're pretty smart, too. Do you think you could arrange to listen to conversations in someone else's house?"

He grumbled incoherently a bit. "You may have a point. But she could hire someone. That's what I would do. There are plenty of people in this world who will do unsavory things for a little bit of pocket change."

He had me there. "Why would she do that?"

He glanced at me like I was daft, and a red blush crawled up his cheeks. "Single men my age are at a premium in this town."

I had to bite my lip to keep from grinning.

"Well, if the person listening to you is Aunt Birdie, then you have nothing to worry about. She may be unkind, but she's not violent."

"No one is violent—until they get caught."

What was that supposed to mean? "She's ornery and cranky and expects everything to be done the way she wants, but she has never harmed anyone."

The judge heaved himself out of the rocking chair, which prompted Fritz to jump to his feet.

"That fire last night was violent on more than one level," said the judge.

I understood what he meant. "I seriously doubt that Aunt Birdie had anything to do with that. She's disagreeable, not stupid."

"I certainly hope you're right about that."

Trixie watched the judge pick up his cane and walk down the stairs without so much as a wobble, with Fritz by his side, matching his pace.

Trixie turned to look at me as though she was thinking what I was—*Did he really need that stick?* "It's not our problem," I said to Trixie. "Maybe he just likes the look of strolling about with a stick."

He crossed the plaza, looking just about as grouchy as Aunt Birdie. Heaven help us all if those two ever got together as a couple.

I opened the door, and Trixie ran inside, wagging her tail. We went straight up the grand staircase and turned right toward Seth's room. The door was open. I stepped inside.

Dave was there alone, looking out the French doors.

"Any luck?" I asked.

"He didn't bring much with him. I'd like to keep the room sealed until we get the results back from the medical examiner. Is that okay?"

"Sure. Can we leave the yellow crime scene tape inside the door so it doesn't scare our guests?" I asked.

He picked up the room keys in a gloved hand and held them out to me. "One other thing. Can you tell me who is in Play?"

The room key in his hand hung from a bronze fob embossed with the word *Play*.

I was stunned. "I never touched it or looked at it because I didn't want to mess up fingerprints. I just assumed they were the keys to this room."

"So, who is in Play?"

"Louisa."

Fourteen

✿ ✿ ✿

Dave studied the key for a moment. "Thanks." He slipped it into a paper bag that had already been labeled.

"They knew each other from college. But why would he have her key?"

"An excellent question. Do me a favor, Holly. I'd like to keep this quiet for the moment. We're the only people who know about this. It could be quite innocent. In fact, it most likely is, considering that he died across town from here. But I don't want Louisa to know about this just yet. Okay?"

"Yes, of course. There aren't that many possibilities. Louisa may have given him her key. Maybe he was planning to visit her room later. Or maybe she was leaving Loki in the room and Seth was supposed to bring him somewhere."

Dave nodded. "Or maybe he stole it from her."

"To what end?" I asked.

"Don't know. But I do know that Seth is no longer able to tell us. So let's not alert Louisa."

He pulled out some crime scene tape, which I took as a clue that we were leaving the room.

I walked into the hallway and waited while he fastened the tape just inside the door. I locked the door to Hike, said goodbye to Dave, and walked downstairs to return the key.

Shadow, our handyman, happened to be walking by with his bloodhound, Elvis. I stopped him and asked if he could change locks on the doors for "old Judge Barlow." I emphasized his age, hoping Shadow would be sympathetic.

"Sure. Can't say I'm a fan of the grump. He used to shout at me when I was a kid and whizzed by him on my bicycle. But he probably doesn't remember that. Everything okay over there?" he asked.

"Yes. But the locks haven't been changed in decades. And you never know who might resent him."

"No kidding. Plenty of people I can think of!"

"Thanks, Shadow."

Rose shot me a desperate glance when I entered the office. Because she was worried that I would blab about her relationship with the judge? I hung up my clipboard and tried to sound cheerful when I said, "Everything looks okay this morning. And there's partially good news. The spot on Seth's back came from an injection, not a bug bite. So you don't have to worry about walking in the woods."

"An injection? In my backyard?" Rose nearly spilled the cup of coffee she held. "What I'd like to know is what he was doing there in the first place. I didn't invite him!"

"You never met him?" asked Oma.

And that was when Rose lied to her best friend in the world. "I may have seen him around town, but it wasn't like I had any connection to him."

Rose's eyes pleaded with me. While Oma and Rose speculated about Seth's death, I couldn't help wondering what was going on with Rose. I left the two of them and headed back to the main lobby.

Footsteps running down the grand staircase caught my attention. Addi avoided looking at anyone as she ran through the library toward her room.

I wondered what to do. I had known her when we were young. Did that friendship transcend the years that had passed? Was I still someone she could confide in? She was traveling with friends who could comfort her. And her grandfather lived in town. I wasn't sure it was my place at all to check on her, but I liked Addi. I followed her into the cat wing and knocked on her door.

It swung open. Addi looked miserable. Her cat, Inky, shot out the door and found herself nose to nose with Trixie. Inky scuttled backward, her back arched like a Halloween cat. Trixie wasn't impressed. She walked into Inky's room as though she lived there.

No dogs were allowed on the cat wing, but we'd made an official exception for Trixie. She had proven that she wouldn't chase cats and appeared to understand that they were guests. Of course, the real reason was that she was constantly by my side. And after someone had tried to steal her, I was more cautious and preferred for her to be close by.

Inky's fur settled, and the confusion on her face was so priceless that Addi began to laugh. "This is so good for Inky. She likes other cats, but she hasn't been exposed to many dogs."

Inky slinked to the doorway and peered inside, looking for Trixie. Prowling like a panther, she slowly walked into the room. I followed her, and Addi closed the door.

The rooms in the cat wing featured cat-size stairs and snuggle perches on the walls. Inky headed for the nearest one, jumped up, and looked for Trixie.

"Is everything okay?" I asked Addi.

"I'm sorry if I disturbed you. My family says I'm far too sensitive and emotional."

"Is it Seth?"

Addi looked up at Inky. "She liked Seth," Addi whispered.

"You did, too."

Addi perched on the edge of her bed, clutching it with both hands. Her entire body seemed rigid. "Do you have a boyfriend in your life who will always be special to you?"

"I guess Holmes falls into that category. It wasn't like I had dated him before he moved away, but he was a special person in my life."

"I heard he had moved back to Wagtail. You first, now Holmes. Before you know it, we'll all be back here."

"Are you considering a move?" I asked.

"Maybe. My grandfather needs someone around who can help him. I know he has Dovie, but she'll be needing help herself soon." She was silent for a moment. "My mom says I always fall for the wrong guys. All I can say is that Seth and I were drawn to each other. We would date, break up, and get back together. We never managed to make it work for long, but we always tried again. He had his share of faults, but don't we all?"

I nodded my head.

She sniffled. "We dated on and off, mostly in secret. Sometimes I wonder if that wasn't part of the attraction. My parents didn't like Seth. You know how it is. As soon as someone tells you not to do something, that's all you can think about. And for the most part, he was good to me."

For the most part? I could hear screeching tires and see red flags waving. I tried to find the right words so she wouldn't balk at answering. "Sometimes he wasn't nice?"

Addi swallowed hard. "He had what my grandmother Theona called *roving eyes.* Except it wasn't just his eyes that roved."

"He went out with other women when he was dating you."

"He didn't just go out with them, if you know what I

mean. That's what finally ended our on again, off again relationship. I wasn't going to take it one more time. I can forgive, but I'm not stupid. I know I'm not gorgeous like Louisa or glamorous like Oriana, but if he had truly loved me, that wouldn't have happened."

"You're every bit as beautiful as they are. Don't short-change yourself."

"Something wasn't working. I felt like he was always looking for someone better than me. Prettier or smarter, more successful or maybe less successful. He, um, wanted to have drinks last night, and I wondered if he was trying to heat things up again."

"Is that what you wanted?" I asked.

She was still for a long moment, but I didn't push her. I watched Inky slither from one perch to another. She finally jumped onto the floor and stealthily neared Trixie, who knew perfectly well that she was there but didn't budge.

"No. I don't think so. I was done with trying to make it work. But Seth was a big part of my life, and I can't believe he's gone. That's the hard part . . . that he'll never be around again. Ever. It's the loss of a friend more than a boyfriend. He loved animals and had a way with them. And he could be so funny! Hysterical, really. I was doing fine this morn-ing, but all of a sudden, I was overwhelmed by the finality."

I understood what she meant. "I'm sure it will hit you for a long time to come. It's hard to lose a friend. Especially one with whom you were once so close."

"Thanks for listening, Holly. I'd better get back to the ballroom. I'm sure Joanne is having a meltdown by now."

"See you tonight at the gala."

"Holly? I have an extra ticket. Do you know anyone who might like to go?"

Suddenly I felt rather like Oma and Rose, who loved matchmaking. "As a matter of fact, I think Dave might be interested in attending the gala tonight."

"Quinlan?" She cheered up a little. "What do you know about Dave?"

"He's a nice guy."

"I suspected *that*. Is he seeing anyone?"

I tried hard not to smile. "I don't think so." I jotted his number on the inn notepad for her before I left.

As I was walking away, I received a text on my phone from the florist, reminding me that my standing order of flowers for family graves was ready. Aunt Birdie had saddled me with that job when I'd moved to Wagtail. I didn't really mind. I hadn't known any of them, but the least I could do was bring flowers to their graves.

I collected the cart I used to transport them, and Twinkletoes appeared out of nowhere like she always did when she heard the wagon.

She sprang along with Trixie as I walked to the florist. The arrangements were stunning, with white and purple gladiolas, pink lilies, tiny white baby's breath, and rich purple wisteria hanging down over the vases. I loaded them into the little cart and walked over to the cemetery, where I found Joanne studying the bell tower on the church.

"Does the bell ring?" she asked.

"Definitely. At Christmas and New Year's almost the whole town comes out to see. Children sing Christmas carols and people hold candles. It's wonderful."

"Flowers for the grandfather you never knew?" she asked.

"Something like that."

She followed me inside the cemetery gate. Trixie and Twinkletoes wandered through the tombstones and monuments, sniffing the ground.

I placed the flowers on four graves.

Joanne stood not far from me, gazing at a gravestone. Behind it stood an angel with a bird perched on her hand.

I walked over to see whose it was. "Theona Barlow," I read aloud.

"She must have been lovely."

"You didn't know her?"

"No. She was already very ill when I started volunteering. I certainly heard a lot about her, though."

"She was loved by everyone."

"So I've heard. They tell me her husband is a bit of a bear."

I laughed. "He's okay. A little grumpy and sharp, I guess. He probably wasn't easy to live with."

"I see graves from the 1800s. Has the church been here long?"

"I don't know how old it is. It was there when I was a child. I remember the bells ringing and singing carols."

"It must have been magical to grow up in Wagtail."

"Probably. My parents divorced. My mom fled to California, and my dad went to Florida. I hated holidays. There was always a squabble about where I would go. I swear I spent more time in airports than by a cozy fire."

Joanne looked at me in surprise. "Funny. I never would have guessed that. I thought you had lived here your entire life." She studied the angel for a long moment. "I admitted my father to a nursing home two months ago. He has early Alzheimer's."

"I'm sorry! That must be so hard for you."

She nodded. "He was a terrible parent. And, yet, I feel guilty about leaving him there. I know it's for his own good. I couldn't possibly manage him at home. But I still feel remorseful about it."

"I'm sure they're taking very good care of him."

"It was strange cleaning out his house. You don't usually do that until a parent has died. It's a curious thing to see the odd bits and pieces a person has deemed worth saving. I hadn't seen him in quite a while. It felt . . . intrusive to go through his belongings." Abruptly she turned toward me. "Well! I have to get back to the ballroom. There's no telling what kind of chaos has befallen the gala in my brief absence. I'll see you tonight, Holly."

I waved at her and watched her walk away. Trixie danced around my ankles and yapped a couple of times.

I petted her and swung Twinkletoes up into my arms. "We're going to a party tonight. Are you excited?"

Trixie twirled in circles and barked. Twinkletoes purred before leaping to the ground and exiting the cemetery with her head held high.

The rest of the day passed quickly. Before I knew it, Casey arrived to babysit the inn, and I ran upstairs to dress.

In my previous life as a fundraiser, I'd attended galas on a fairly regular basis, and I had kept most of my gowns. I knew it was silly, but I wore a pale pink silk gown to match the bling Trixie and Twinkletoes wore. I swept my hair up into a French twist, pinned it, and added dangling rhinestone earrings.

Trixie and Twinkletoes seemed to know something special was afoot. I carried Twinkletoes's tiara in my small purse. I could slip it on her head when we arrived at the gala.

They followed me out the door. I locked it and walked down the grand staircase, feeling ridiculously princess-like.

It was the first time in my life I had seen Holmes in a tuxedo. "You clean up very well," I teased. Holmes had recently moved back to Wagtail from Chicago. He was the first boy I had kissed, and I'd been goofy for him ever since. College and jobs had taken us in different directions. I had lived in northern Virginia and hadn't seen him for a decade until I returned to Wagtail. He'd been engaged then, to a rather spoiled and high-maintenance woman if you asked me. I knew better than to try to break them up. After all, he had chosen her. I did my best to be supportive of his decision. But, as it turned out, he changed his mind about marrying her and decided to move back to Wagtail.

He lifted my hand and kissed it, making me giggle.

Trixie sat at his feet and raised her right paw, sending us into gales of laughter. She wore a pink collar adorned with a double line of rhinestones. A teardrop-shaped diamond hung off it.

Twinkletoes wore a rhinestone collar with a pink stone embellishing it.

They walked with us to the Wagtail Springs Hotel, darting around to visit with dog and cat friends they encountered along the way, then racing to catch up to us.

People on the sidewalks had never looked lovelier. The beauty salons must have been busy. Not only did ladies have their hair styled in amazing ways but two black poodles passed us with fancy flouncing haircuts adorned by jewels that looked real.

We spied Oma and her favorite date, Thomas Hertzog, owner of the Blue Boar restaurant, stepping out of a Wagtail taxi. She wore a sequined shawl-collar jacket in black with a long skirt. Gingersnap had ridden in the taxi with them and pranced proudly in her fancy faux-sapphire collar, which was so bright that it glittered as she moved.

I fastened the tiara to Twinkletoes's long fur and hoped it would stay on. She seemed a little miffed about it, but, ever a good sport, she joined the dogs and raced up the stairs ahead of us. Holmes and I waited for Oma and her date. We followed them through the lobby and into the ballroom. It was gorgeous but packed.

People immediately descended on Oma. No doubt they were complaining or pitching some idea to her. Holmes went off to find the champagne, and I spotted Aunt Birdie moving in on Judge Barlow and Fritz.

I sighed. It wasn't easy being related to a woman who deemed herself queen of everything and boss of me.

Fifteen

✿ ✿ ✿ ✿

It irked Aunt Birdie no end that I lived and worked with Oma. She'd taken my parents' departure from Wagtail as a personal slight. She may not have been far off, considering that my mother hadn't been back to visit her in years.

Birdie had never married, which came as a surprise only to Birdie. She was family, and I was stuck with her, but she was probably the most disgruntled person in all of Wagtail and a good bit beyond. Her age and snippy disposition didn't prevent her from chasing men, though, and I suspected she now had designs on Judge Barlow.

Birdie was well known in Wagtail as a clotheshorse. No ratty garden duds for her. The fabric of her black dress followed the contours of her slender figure. It was simple and basic, except for a white satin stand-up collar in an oval shape that extended to her shoulders, setting off her remarkably firm neck and face. It was reminiscent of Audrey Hepburn. Birdie's hair remained black, with some help from a bottle, no doubt, but a swatch of silver rose from her forehead and gracefully curved along her face.

I sidled over to them. "Good evening, Aunt Birdie, Judge Barlow. How's Fritz doing?"

"Splendid! You'd never imagine that he was lost. He's perfectly content and acting like his old self. Look at him over there, sniffing a biscuit on a plate. I think he's waiting for me to tell him he can eat it."

Aunt Birdie smirked. "If Fritz is so well trained, why didn't he come home?"

"There is speculation, as Holly can confirm, that Fritz responded to trouble, sort of like Trixie does."

"Good grief. Not another dog who smells corpses." Aunt Birdie didn't bother to hide her disdain.

If Birdie was trying to impress the judge, she wasn't on the right track by criticizing his dog. He huffed a little, and finally said, "Not all troubles are related to murder."

I couldn't exactly come out and ask in front of Aunt Birdie if he'd experienced any more unusual events. "Is everything okay?" I asked.

He blinked a few times and looked away. "I don't want to be here."

"I think everyone would understand that it's too soon for you," I said. Aunt Birdie and I shared a glance.

"Not Theona," said the judge.

Birdie and I looked at each other again. He was talking about his dead wife!

He didn't seem to notice our shock and rambled on. "This was important to her. Theona would have been in her element, mingling and greeting people. She was like a graceful hummingbird. She would have flitted by me occasionally, just to remind me to smile and at least *try* not to appear miserable."

"She sounds lovely," I said. "No wonder Oma enjoyed her company."

"I was surprised that she married me. I had to chase her, you know. She could have married any one of her suitors."

"But she chose you," I said kindly.

"I have never understood why. She truly was my better half, always reminding me not to be brusque. I saw the monstrous side of people every day in my courtroom. Then I would go home, and Theona would have brought home some pitiful animal to restore its trust in people. 'How could anyone have been cruel?' she would ask. And I always thought to myself that she had no idea of the inhumanity that permeates our world."

"You spared her that?" asked Birdie. "I would have wanted to know."

"I loved Theona. I did everything I could to shield her from the dark side of life. And now there is nothing left. Theona took my spirit with her when she departed from this world."

"But you have children and grandchildren," I protested. Not to mention Rose. Did she mean anything to him at all? It didn't sound like it.

His nostrils flared and the corner of his mouth twitched. "When your children are small, you do everything for them. They leave you as soon as they can. I lost two of my children, but do the others come around? Of course not. They're too busy for their old dad. Have you met Addilyn Lieras? She's right over there in the blue dress. Looks kind of like Little Bo Peep." He pointed in her direction. "Her mother is one of my daughters."

"Addi is a delight. You may not recall, but we played together as children," I said.

"She has Theona's kind disposition."

"You see? Addi will keep your spirits up."

He watched Addi, who flitted about in a blue-and-white dress that was fitted at the top with a gauzy skirt that consisted of four layers of long ruffles. Giant gold-and-silk earrings hung from her ears. She looked every bit the free spirit I knew she was. Her black cat, Inky, wore a bright pink dress with black dots, a black-and-pink-checkerboard belt, and a pink tulle skirt. She had hopped onto a chair and was currently reaching for a fish treat, her fluffy black tail waving back and forth.

Dovie approached us. Thick makeup covered her face, and she had used a heavy hand on her eyeliner. Once again, her fake eyelashes reached nearly to her eyebrows. She had styled her bottle-blond hair high in loose curls.

"Hello, Dovie," said Aunt Birdie in a most unwelcoming tone.

Dovie's curt "Birdie" left no mistake that the two of them didn't care for each other. Given that they were both about the same age and clearly took great pains with their appearance, one might have expected them to be friends. But that was not the situation. In fact, I wondered if the two of them were some sort of rivals. Maybe it went deeper than chasing after the same man. Aunt Birdie had been hostile toward Dovie in her time of need when her shed was on fire. I had a bad feeling the animosity between them went back years.

In a much sweeter voice, she said, "Now, Judge, don't you forget to enter the silent auction."

"I don't need any of that junk," he grumbled.

"Really?" she asked. "What about the two bottles of Scarecrow Cabernet Sauvignon 2015? Or the seven-course dinner for two at the Blue Boar? I'll gladly accompany you to the dinner if you win."

Aunt Birdie bristled, confirming my suspicion that she had more than a passing interest in the judge.

But whatever Dovie and Birdie planned, they were sunk as soon as Addi joined us. Her earlier melancholy had vanished. Smiling as though she'd never been happier, she held out a glass of champagne to her grandfather. "A little bubbly for you. Grandmum would be so happy if she could see this. In fact, it wouldn't surprise me if she were watching us right now. Don't you think so? The WAG Ladies have done her proud."

The judge's lips curled up in a smile. "This is Theona's project. If she were here, she would expect me to bid and be generous. Thank you for that reminder, Addi. Excuse me, ladies." He toddled off with Addi to examine the silent auction items, leaving Dovie and Birdie behind in a huff.

"You certainly know how to handle him," I said to Dovie.

"He's not the first cantankerous man I've met. Don't let him fool you, he can be quite dear. Or he was toward Theona anyway. And now he dotes on Addi. Oh my! Who is *that* man?" She hurried off at the same time that Holmes handed me a glass of champagne.

Birdie seemed put out. She frowned. "What kind of person wears jeans to a gala?"

The man speaking to the judge and Addi wore a very dignified tuxedo. What on earth was she talking about? "Thanks," I said to Holmes. "Have you bid on anything?"

He wiggled his eyebrows. "I have. My secret, though."

I laughed at him. "Now I have to go snoop and see if I can find it."

"You wouldn't want to spoil the surprise," he said.

"What if I accidentally bid against you?" I feigned innocence.

Yates Garvey joined us and pumped Holmes's hand. He kissed me on the cheek. "I was hoping to see you here, Holmes. You don't mind if I steal him for a moment do you?"

I took a few minutes to peruse the silent auction offerings and placed bids on two of them. When I looked up and gazed around the room for my little rascals, to my complete horror, I realized that Trixie, Twinkletoes, and Loki had taken seats at a table and were investigating treats. Only inches from their little noses were martinis! I dashed over to them at the precise moment that Trixie gave Loki a dirty look and intentionally spilled the martini in front of her as though she thought it was poisoned.

I grabbed the martini glasses.

Oriana gracefully floated over to me. She pointed at a little card that stood on the table. "It's okay, all the ingredients are dog- and cat-friendly. The—" she made little air quotation marks with her fingers "—*martinis* are made of fresh Wagtail spring water. And a baker in town fashioned the olives and the toothpicks out of fish paste. They're absolutely brilliant and completely edible. Honestly, the woman is an artist."

"You're kidding." I examined them more closely. "I hope no people think they're the real thing and try them."

Oriana laughed gleefully, "It won't hurt them, but they may not like the flavor. Dogs and cats can't get their own water, so we thought it would be cute to have it waiting for them at the tables. And the martini glasses are recycled plastic, so they won't break if they fall to the floor." She frowned. "Does Trixie have something against Loki? She's clearly not pleased that he's sitting next to her."

"I noticed that."

"He's a bit of a handful. Maybe he's too lively for Trixie's taste. I've noticed that Garbo has distanced herself from him, too. She's sitting with Inky and Fritz tonight."

Oriana's watch dinged. "That's my cue. We drew straws so Joanne wouldn't appoint herself queen of the ball. I get to welcome everyone."

Oriana swished away in her exquisite eye-catching red gown with a bateau neck and long sleeves. She looked positively regal as she took the microphone. Garbo, her saluki, stood by her side. The microphone squealed when she said, "Welcome to the There's No Place Like Home Gala."

Loki and another dog howled, bringing on laughter.

Nonplussed, Oriana continued, "Thank you for that introduction, Loki. And thanks to all of you, both two- and four-legged, for coming tonight. This is a bittersweet occasion. As you know, this gala was the idea of our beloved Theona Barlow, who sadly passed away only six months ago. I have no doubt that she's watching and having a glass of champagne in heaven. Whether it's to honor Theona's memory or to help save desperate cats and dogs, your generosity is most appreciated. Please note that Wagtail residents have volunteered to attend with cats and dogs from WAG that are currently up for adoption. They are all wearing special There's No Place Like Home bandanas, and Paige McDonaugh is in the rear taking adoption applications right now! Please mingle and place your bids for the silent auction items. Dinner will be served shortly, and we'll have a live auction with our dessert! Enjoy!"

The microphone squealed again as she put it away, bringing on more howls and barking.

Brenda sidled up to me. "Have you seen Louisa? She's in charge of the champagne. It looks like we're running low."

"I'm afraid I haven't seen her, but I think you win for loveliest gown."

Brenda smoothed the fabric of her dress, which looked to be silk and organza printed with turquoise flowers that matched the color of an organza swath that was wrapped around her bust and cascaded to the floor on one side.

"It's vintage. It belonged to my grandmother. Frankly, I think it's much prettier than most of the dresses I see today." She glanced around and lowered her voice. "It was a little bit awkward. Oriana brought a closet full of dresses in case one of us wanted to wear one. I have no idea why she would think we didn't have appropriate gowns. But they were not my taste. Horrible sleek black things that Morticia Addams would have liked. My mother and grandmother were such clotheshorses. Back in their day, clothes were so important. No one dared leave the house in jeans, or pants for that matter. My mom was always perfectly dressed. Even if she didn't have plans for the day. I suppose I should have gotten rid of their clothes after they passed, but they're so much better quality than they make now. And the price is certainly right! Oh! There's Joanne. If anyone would know where Louisa is, it would be Joanne. Have you ever in your life met anyone quite so bossy? The woman thinks she's in charge of everything."

A little bell tinkled, indicating it was time for dinner. Twinkletoes and Trixie were nearby, but Holmes was across the room. He made his way over, and we sat down to dinner.

"What did Yates want?" I asked.

"I wasn't planning to tell you about it tonight, but I might as well. You know the big house on the corner of Pine Street?"

"The one with plants growing in the gutters?"

Holmes laughed. "That's the one. I made a low offer for it, and the owner grabbed it."

"But you have a house. Is the A-frame getting too small for you?"

"I actually like being up the mountain, away from everything. In my Chicago condo I felt like there were people everywhere. Over me, under me, next to me. I like having my coffee outside in the morning and not hearing anything but birds. I'm going to renovate the house on Pine and flip it."

"That's terrific! You're the perfect person to do it, too."

"I think it might be fun."

I raised my glass of champagne. "Congratulations!"

Our conversation moved to food as the banquet was served. The entire meal was cat- and dog-friendly. The appetizer was a scrumptious morsel of filet of beef on toast. Twinkletoes skipped the toast, but Trixie ate it for her. Holmes wanted more.

Fish stew served in small bowls followed.

The entrée of chicken breast with sweet potato puree and sautéed summer squash was perfect. Light and a little bit different from the usual banquet foods. Twinkletoes turned her nose up at the squash. When Loki showed an interest in it, Trixie hastily leaned over and snarfed it. There was something going on between those two!

As promised, a live auction commenced with dessert, which was dog- and cat-friendly ice cream topped with carob sauce for humans and dogs.

A local auctioneer had volunteered his services. He took his place at a podium. As he swung into a coaxing rhythm, I could see people becoming frenzied as they bid on paintings, sculptures, jewelry, and fancy vacations.

Most of the cats were following proper feline etiquette and doing their after-dinner grooming. The dogs, even Loki, looked sleepy.

The pitch in the room became frenetic as people bid outlandish amounts to outdo one another.

In the middle of a bidding war, Loki watched Louisa leave the room. He jumped from his chair and sprinted after her. Twinkletoes stopped licking her paws and observed.

Without so much as a yelp, Trixie leaped from her chair and raced out of the ballroom with Twinkletoes right behind her.

Holmes leaned over to me. "What's that about?"

"I don't know. Maybe I should check on Louisa."

Sixteen

❁ ❁ ❁ ❁

I stood up, hoping not to attract too much attention. Dave, who sat on the other side of the room, watched me. I was pleased to see him seated next to Addi.

I quietly left the ballroom and found Louisa outside on the stairs. "Are you okay?" I asked.

"I just needed some air."

"Is it Seth?"

She inhaled deeply and swayed. I held out my arm to steady her, wondering if she'd had too much to drink.

"I have to sit down."

I helped her to a bench in front of the hotel. Night had fallen while we were in the ballroom. Lights glimmered in restaurants along the green. All was well and peaceful in Wagtail.

Loki sat at her feet and insisted on attention, pawing at her. Twinkletoes jumped on my lap and purred. But Trixie maintained her distance, watching Loki with a distrustful look.

Louisa stroked Loki's head. "I feel horrible."

"Are you going to be sick?"

"I don't think so. I have terrible allergies to grass and trees." She waived her arm in a big arc. "To just about everything in nature that's beautiful. They call it allergic rhinitis and asthma syndrome. Ugh. My heart is racing. And I'm so hot. But I meant about Seth. I'm supposed to feel sorrowful that *anyone* has died, but I'm not sad about Seth. Isn't that awful?"

It was appalling. But I didn't think I should tell her that. "I thought he was a friend of yours."

"I knew him in college, but not terribly well. He was really my husband Tom's friend. Seth never appealed to me. Have you ever gotten bad vibes from someone? He never did anything awful, I just didn't like him. And then, when Tom was sick, Seth showed up one day to visit him, which I thought was very considerate. That turned out to be completely wrong. He had an agenda. When he left, I learned the real reason he had been there."

"What was that?" I asked.

"When Tom and Seth were sixteen, they went out one hot summer night with Brenda's brother, Wallace, who had taken alcohol from his dad's stash and borrowed a car without permission. The three of them were loaded when their car hit another car, killing the woman who was driving. Seth had been driving, but he'd been in trouble for driving drunk before, so he begged Tom to say Wallace had been at the wheel. Wallace protested, but Tom went along with Seth's deception."

"Tom lied about who was driving," I said, to be sure I understood.

"He thought they would go easy on Wallace because it was his first offense. As it turned out, they were right. Because of his age, and probably a really smart lawyer, Wallace avoided prison by participating in a diversion program aimed at rehabilitating teens."

"Which meant Seth killed someone and got off scot-free."

"Exactly. Wallace denied that he was the driver, but given Tom and Seth's statements, the authorities believed that Wallace was lying to protect himself."

"Seth visited Tom to thank him?"

Louisa laughed bitterly. "He was afraid Tom would spill their secret to clear his conscience. It was a totally self-serving, narcissistic thing to do. For heaven's sake, Tom was dying, and all Seth could think about was himself."

Seth had seemed so friendly. Of course, that accident had been a long time ago, probably twenty years back or more. Clearly, it still weighed on his conscience. I imagined something like that would plague a person forever. "Did you tell anyone else?"

"I told Brenda about it. And I mailed the letter that Tom dictated and signed before his death to Judge Barlow a couple of months ago. I thought Brenda should know that her brother hadn't killed anyone." She sighed heavily. "The driver of the other car was Judge Barlow's daughter. He had a right to know."

I barely heard what else she said. That information changed everything.

"There were so many things to take care of after Tom's death, and then I threw myself into the gala." She looked back at the hotel. "Where I should be right now instead of out here. To be honest, it had kind of gone out of my mind until yesterday when Seth helped us catch Loki. It all came flooding back."

She stood up abruptly and wobbled a little. "I don't dare linger out here much longer." She smiled at me. "Joanne is probably taking roll."

"If she gives you any trouble, send her to me. I'll tell her you weren't feeling well."

"Thanks, Holly. Loki, are you ready to return and bid on something?"

He walked beside her slowly, as if he was concerned about her. I watched them trudge up the steps and inside.

Trixie jumped up on the bench next to me in the spot Louisa had vacated.

"May I?"

I looked up at Dave. "Of course. I must say, you're quite dapper in your tuxedo."

"I don't get many chances to wear it."

"I see you're here with Addi."

"Don't start with me."

"You're very sensitive about the women in your life."

He snorted and looked away for a moment. "Too many of the interesting women I meet are here for a week. Then they go home, never to be heard from again. It's the curse of working in a resort town. I know most of the resident women my age. I went to school with them. It's not easy to find the right person for a relationship."

"Addi doesn't live here, either."

He shrugged. "I needed a date, and she happened to have an extra ticket. Besides, she's kind of cute."

I didn't try to hide my grin. "She is at that."

"You won't believe this, but I bought one of her paintings a few years ago. It's of Dogwood Lake in the fall when the leaves turn colors. I'm not much of an artsy guy, but I really liked it. I was pretty surprised to realize that the artist was Addilyn Lieras."

"It was meant to be."

He tilted his head, "Maybe. Who knows?"

"She's probably wondering where you went," I pointed out.

"I'll get right back to her. That was an interesting conversation you had with Louisa."

"You were eavesdropping?"

"I prefer to think of it as doing my job. I guess we now have two people with a motive. The medical examiner's office called shortly before the gala commenced. "Seth died from aconite poisoning, which likely caused the cardiac death."

"Wolfsbane?" I asked.

"Exactly. Plenty of it around here. It would appear that the killer collected some roots, made them into a fine mash, and injected it into Seth's back, fairly close to the heart."

I leaned back against the bench, sagging at the thought. "He was here for less than twenty-four hours." I gasped. "It was Dovie who called him to come."

Dave nodded. "Almost too obvious. I'll be having a chat with her tonight after the gala. And now your little conversation with Louisa has pointed out more suspects."

"Do you think Wallace is in Wagtail?"

"Another possibility, thank you."

"Seth had Louisa's room key. That's a definite tie. But I'm not sure about a motive. I hardly think she would kill him because he wasn't sufficiently upset about her husband's illness."

"I find it intriguing that Brenda quickly denied that any of the WAG Ladies had close ties to Seth. Yet her brother, Wallace, paid the price for Seth's sin. Two more things. Seth had meringue on his clothes, and, apparently, someone slapped him before he died."

"Brenda." The name escaped my mouth like a hiss. "Her dog got into a berry meringue pie that Rose had made and planned to serve for dessert. And she definitely returned to the house with her dog to wash him off."

"Brenda. Means, motive, opportunity." Dave rose to his feet and offered me his hand. "Shall we return to the gala?"

I took his hand and stood up. We walked to the bottom of the stairs. At that moment, the doors to the hotel opened and elegantly clad people ambled out, some carrying items they had won, most accompanied by a dog or cat. The majority of them walked right by us without even noticing our presence. A few waved but hurried on their way.

We passed Oma on our way inside. She motioned to me and said something to Thomas. I followed her to a quiet spot in the lobby.

"What has happened?" she asked.

"Seth's death was definitely murder, Oma."

Oma grasped my hand. "No! Who would do such a thing? He seemed like a nice young man."

"Surprisingly, there are several suspects already."

"This is terrible. What a tragedy."

"Come, Liesel." Thomas gently took her elbow. "I will make you a cup of tea with rum."

Oma nodded and walked away with him, but before they were out the door, Dave caught up to them and had a little conversation with Oma.

Holmes made a beeline for me. "Where have you been?"

"Louisa stepped out for a moment, and I went to check on her."

"Is she okay?"

"I'm not sure."

Holmes glanced around. "I'm going inside to see if I won my silent auction bids. Want to come with me?"

I nodded. But when we entered the ballroom, Louisa stood nearby, holding tightly on to Loki's leash with one hand and grasping a table with the other. She appeared almost trancelike. As if she couldn't comprehend what had happened or how to move forward.

"What's wrong with Louisa?" whispered Holmes. "Too much to drink?"

"You go ahead, I'll follow in a minute. I want to check on her." As I walked toward Louisa, I noticed Dave escorting Brenda out of the ballroom. If I hadn't known better, I would have assumed they were friends. I gave him a lot of credit for not embarrassing her. But it was apparent to me that he was taking her in for questioning. Oriana looked worried as she watched them leave. She was holding Fagan's leash.

"Are you all right?" I asked Louisa.

She turned her head slowly. "I'm a little woozy."

I didn't want to offend her, but I had to ask, "Maybe you had too much wine?"

"I feel like I'm coming down with something. Hot and very tired."

"Dr. Engelknecht was here earlier. Maybe I can find him."

"That's not necessary. This was all too much. Too soon after Tom's death. Seeing Seth dead yesterday brought back so many memories of the days around Tom's death. What I should have done. What I could have done. What things I should have handled differently." Her shoulders sagged like she was about to wilt. "I probably ought to go back to the inn."

I suspected I should go with her to make sure she got back safely. I asked her to sit down for a moment while I ran over to Holmes and told him what was going on. I insisted he stay.

Louisa, Loki, Twinkletoes, Trixie, and I took a Wagtail taxi back to the inn. Louisa was silent at first, but then she said, "I turned Seth down."

"What do you mean?"

"He wanted to have a drink or a meal with me, but I was so angry with him that I turned him down. And now he's dead. In the blink of an eye, he was gone. Forever. Never again. I should have had dinner with him. Or at least a drink or lunch . . ." She trailed off. "Why didn't I?"

"He told me you were the girl who got away."

Her shocked eyes met mine. After a moment they relaxed. "That's not true. Not even remotely. He once told me he felt like he only got Tom's leftovers. It's a terrible way to talk about women, but I knew what he meant. Now I'm one of the leftovers."

What she was telling me made me dislike Seth a little more. But whether he had loved Louisa was now unimportant to anyone except her. I suspected it might have been true, because I couldn't imagine why he would have said such a thing to me. It would have been easier, though less dramatic, to simply tell me they went to college together, but he chose to tell me she was someone important to him.

Seventeen

❀ ❀ ❀ ❀ ❀

Although I had been up late, I had slept fitfully. As the first streaks of sunlight broke over Wagtail, I hopped out of bed, annoying Trixie and Twinkletoes, who were worn out after their gala night. They grabbed a few more minutes of sleep while I showered and dressed.

Twinkletoes heard me dishing catfish breakfast stew into her bowl. Or maybe she smelled it. The odor was powerful. She joined me in the kitchen, meowing and rubbing her head against my legs as though she was eager to eat.

I made sure the pet door in my dining room was open so she could stroll around the inn if she felt like it. Then I called Trixie and locked the door behind us.

The smells of brewing coffee and sizzling bacon wafted up to us. Trixie raced downstairs as fast as she could. I found her with Mr. Huckle, who was eating his breakfast in the dining area. Not another soul was up yet.

Mr. Huckle had been a butler to the richest man in Wagtail most of his life. When his employer fell on hard times, Oma hired the elderly butler as a kindness. But her thoughtfulness had turned out to be a terrific business decision. Mr. Huckle insisted on wearing his butler's uniform, an old-fashioned waistcoat and bow tie. Not only did he give the inn a little class, but he always had time to help a guest. He walked dogs, delivered food to rooms, arranged buffets, scheduled appointments for people, and much more. We were convinced that he was everyone's favorite at the inn.

He stood up when he saw me, but I motioned for him to be seated and took Trixie outside to do her business.

Trixie and I left through the main lobby. The rocking chairs on the front porch were empty. Birds sang joyously in the trees. We were among the first to be up and about in Wagtail.

I didn't even see any joggers yet. The gala attendees must have been sleeping in, but that made it all the more obvious when I spied Joanne outside. It was the first time I had seen her in casual clothes. She wore black leggings and a shapeless long-sleeve black top.

"Good morning," I called.

She jogged toward me. "I'm so used to getting up early that I can't sleep late when I need to. You, too?"

Not really, but I nodded. "It's pretty quiet out here."

"They're all worn out. We brought in an unprecedented amount of money. Jaw-dropping!" Joanne leaned over to stretch, and I noticed a price tag still hanging off her top.

When she stood up, I said, "Thanks in large part to you."

"It was nothing. And I'm so glad to be able to help all those beautiful animals." She checked her watch. "I wonder if the others will be available for our bottle-feeding times today. You wouldn't believe how those kittens are thriving."

It was probably mean of me, but I asked how Rose had liked her gift.

Joanne started for the briefest moment, "She loved it. What was going on with Louisa last night?"

I supposed it had been unreasonable of me to expect Joanne to explain what happened with her credit cards. Had it been me, I might have blathered a funny story. But maybe it was Joanne's pride that caused her to switch the subject so abruptly.

"Everyone is having a hard time coping with Seth's death," I said.

"What did she tell you?" demanded Joanne in a tone so sharp that I wondered what she was afraid of.

I fudged. "Not much. He had asked her to lunch, and she turned him down. She was ruing how his death happened so fast, and she felt terrible that she hadn't taken that small amount of time to spend with him. It's something we all think about when a person passes on."

"I see. Perhaps we do."

"How well did you know Seth?" I asked, trying to sound casual.

"I barely knew the man at all. Certainly least among my friends. To be honest, I wouldn't have known him had he approached me on the street. None of us knew him very well."

That was a bald-faced lie. And quite unnecessary. Yet she felt compelled to say it. Either she hadn't received the memo about Addi's and Louisa's relationships with him or she was determined to protect someone. I looked at her in a different light. When you were always on top of things, it must be hard when something happened outside of your control.

Garbo, the elegant saluki, appeared. She nuzzled Trixie politely.

Oriana strode toward us from the direction of the lake. "Where is your husband?" she demanded of Joanne.

I would have sworn that Joanne stood more erect than usual. But the color drained from her cheeks.

"I was counting on him to keep my husband busy today," said Oriana. "Fortunately, that adorable Mr. Huckle lined us up with a boat and fishing gear. My hubby acted like a child. I have to remember that for gifts in the future. He was thrilled to be off on his own for a day on the lake.

Mr. Huckle even supplied a lunch and snacks. Holly, that man is a gem. I've told him that I'm ready to hire him. He can come whenever he wants."

"I hope he doesn't take you up on that!" I didn't think he would, but it probably made him feel good to know he was still appreciated.

"So, where is your husband?" Oriana asked again. "I didn't see him last night."

Joanne was silent for a few notable seconds, as if she was considering what to say. "Something came up. He wasn't able to make it."

"That stinks. At least you don't have to figure out how to entertain him today. Are we ready for breakfast? Shall we go in?"

I couldn't imagine Oriana fishing. She was dressed all in white, with double bell sleeves on her top, and trousers that fit like they had been made just for her. They probably were.

When we returned to the dining area, Brenda was yawning and Addi was chugging coffee. Oriana and Joanne joined them at their table.

I helped myself to a cup of hot tea before taking a seat across from Mr. Huckle.

Shelley swept by me and whispered quickly, "The great debate this morning is what happened to Joanne's husband."

"Did I miss something?" asked Mr. Huckle. "Gossip from last night, eh?" he asked, looking at me with disapproval. "You know how I feel about that."

I changed the subject. "Thank you for lining up a fishing day for Oriana's husband. They're delighted."

"My pleasure. They're such fine people. I do hope they'll come back to the inn sometime. But I'm quite concerned about Joanne. No one knows why her husband didn't arrive for the gala."

I sipped my tea so he wouldn't see my grin. Mr. Huckle insisted that he didn't gossip. He was even known to frown on such behavior. But the truth was that not much got by him. He was so proper and dignified that everyone in town confided in him. Guests at the inn disclosed all sorts of information to him. And despite his protests about the evils of gossip, he didn't hesitate to share what he learned.

He dabbed his mouth with a napkin and leaned toward me. "I gather they had a rather heated discussion on the phone yesterday."

I wondered if that had anything to do with the credit card issue.

At that moment, Trixie yipped, demanding my attention. She looked up at me with those big, innocent eyes. Sometimes I thought she understood what we were saying about her. But this morning, I suspected she wanted breakfast.

Shelley was laughing when she came for our order. "Somebody is hungry! Our specials this morning are cinnamon-buttermilk pancakes or a croque madame with cheese, ham, and an egg."

"Who could resist cinnamon-buttermilk pancakes?" I asked. "Twinkletoes has eaten, but I'm pretty sure Trixie would like the dog version of the croque madame with chicken instead of ham."

When Shelley brought our breakfasts, she pointed at the grand staircase. Twinkletoes sat on a step quite regally, but she was stretching her neck to watch Inky stalk Fagan.

Shelley giggled. "They're as bad as we are, spying on one another."

Trixie ate her breakfast with gusto. Mr. Huckle left to take care of a guest request, and I ate alone, listening to snippets of conversations between guests.

Half an hour later, I heard Oriana say, "She isn't answering her door."

I didn't think much about it until Brenda speculated that Louisa might have gone out early. Maybe to exercise Loki.

That made perfect sense to me. They continued eating while I dashed upstairs to brush my teeth, then headed to the office for my handy clipboard. I started my rounds on the second floor of the main building where Louisa's room was. No *Do Not Disturb* sign hung on the door, but I could hear Loki crying inside.

I hesitated. Maybe she had left him there while she went for breakfast. Or maybe she was in the shower and he needed to go out. I knocked gently. "Louisa?"

There was no response. I checked my watch. I would make my way through the hallway and then come back and look in on her. Trixie gazed up at me as though she wondered what was going on.

"Can you tell what Loki is saying?" I asked. Trixie sat at the door and stared at me. Her little tail wagged the tiniest bit, like she was acknowledging what I had said.

I walked on but realized that Trixie wasn't coming with me. She had parked herself by Louisa's door. She yelped at me.

Trixie didn't like Loki. But maybe she sensed something in his cries? Trixie had different barks, and I recognized most of them. It probably stood to reason that she would understand the nature of another dog's whines.

Oriana walked along the corridor toward me. Garbo ran to Trixie and then sniffed the crack at the bottom of the door.

"Do you have a key?" asked Oriana. "I'm getting worried about Louisa. We all had a late night, but I'm sure Loki is desperate to go out by now. I hear him whining."

"I'll be right back," I said. I could hear Oriana banging on the door and calling out Louisa's name. The room was close to the inn office. I explained to Oma, grabbed the key, and sped back. Trixie had remained there the entire time. It wasn't normal. Not at all. I shivered a little bit and fervently hoped we wouldn't find a disaster when we opened the door.

I slid the key into the lock and twisted it. I opened the door slowly, afraid Loki might bound out.

But he didn't. I stepped inside with Oriana right behind me. Oriana screamed.

Eighteen

❀ ❀ ❀

Louisa lay on her bed, one arm flung out and hanging off the side. She had thrown the comforter on the floor. Loki sat near her arm, whining.

"Louisa!" I rushed at the bed.

She was flushed and sweaty. Tiny beads of perspiration oozed on her face. Her eyes were open. I checked her pulse. It was racing. "She's alive. But something is very wrong."

I stepped back, pulled out my cell phone, and dialed Dr. Engelknecht's number. He didn't answer. I left a message and called 911. Oma was working in the office, so I let her know where to send the emergency medical technicians when they arrived.

When I ended the call, Oriana was holding Louisa's hand. "She's burning up!"

I rushed to the bathroom and wet a washcloth with cold water.

"No, no, no, Louisa! No! Holly!"

I folded the washcloth and ran back in time to see Louisa's body tense and contort. "Is she having a seizure?"

"I don't know. It's horrible. Louisa! Can you hear me?"

We watched as Louisa's body relaxed and slowly laid back.

I pressed the cold cloth across Louisa's brow.

"Louisa, can you hear me?" asked Oriana again.

"Tom?" murmured Louisa, "Can you take Loki out?"

My eyes met Oriana's in horror.

"Louisa," she said in a soft sweet voice, "it's me. Oriana."

"Oriana? It's okay. I promise I won't tell anyone your secret."

Oriana was looking at Louisa, but I could see her stiffen again. "I think she's delirious."

Someone knocked on the door, and it swung open. "Have I got the right room?" Dr. Engelknecht walked in.

Oriana left Louisa's side to make room for him.

"Who have we here?" he asked.

"Louisa Twomey. We found her like this, and we think she just had a seizure."

He took her temperature. "One hundred four. Have you called the ambulance?"

"Yes. Right after I phoned you."

He continued to examine her. "Has she eaten anything today?"

Oriana responded, "Not that I know of. She didn't come down to breakfast."

I noticed a glass of a clear liquid, probably water, on the nightstand, but I didn't see signs of anything else. I peered in the trash. No empty chip bags, cookie boxes, or the like. I wandered into the bathroom, and found one medicine bottle by the sink. I picked it up and carried it into the bedroom. "I found a prescription bottle of Levocetirizine."

Dr. Engelknecht reached for it. "That's an antihistamine for allergies. It shouldn't be causing a problem."

"She told me she has severe allergies to almost everything. Plants, trees, all sorts of things." I thought for a moment. "Allergic rhinitis and asthma syndrome?"

Dr. Engelknecht nodded. "Thank you, Holly."

The emergency medical technicians arrived, their gear clanking as they entered the room. Loki, who had been fine with Dr. Engelknecht, growled at them as they neared.

The one in the lead stopped. "Can someone remove the dog, please?"

It was an understandable request. I located Loki's halter. He didn't object when I slid it over his head and fastened it, but he clearly didn't want to leave Louisa. With Oriana's assistance and a handful of bison treats she happened to have in her pocket, we managed to coax him out of the room. I led him toward the stairwell, where he readily followed Trixie down to the lobby. I figured he hadn't been out that morning, so we headed for the dog potty area near the registration entrance where the ambulance was parked.

Trixie was not particularly happy about Loki's presence. She glared at him as though she was annoyed. I was wondering what to do with Loki when the EMTs brought Louisa out on a gurney and loaded her into the ambulance. Dr. Engelknecht followed them. I heard him say, "I'll meet you there."

The ambulance pulled out of the driveway, and Dr. Engelknecht walked toward me.

"Any idea what's wrong with her?" I asked.

"Nothing that's immediately obvious. A lot of things can cause seizures, but I can't discuss a patient's condition with you anyway." He smiled at me when he said that.

"Okay. Have you ever had a patient display similar symptoms?"

He was thoughtful. "Not exactly. Holly, I don't have a

handle on it yet. It could be any number of things. I'd better get over to the hospital."

"Thanks for coming so quickly when I called."

He waved and took off across the green at a good jog, and I went in search of Oriana. I found her in the Dogwood Room, filling in the rest of the WAG Ladies.

"Loki!" Addi scooted forward in her chair and held her arms out to him. "I forgot all about you!"

Loki readily went to her. I handed over his leash. "Can you take him while Louisa is in the hospital?"

Before Addi could respond, Brenda said, "I'll take him. I have enough room in the car and plenty of fenced-in space for him at home."

Addi gasped. "Surely you're not planning to leave without Louisa?"

Oriana sighed. "Tomorrow is Sunday. I've been away from the business all week."

I wondered if the others noticed that Joanne seemed particularly uncomfortable. "Yes. There are matters I should tend to as well."

"That settles it," said Brenda. "Our vacation ends tomorrow. Oriana isn't able to tell us much about Louisa's condition. What do you think, Holly?"

"She was confused and very hot. I don't know what that means."

"We should visit her in the afternoon," said Joanne. "Perhaps the doctors will have a better idea of what's wrong with her then."

I left them to their musings, noting that Trixie had a spring to her step again when we left Loki behind. We were walking into the reception lobby just as Rose arrived.

She seized my arm and propelled me to the corner. "I can't believe this. I was going to bring a picnic lunch to Grant today that we could eat in his backyard, but this morning I received an email from him saying that he had other plans and not to phone him. He claimed that last night was hard on him and made him think of Theona too much and that he had to call everything off. He would contact me if he ever wanted to see me again. Isn't that peculiar?"

My initial thought was that Rose might have pushed too hard. Everyone knew how easy it was to scare away men. And the judge probably wasn't used to being pursued. "I'm sorry, Rose."

"Sorry? Can't you see that something isn't right?"

It broke my heart. She was such a dear. She deserved to have someone special in her life. "Rose, give him a little time. Everyone was talking about Theona last night. It probably brought back a lot of memories. He might need a little time to himself to think of her and mourn her passing."

Holmes walked through the door.

Rose scowled at me and hissed, "Not a word, please!" She changed her tone and said, "It's almost lunchtime. Would you like a turkey and brie sandwich? Or how about egg salad? Holmes loves egg salad."

I wanted to do about a dozen other things, but I would probably stop for lunch at some point. I might as well do it now when Holmes was going to join us. "Sounds lovely, Rose."

At that moment, my phone chirped, indicating a text had come in.

Congratulations on your silent auction win last night. Please pick up your certificate for "A Day of Sailing on Dogwood Lake" at Tall Tails Bookstore no later than noon tomorrow.

I had been so concerned about Louisa last night, that it didn't occur to me to see if I had won anything.

I walked to the inn office. Oma was thrilled with the idea of a picnic lunch. While she oohed and aahed over Rose's picnic basket, I threw open the French doors so we could eat outside overlooking the lake. It was a perfect day with a bright sun and low humidity.

Oma and Rose added a nip of vodka to the lemonade Rose had brought. I tried to be cheerful, but Louisa weighed heavily on my mind. I passed on the alcohol, worried about what had happened to her.

I bit into a turkey and brie sandwich. It was a heavenly combination. Rose had softened the brie and added a dollop of apricot preserves for a delectable sweet and salty contrast. The three of them chattered about the success of the There's No Place Like Home Gala, but I noticed that Rose never once mentioned the judge. What was the deal there? She was Oma's best friend, yet she'd confided in me?

When my cell phone rang, I nearly jumped out of my seat. As I'd hoped, it was Dave.

"Still at the hospital, but we've got a problem," he said. "Doc Engelknecht was suspicious about the pills Louisa was taking."

"The allergy pills," I said to be clear.

"Right. Turns out they're thyroid pills. They're meant to boost a low thyroid, but since Louisa apparently has no issue with her thyroid, it was like an overdose. That's why she's so hot and a little delirious. She's probably been taking them for days. We're lucky she didn't have heart failure."

"Is she still having seizures?"

"I don't know. All Doc will say is that he expects her to improve and that it appears someone swapped her meds on purpose. Seems the two pills look very much alike."

"I know pharmacists are well trained, but couldn't that have been an error in the pharmacy?"

"We don't think so. The bottle held a thirty-day supply, and she was near the end. If she had taken the wrong thing for that long, she'd likely have been dead already. Listen, Holly, I need you to block off her room. Oh! And don't let any of those WAG Ladies check out. Got it?"

I hung up. I hadn't bothered telling him I couldn't keep

them here against their will. He knew that better than I did.
Besides, unless they had changed their plans, they were
intending to stay until the following day anyway.

"Holly?" Oma placed her soft hand on my arm. "Is it
about Louisa?"

I took a big sip of lemonade before telling them what
little I knew.

Holmes put down his sandwich and sat back. "Louisa is
the pretty redhead? Why would anyone want to harm her?"

"There's one person who might want to, but he's dead."
I told them the story about Seth driving the car that killed
the judge's daughter but claiming it was Wallace, Brenda's
brother, who drove.

Rose gasped and slapped a hand against her chest. "Poor
Bobbie! What terrible young men they were."

"Seems pretty straightforward to me." Holmes brushed
sandy hair off his forehead with one hand. "It's either the
judge, Brenda, or her brother. Do we know if he's in town?
Could he be staying here under another name?"

"It's possible, I guess, but wouldn't the WAG Ladies recognize him? It sounds like he's not very nice, so he would
surely have made a fuss about something by now."

"But that doesn't mean he's not staying elsewhere in
Wagtail," Oma pointed out.

"Wait a minute," I said. "I have trouble imagining that
Brenda or Wallace would want to harm Louisa. She might
be the only person who knows the truth, namely that it
wasn't Wallace who was driving the car that night. Why
would either of them want to get rid of her? I would want to
keep her around to tell everyone else the truth."

"Then it must be one of the other WAG Ladies," said
Oma. "That should not be so difficult to uncover. Is it Oriana, Joanne, or Addi?"

"Clearly we can eliminate Addi," said Rose. "We've all
known her since she was a child. She's very kind."

"Oriana," I said. "Louisa was definitely confused. She thought her dead husband was in the room. And then she told Oriana not to worry, that Louisa would keep Oriana's secret."

Oma clapped her hands. "There you have it. Oriana has a secret and feared Louisa would tell, so she attempted to kill her."

Holmes asked, "Could Oriana have murdered Seth?"

Nineteen

   ❀ ❀ ❀

"Are you suggesting that he and Louisa knew Oriana's secret?" I asked.

Holmes shrugged. "I'm just saying that there could be a connection."

"She's so lovely," said Rose. "I can't imagine her doing anything so crass."

"Was she at your party that night, Grandma?" asked Holmes.

"All of the WAG Ladies were present. But then the fire at Dovie's place drew us out on the street. I had assumed that he was sickly and had stumbled into my backyard. Are you proposing that someone killed him right then and there?"

"Not necessarily," I said. "I'm not sure how long it would have taken for the poison to throw his heartbeat off. But if he had encountered someone, surely he would have asked for assistance. 'I need help. So-and-so just pricked me in the back,' or something like that."

"I presume he was not on your guest list?" asked Holmes.

"You don't have to look so put out. No gentlemen were invited. Just the WAG Ladies, Liesel, and Holly."

"When the fire broke out, I was focusing on Dovie and looking for Trixie and Twinkletoes. I paid no attention at all to the WAG Ladies. Oma? Rose? Did any of them disappear?" I asked.

"I don't know about Rose, but I did not take attendance," said Oma.

"She's right," agreed Rose. "It's not as though the WAG Ladies were lined up like children. Any one of them could have gone for a jacket, or to retrieve a phone, or to use my bathroom for that matter. My eyes were on the fire."

I munched on a soft chocolate chip cookie. "These are good, Rose. Okay, Oma and Rose, it's your job to talk with the WAG Ladies and see if you can weasel any information out of them. Do they know Oriana's secret? We know Brenda went back to the house, but did any others go back to Rose's house or disappear during the fire? They're planning to visit Louisa at the hospital. Maybe you can catch them before or after? Thanks for lunch, Rose."

"And while they're sleuthing, where might you be off to?" asked Holmes.

"I have an auction win to pick up," I said with pride. I excused myself and headed for the green.

Trixie ran ahead of me, stopping to sniff now and then. We crossed to the sidewalk and were about to turn left when I heard someone calling my name.

I turned to see Dovie hustling toward me. "Now she's gone and done it!" Dovie wiggled her finger at me. "I've lost my job! After all these years, she waltzes in and changes everything. I've a mind to tell everyone and embarrass them both."

"Dovie, I'm afraid I'm not following you."

"Rose! Oh, she looks so sweet, doesn't she? That wicked woman talked the judge into firing me. Where am I going to find a job at my age? She just wants him all to herself."

That last part might be true. But would Rose really do that? "The judge told you that Rose doesn't want you working for him?"

"Judge Barlow isn't delicate. He comes right out and says exactly what he means. But the old coot didn't have the courage to tell me himself. That's what I get for dedicating my life to him and his wife. They were my family! I helped raise their children. I took care of Theona when she was ill and during her last days. And *this* is how he shows his gratitude."

"If he didn't tell you that you were fired, then who did? Rose?" Surely not. That would be completely out of character for her.

"He sent me an email. Nice and formal-like." She looked up at the sky like she was reciting something she had memorized. "'Dear Ms. Dickerson, you are hereby released from your duties as my cook and housekeeper. Your services will no longer be needed. A final paycheck will be sent to you in the mail. Sincerely, the Honorable Judge Barlow.' Now I ask you. Was that honorable or sincere? Because I'd like to know which part of that was honorable or sincere!"

A queasy wave washed over me, making me shudder. Aunt Birdie. Of course. She didn't just have Rose to contend with, she had to get rid of Dovie, too. At least she hadn't murdered them.

I reached out for Dovie's gnarled hand and took it into both of mine. I didn't dare tell her the truth. I tried to smile and choked out the same old tired explanation I had given Rose. "Dovie, last night was very hard on Judge Barlow. Everyone was talking about Theona, and it took the steam out of him. I think he might just want to be alone today. I bet you're not fired at all. You hang in there. Maybe have a cup of tea and a nice piece of cheesecake. I'll go see what's going on."

"Would you, darlin'? You'd do that for me? I don't know what to say. I'd be ever so grateful."

I steered her toward the bakery, which had a section in back with tables. "I'll let you know what I find out." I waited until she disappeared inside before I said to Trixie, "Aunt Birdie has done it this time."

I picked up my auction win in a hurry. It turned out to be a small crystal sailboat and a square slip of paper with instructions. Afterward, Trixie and I walked to Birdie's house. It was a lovely old home with a porch across the front. White wicker chairs with bright blue and white cushions practically asked people to come and sit for spell. A decorative birdcage sat on the table between them along with a bowl of summer peaches. Pink petunias cascaded from hanging baskets. Aunt Birdie might have some issues, but she had an eye for decorating.

I braced myself, marched up the stairs, and knocked on the front door. Aunt Birdie threw it open, crying, "I knew you'd come!"

She stopped abruptly and looked past me. "Oh. It's you."

Aha! She was undoubtedly expecting Judge Barlow. She wore a long-sleeve black scoop-neck top with a single strand of pearls and mabe pearl earrings. Her trousers were white. I had to admit that with her dark hair and the silver streak in the middle of her forehead, she looked chic. I suddenly felt frumpy. "You're lucky it's not Rose or Dovie standing here."

Aunt Birdie toyed with her pearls. "I'm sure I can't imagine what you're talking about."

"Maybe we should sit down."

"Has something happened?"

I gestured toward her chairs. The moment I sat down, Trixie leaped onto my lap.

"Aunt Birdie, what have you done?"

"I suppose you mean my extravagant bid last night for a hot-air balloon ride. My finances are none of your business, young lady."

"Did you win?" I was actually amused by her revelation. Aunt Birdie had a spark of adventure in her that I never knew about.

"With that bid? I should hope so! I thought Grant Barlow might come with me. We're at that age, you know."

"What age is that?" I asked, fearing the answer.

"Bucket list. There isn't much we haven't done in our lives. A hot-air balloon seemed so romantic."

"When I knocked on your door, you thought I was the judge."

"I do enjoy your exceedingly rare visits. It wouldn't hurt you to come by more often. But I was expecting Grant."

She avoided my eyes and studied her hands. I waited quietly with great certainty that she would confess to sending the emails to Rose and Dovie.

When she finally looked up at me, some of the fire had gone out of her. "I hope you marry Holmes and grow old with him."

I had to hold on to the arms of my chair. In the first place, we were nowhere near marriage. And secondly, it broke my heart to hear the sadness in her voice.

"I have been a very strong woman in my life. I have struggled to maintain respect and be self-supporting. I'm not sure I ever actually wanted to marry. Well, maybe a couple of times. But now I would like to have a companion. A gentleman friend with values and virtue. Someone to have a laugh with or go to dinner with. I guess I wasn't the only one who thought Grant Barlow might fit the bill. Of course, I planned to wait one year after Theona's passing. It never occurred to me that anyone would violate that rule of decorum. Dovie had an advantage, being there with him all the time. Small wonder that he developed a fondness for her. She waits on him hand and foot."

I admit that I felt a teeny bit sorry for her. "Pretending to fire her was hardly a virtuous thing to do."

"Fire her? Grant fired Dovie? When did this happen?"

"There's no point playing dumb. It doesn't become you."

Aunt Birdie tilted her head. "I know nothing of this."

I didn't believe her. "Oh, Birdie! I know what you did. You need to correct it, and I mean *now*."

"Grant let her go!" Aunt Birdie stared around, but I didn't think she was seeing anything. She frowned at me. "Are you sure about this?"

"Quite."

"Stay here." She rose and went into her house, returning with a letter, which she held out to me.

Dear Birdie,

I am afraid I must call off our plans. Last night at the gala was hard on me. The tributes to Theona brought back memories and made me realize how very much I miss her. Please do not contact me as I need some time alone.

Sincerely,
The Honorable Grant Barlow

"Isn't that peculiar?" asked Birdie. "Who calls himself 'The Honorable?'"

"That's a little odd. Not in a business letter, maybe, but it's absurdly formal in personal correspondence." What was even more strange was the fact that it sounded very much like what Rose and Dovie had described. "When did you receive this email?"

"This morning. I always check my email when I have

my second cup of coffee." She leaned toward me. "I prefer to sit outside with my first cuppa, assuming the weather is nice. It's most interesting to see what's going on in the world. People walk their dogs and cats. Some are on their way to work. A few zoom by on bicycles, going much faster than they should. Mr. Stashhollow wears a backpack when he pedals by on his bike, and the cutest little dog is inside. His face is visible and you can see how much he loves his morning ride."

"What is this plan to which the judge refers?"

She closed her eyes tightly before opening them and saying, "Clearly I have made an utter fool of myself. During the live auction, I bid on a dinner for two at Chowhound and won. I thought it would be a lovely gesture to invite Grant to accompany me."

"He accepted?"

"Yes. I thought he was a gentleman. But he's clearly a coward who had to hide behind his computer to weasel out of it."

"It can be awkward to turn down a person's kind invitation," I said.

"Not for me. I just say *no*."

"And that's why you're so beloved."

"Was that sarcasm?"

Naturally, it was. I didn't respond, allowing her to think what she wanted. It crossed my mind that Birdie could have sent all three emails. She was just sneaky enough to send one to herself to throw off suspicion. But I didn't think she was acting. "May I keep a copy of this?"

"Yes. Why would you want it?"

I debated the wisdom of letting her know that Rose and Dovie had received similar letters. I didn't think there was anything to gain by revealing that information. "I'm glad you shared this with me. I find it interesting that you received this on the same day that the judge fired Dovie."

Aunt Birdie gasped. "Rose!" She uttered Rose's name in a deep tone, like it meant her doom.

"I'm afraid not. I spoke with her this morning." I fudged a little to maintain Rose's privacy. "She brought lunch to Oma and me."

Aunt Birdie's perfectly shaped eyebrows arched. "My, my. What can Grant be up to?"

"I'm not sure. That's what I plan to find out."

Trixie and I left Aunt Birdie sitting on her porch and hurried toward the green. As we walked, I pulled out my phone and called Dave.

I could hear it ringing on his end, and at the same time, I thought I heard a phone ringing near me. His phone rolled over to voice mail, so I left a message to call me. On a hunch, I dialed again, and just like before, I could hear a phone ringing somewhere nearby.

It was Trixie who led me straight to Dave. I found her sniffing his feet.

He was so absorbed in kissing Addi that he didn't hear Trixie's shrill, insistent barks, nor did either of them notice me.

I cleared my throat and mock-coughed. Still nothing. "Excuse me! Hello?"

Dave came out of his romance-induced fugue. "Holly."

Addi flushed like a schoolgirl caught in the act.

"So sorry to interrupt, but I happened to be passing by."

Addi held on to Dave's hand like she didn't intend to let go. The trouble was, if neither Rose, nor Dovie, nor Birdie had sent those letters, then who did? The judge was most likely. Maybe he really didn't want them all buzzing around him. But after the judge, Addi had to be my primary suspect. I didn't know what might have motivated her unless she wanted the judge to think he needed her.

I gazed at Addi. She looked so happy. Of course, one did when one was in the fresh thrill of a new infatuation. I couldn't hold that against her. But I also couldn't help wondering if she was the one who had been spying on her grandfather. Could she be jealous and want him all for herself? Had she set him up to be alone so he would beg her to come live with him? Or both!

No, I couldn't mention a word about the judge's problems in front of her. As much as I liked her, I now had to be cautious. I smiled brightly, "Have you heard anything about Louisa?"

Dave suddenly appeared uncomfortable. "She's improving. The doctors expect her to make a full recovery."

"Great! I am very relieved to hear that."

He gazed at Addi for a moment before facing me. "I was going to call you, Holly. The fire chief from Snowball has determined that the fire at Dovie's shed was intentionally set."

Twenty

❀ ❀ ❀ ❀

My blood ran cold.

Addi still clutched Dave's hand and looked at him like he was wonderful. I had no reason to imagine that she had set the fire. But it was beginning to appear that someone wanted to be rid of Dovie.

In fact, it opened a whole other realm of possibilities. The most important one, perhaps, being that the person who set the fire might have sent Dovie the email firing her and added the other two as a cover.

"Do they have any suspects?" I asked.

Dave tore his eyes away from Addi's. "Um, no. Not that I'm aware of." He stared at me for a moment, as though he was thinking. "Did Judge Barlow call you?"

"No. As a matter of fact, I'm just headed that way."

He glanced at Addi. "I was there this morning. Be sure he tells you about it."

I squinted at him. He didn't want to say more in front of

Addi? Before she could ask, I changed the subject. "Are you still planning to visit Louisa today, Addi?"

She glanced at her watch. "I'm late! They'll be waiting for me."

She stumbled in her hurry to rush back, but Dave caught her. "I'll walk over to the inn with you."

They were sweet together and clearly had a strong mutual attraction. I liked Addi so much. But it worried me that she had ties that linked her to everyone in this mess. She'd been in love with Seth. Of all the WAG Ladies, she had the strongest connection to Wagtail. And her main contact in Wagtail was the judge, who was having mysterious issues of his own. As fond as I was of Addi, I couldn't help feeling leery. She seemed to be in the middle of the peculiar things that were happening.

I watched them walk off, wondering if Dave had the same reservations.

Trixie and I continued to Judge Barlow's house. I was a block away when I spotted Dovie behind a tree in the yard across the street from Judge Barlow's place. Trixie raced toward her. As I neared, I heard Dovie saying, "Shoo, Trixie! You'll give me away!"

"What are you doing?" I asked.

"You wouldn't have seen me if it hadn't been for Trixie."

That wasn't true, but there was no point in squabbling about it. "Are you spying on the judge?"

"I want to see who's in there. Do you think he hired a new housekeeper? And by the way, it's not Rose. She has walked past me four times."

Good grief. All his admirers had come to spy on him. Sure enough, Aunt Birdie marched toward us and nearly collided with Rose.

Mae Swinesbury, the judge's neighbor, emerged from her house and watched us from her porch. After a moment, she joined us. "What's going on out here?"

I tried to make light of the situation. "Everyone is worried about the judge, but no one wants to admit it."

"Worried? Well, I must say I wondered why Dovie didn't arrive for work this morning."

"Dovie, come out from behind the tree."

Mae raised her eyebrows. "Are you hiding from someone?"

I waited for Birdie and Rose to reach us. "I'm sure he's fine, Mae. It's just that no one heard from him today, so we're going to check on him. Now, ladies, I'm going in there to have a chat with the judge. And you may *not* come with me."

They protested quite vehemently, but their pleas didn't sway me one bit. I crossed the street and knocked on the judge's door.

He swung it open eagerly, but then his expression turned to disappointment. "Oh, it's you."

I seemed to be getting that unenthusiastic greeting a lot. Fritz was far more welcoming toward Trixie.

"Well, I'm glad you're here anyway," he said. "I had a hostile visitor. It was horrible. I had to call Dave."

"Are you all right?" I asked.

"My nerves are shattered, I can tell you that."

"Who was it?"

"We don't know. He banged and made sinister noises."

The judge looked quite fine. Fritz stood beside him, wagging his tail.

"May we come in for a moment?" I asked.

He looked right past me and waved at his trio of admirers as though he was thrilled to see them.

"I'd like to have a quick word alone before they come in."

His smile faded. "If you must."

Trixie and Fritz engaged in canine social niceties, but I followed the judge into the kitchen. It looked like a hurricane had blown through. "What happened in here?"

Fritz and Trixie trotted in, skidding on what appeared to be flour on the floor. Noses down, they sniffed out a cracked egg with a broken yolk flooding out of it, a blackened slice of toast that had been ineffectively scraped, and the entire contents of a can of tuna, which they politely shared.

"Dovie didn't come this morning, so I fixed breakfast for Fritz and me."

"You had tuna for breakfast?"

"To be honest, we didn't have much breakfast. The toaster is impossible. Everything comes out charred. I tried my hand at pancakes, but that didn't go very well, either. I thought I'd move on to tuna for lunch."

"So you didn't fire Dovie?"

"No, of course not."

"Did you write emails to Rose and Birdie asking them not to come around?"

"Why would I do that?"

It dawned on me that if someone were listening to his conversations, they could hear every word we were saying. That might not be a good thing.

I signaled for him to go into the forest-like conservatory. "Wait for me here, please." I returned to the foyer, where I opened the door and gestured for the three ladies to come in. I held my finger up to my lips, just as Rose had when I had visited before.

There was no stopping the gasps and shrieks when we walked into the kitchen. They followed me into the conservatory, and I closed the door. Fritz and Trixie came, too, with a good bit of flour dusting their noses and tuna breath when they panted.

"The judge denies having sent you emails. Dovie, you are not fired. Aunt Birdie and Rose, you are welcome here."

"One of you two must have fired me!" Dovie pointed at Rose and Birdie.

An indignant squabble ensued that was so annoying I was tempted to throw them all out. "Please! Quiet, everyone!"

They settled down but threw nasty glances at one another.

"If it should turn out to be one of you who sent the emails, the rest of us will be sorely aggravated, and rightly so. I suggest you confess now so we can put it behind us."

They eyed one another but didn't utter a peep. I felt like a schoolmarm trying to find out who threw the ball at another pupil. "All right, then. We will assume that none of you sent the emails. But that means someone else did."

Rose frowned at me. "I hate to be stupid, but how could anyone send an email with Grant's name and email address on it?"

"There are programs that make that possible." No sooner were the words out of my mouth than I realized that was proof that none of them had sent the emails. The judge could have, of course, but he was crotchety by nature and wasn't likely to have denied it. Not to mention the fact that he seemed quite relieved that his lady friends were there. None of them were dense, but they probably weren't sophisticated computer-wise, and pulling a stunt like this would have been a big effort for one of them.

The culprit had to be younger and more computer savvy. Just like the person listening in on the judge's conversations. In fact, it was very likely the exact same person, oddly intent on disrupting the judge's life.

They all stared at me, expecting me to clear it up for them. "I'm going to ask you not to speak of this with anyone else. Someone is trying to manipulate you, but I have no idea why. If you suspect anyone or notice anything odd, I want you to tell D—" I broke off. "—me right away."

Dave's name had been on my lips, but his new love for Addi was worrisome in this regard. Maybe it was best not to mention it to him. "All right?"

The three women began to chatter as if they were

friends. Which they were, I supposed. And there was nothing like a common enemy to unite people. But Rose's secret would be out of the bag now that Aunt Birdie knew about it. Had she given up on her privacy?

One other thing still bothered me. "Judge Barlow, why didn't you phone Dovie when she didn't come in this morning?"

A bit sheepishly, he said, "I thought she had quit. I was harsh with her at the gala."

Dovie wrapped an arm around the judge. "We've had words before. Last night wasn't any different. Both of us are opinionated and say what we think."

He smiled. "It was Theona who kept us levelheaded."

"Now that's the truth! She always helped us find a way around our differences."

I said goodbye, but Fritz was the only one who noticed Trixie and me leaving. He walked us to the front door like a proper host. He sat down, not at all interested in zooming outside. I closed the door behind us and wondered again about the day he'd gone missing.

Had Dovie accidentally let him out as the story went? Or had someone else intentionally let Fritz out to upset the judge? Had that been the first stunt?

At this point, I wasn't sure I could eliminate anyone completely. But I now worried that the person who was trying to upset the judge might be closer to him than anyone had imagined.

I walked back to the inn, knowing I should be concentrating on Seth's murder. But part of me felt like the pranks on Judge Barlow should be easier to figure out. I couldn't drag Rose away from the judge right now, but I needed some information from her.

Oma texted me as I walked. Trixie and I headed for the reception lobby. Oma was in the office.

She held out a check.

It was written by Joanne Williams. "Did you cash it for her?" I asked.

"Zelda gave her the money. It wasn't an enormous amount, so it didn't concern me very much."

"Have you tried to deposit it?" I asked.

"Not yet. I should like to know more about the circumstances in which she finds herself first. Perhaps it would be wise to inquire about her situation before shopkeepers and restaurateurs line up at my door with complaints."

"I gather that job falls to me?"

"You seem to be friends with them."

I nodded. That wasn't exactly the case, but it was part of the job.

As I walked by the registration desk, Zelda called out to me.

"Hey, Holly! You'll never guess who claimed that grubby T-shirt. Louisa!"

"The one with the Walley World logo on it?"

"The very same. She saw it when I was straightening the lost-and-found box and seemed sort of upset about it."

"Thanks, Zelda." Could there be a connection between Walley World and Brenda's brother, Wallace? Unlikely, I thought. But if my name were Wallace, I might wear a shirt like that as a joke.

I walked through the hallway to the main lobby, Trixie at my heels.

As it turned out, the WAG Ladies hadn't left for the hospital yet. They were gathered in the Dogwood Room with Dave. Had one of the shopkeepers complained to him about Joanne?

It appeared that all of them were talking at once. I caught mention of Louisa.

"What happened?" I asked. "Is Louisa okay?"

"It's Hershey!" wailed Joanne. "He's gone! I can't find him anywhere."

"She let him off leash because he was having so much

fun exploring the inn," explained Dave, "but now she can't find him."

"Do you have a photo of him?" I asked. "I can put it online so residents can let us know if they see him."

"Would you?" She asked for my email address and sent a photo immediately.

"You go ahead and visit Louisa. We'll be on the lookout for Hershey on this end."

"I think I should pass." Joanne's impeccable composure began to crack.

I understood what she was going through. I had lost track of Trixie a few times. "You stay here with me. I'll make you a cup of coffee. Give me a minute to post Hershey's picture. I'll be right back."

I hurried to the reception lobby and posted a missing-cat notice to the residents of Wagtail along with his photo. He was gorgeous, with ruddy fur and a fluffy plume of a tail. His copper eyes looked like they glowed.

When Trixie and I returned to the lobby, Joanne was gazing out the window, her arms wrapped around herself so that her hands clutched her elbows. Almost a self-hug.

"He's so distinctive," I said. "I'm sure someone will spot him and contact us."

She continued to stare out the window. "Have you ever gone through a phase in your life when everything went wrong?"

I had to stop myself from laughing. She probably wouldn't appreciate that, and it might sound like I was making light of her troubles. Had I ever gone through a bad patch! "When I came back to Wagtail, Oma was sick, I thought I hit a man on the road, I had lost my job, my boyfriend was being a total jerk, and then he *texted* a proposal to me. Oh! And Trixie jumped into his car wet, spilled coffee all over the carpet, then tore open a bag of nacho chips, and mashed them into the wet carpet while she was snarfing them. Nothing was going right."

She finally turned to look at me. "You seem to have landed on your feet. Are you still with the boyfriend?"

"No. But I have a new one who is far more wonderful."

She took a breath so deep it must have been painful. "I've lost everything. Hershey is all I have left."

Mr. Huckle cleared his throat. "Excuse me. Your grandmother has suggested I bring you some tea."

"That would be lovely! Thank you. Perhaps in the private garden?" I asked.

"You ladies go right ahead. I'll only be a minute."

"This way." Joanne followed me through the private kitchen and out to Oma's garden. A small table and chairs were surrounded by zinnias, petunias, herbs, and tomato plants.

Mr. Huckle was right behind us with a tray of tea and a tiered server loaded with tiny sandwiches and cakes.

When he left, Joanne leaned toward me. "I must say you have the good life with your own butler."

"There's another story of being down on your luck. Oma hired Mr. Huckle when he lost his position. Now he's like family and spoils us terribly."

Joanne sipped her tea. "It's nice being out here in the mountains. It's as though time has stopped and other things are important. No one is running to meetings and trying to fit more into an already packed schedule."

"I'm glad you feel that way. That's how life should be when you're on vacation."

Her hand shook as she lowered her teacup to the saucer. Her voice was a mere whisper. "I don't know what I'm going to do when I go home. I'd like to stretch out the days as long as I can. I'm afraid to go."

I had a feeling we were getting around to her financial

problem. "Why would that be?" I picked up a cream puff and bit into it.

"My husband took everything and left me. He was supposed to come here with Oriana's husband, but instead, during my absence, he wiped out our bank accounts, both business and personal. It's all gone. I'm going to have to sell the house, but it's mortgaged, so there won't be enough proceeds to save the business. He closed our credit cards and cashed out our investments."

Her breath shuddered. "You know what really gets me? How long he must have been planning this. I started the business all by myself. When we married, I thought I had a partner. He was so helpful, so interested in every facet of the business. Now I have to wonder at what point he decided to steal everything I had worked for. Was it before the marriage? Was that why he married me? Was he a con artist all along? Or did there come a day when my dear husband thought to himself, *I'm out of here and I'm taking it all*?"

Twenty-One

✿ ✿ ✿ ✿ ✿

"That's awful," I said. "What are you going to do?"

"Zelda very kindly cashed a check for me. Just enough for dinner tonight and gas for the drive home. Don't worry. I'll make sure it's covered. Unlike my husband, I don't leave people in the lurch. And then I'll have to patch things up the best I can. I don't know if anyone will give me a loan to keep the business afloat. I'll probably have to let employees go. That worm! What he did to me is awful, but didn't he realize that he was impacting other people's lives, too?" She held up her palm. "Don't answer that. He never gave them a single thought."

She picked up a sandwich and looked at it. "It's like being a child again and dealing with my father. I didn't grow up wealthy like Addi and Brenda. There were no trust funds or ponies. Louisa and Oriana came from middle-class families. But I was dirt poor. I didn't have a single birthday party when I was a child. My father couldn't hold a job, so we moved constantly, but it was always the same thing. Another dingy little hovel in a succession of forgotten towns. I was determined to claw my way to a better life. And now the one person I trusted has turned on me and taken everything. Wiped me out."

"You still have the business, though. So you'll probably have some money coming in," I said hopefully.

"Between rent and employees, the overhead is staggering. But maybe the worst thing of all is that I feel like such a fool. I married someone worse than my father! He had plenty of problems, but he wasn't a thief. I can't begin to tell you how many paychecks he squandered at the bar while there wasn't a morsel of food in the house. Some days all I had to eat were those little boxes of raisins. I can't stand raisins now. The sight of one sends me back to my childhood, and I can feel the hunger in the pit of my stomach. You've heard of children who don't have any food if they don't get it at school? That was me. I was the only kid I knew who cried when school ended for a vacation. I begged to go to summer school, and they all thought I was so smart and such a dedicated student." She leaned toward me. "I was hungry, and not for knowledge."

"That's terrible! What an awful childhood."

"I don't know whether to cry or be angry," said Joanne. "The first time I called my husband, I thought I could hear a woman in the background. I tried to brush it off as the TV. The second time, I didn't understand why he wasn't answering the phone. It wasn't until the credit cards were all closed that I started to worry. I checked our personal bank account and couldn't understand why it was empty. But when I looked at the business bank account, I realized what he had done. And now I don't want to go home and face it." She looked down at her manicure.

"I'm so sorry, Joanne."

"I have every reason to be furious with my husband. But

you know who I'm most angry with? Myself. How could I have been so thoroughly deceived? How did I allow myself to trust another human being?"

"I understand why you feel that way. But we all have to trust other people at some point. None of us go through life all by ourselves."

"I have. No one was ever there for me, except for my husband. And look how that turned out. All I have is Hershey. And now he has left me, too."

"Why is he named after chocolate when he has that beautiful reddish fur?" I asked.

"He's named after Milton Hershey, the founder of the chocolate company. Milton failed miserably at two businesses before he came up with a recipe for chocolate that was a success. I admire people like that. They keep trying and don't let their failures stop them."

"You're like that."

She looked at me in surprise. "Yes, I guess I am. I'll pull through this. There are always blue skies after a storm. Unfortunately, in my life, it has only begun to thunder. It will be a long time before I see the sun again."

"I have every confidence in you. If there's anything Oma or I can do to help, please let me know. Now let's have a good look around the inn. Hershey might be contentedly sleeping in a nook somewhere."

I sent Joanne to check the main floor, especially the library, which was often quiet enough for a good cat snooze. Meanwhile, I took the tray of dirty cups and plates to the commercial kitchen. That done, Trixie and I walked up the grand staircase to our quarters. Twinkletoes appeared annoyed when we entered and disturbed her afternoon catnap. She curled herself tighter and placed one paw over her face, the cat equivalent of a *Do Not Disturb* sign. The pet door was open, but a quick sweep of the apartment didn't turn up any sign of Hershey's presence.

I locked up. Trixie and I strolled the entire length of the second floor quietly, in case Hershey had been accidentally locked into a guest room. If he had been, he wasn't yowling or scratching to get out. We ended our tour on the first floor of the cat wing, where Joanne spoke with our housekeeper, Marina.

Marina shook her head when she saw me. "Hershey has always been very friendly to me. He is a very curious cat, watching everything I do. I am sorry that he is missing, but I haven't seen him anywhere."

"Thank you, Marina." I said. She opened the door to Pounce, and an object flew into the hallway, followed by Inky, who moved so fast all I saw was a black streak.

Marina was on the ball. She quickly swatted the cylindrical toy inside the room, and Inky followed at lightning speed.

Marina, Joanne, and I entered the room and shut the door before Inky could slam her toy into the hallway again.

Marina laughed. "You are a silly kitty." She leaned over and picked up the toy, quickly replacing it with a fuzzy catnip-filled ball.

Holding the toy out to me, she scanned the floor. "It's a medicine bottle. Is the cap secure? I don't see any pills."

I didn't either. But my heart fell. The medicine had been prescribed to Addi Lieras. It contained levothyroxine, the thyroid medicine that had nearly killed Louisa.

Twenty-Two

❧ ❧ ❧ ❧

"Is something wrong?" asked Marina.

"No." I forced a smile. "I'll just tuck this into the drawer by the bed so Inky won't play ball with it again." I plunked it into the drawer and shut it firmly. I couldn't believe that Addi would have tried to murder Louisa with her pills. Why would she do that? It wasn't like Addi at all. Surely she couldn't have changed from the sweet, fun girl I knew into a killer?

Joanne and I left the room, taking care to be sure Inky remained inside.

My phone trilled at me. Texts about Hershey were coming in. "Great news, Joanne! Hershey has been seen by several people on the green. Looks like he's heading northeast." I showed her a photo someone had snapped of him.

"That's definitely Hershey! Where is he, exactly?"

"Go out the front door and walk straight ahead. Keep going, but veer to your right."

"Thank you, Holly. What a relief. At least he's okay." Joanne hustled down the hallway toward the main lobby.

I trailed behind her.

"There you are!" Holmes walked toward me.

Trixie beat me to him. Holmes picked her up and cuddled her. Her little tail wagged so hard it fanned me.

"Could I interest you ladies in dinner this evening?" he asked.

"Sounds lovely. I wanted to talk with you anyway."

"I'll pick you up around six?"

"Perfect." When Holmes left, I made my way to the inn office, hoping Oma didn't have any big plans and could babysit the inn. She was locking the office door when I arrived.

"Holmes was here looking for you," she said.

"He invited me to dinner."

She smiled at me like only a grandmother can. "Don't mess things up with him!"

I laughed at her. "Do you mind staying in tonight?"

"Liebling, that was my plan anyway. Feet up with a good book."

"Thanks, Oma."

"Holly? Have you noticed anything different about Rose?"

Uh oh. "How do you mean?"

"She seems troubled."

I fudged. "Probably about Seth. It must be awful for her to know that he died in her backyard. She probably looks out the kitchen window and imagines him there in her mind."

"Yes, of course. I should have realized that. That would be very upsetting, indeed. We must consider how to change that."

"Good idea."

"Put on something pretty this evening. Yes?"

"Oh, Oma."

She waggled her finger at me. "Don't take him for granted. I'm not having you go back to the Ben."

I giggled and walked away. Oma disliked my previous boyfriend, Ben, and insisted on calling him "the Ben" to make sure everyone knew just how she felt. Trixie and Twinkletoes hadn't cared for him, either. And in the end, I knew he wasn't right for me. Maybe I *should* gussy up a little bit for Holmes.

At a quarter until six, I had showered and changed into a dusty-pink-plaid linen dress. It was casual, but about right for most places in Wagtail. Trixie and Twinkletoes wore matching gingham bows. I stashed the sailboat from the auction in my pocket. Holmes arrived just as the daily pet parade was ending on the plaza.

I began to suspect something was up when we walked past shops and restaurants and turned left into the residential area. Two blocks down, Holmes said, "Ta-da!" in front of a Queen Anne Victorian in desperate need of repair.

"This is the house you're going to renovate?" I asked.

"I wanted you to see it. I think it'll make a terrific bed-and-breakfast."

It had a huge porch around the front and sides, with beautiful rounded railings at the corners. I could imagine tables and chairs for dinner in those curved spots.

The door creaked horrifically when he opened it.

"Sounds like a haunted house. Is there any place in here where Trixie or Twinkletoes could get hurt?"

"Nope. It's a mess, but it's safe."

He gave us a tour through the immense foyer, a front parlor, a huge dining room with a grimy yet impressive chandelier, a butler's pantry, a charming old kitchen, and then up the stairs to six good-size bedrooms. We returned to the main floor down the back stairway, and he guided us outside.

The vast yard was hopelessly overgrown, except for a brick patio. Holmes lit tiny candles on the tables, and he had strung fairy lights from the branches of a large tree that extended overhead.

"There's no electricity yet," he apologized, gesturing to one of two chairs at a small table with a cluster of candles flickering in the middle.

"I think I prefer it like this. It's so romantic."

Holmes unpacked our dinner. "Salmon for Miss Twinkletoes because we all know that's her favorite." She purred and rubbed against his arm. He set her little bowl on the ground, and she immediately tucked into it.

Trixie looked on nervously, like she thought he'd forgotten her. She paced the brick floor, alternating between watching Holmes and sniffing the air near Twinkletoes's dinner.

"We are having pineapple slaw," said Holmes.

"Very interesting. I can't say I've eaten that before."

"Tomato, corn, zucchini, and quinoa salad. And steak with balsamic vinegar."

Trixie was getting impatient and yelped at him.

"I could never forget you, Trixie." He pulled out a bowl and set it in front of her. She began eating immediately, like she was starved. She didn't wait to hear him say, "Steak feast for my favorite pup, with corn, zucchini, quinoa, and barley."

Holmes handed me a plate. "Courtesy of our friends at the Blue Boar."

"Thank you!" Someone had thoughtfully presliced the steaks and drizzled the sauce over them.

Holmes produced two old-fashioned glasses, plunked crushed ice and straws in them, and filled them from a large insulated bottle. "Firefly Sparklers."

"They really sparkle!" I tasted sweet mango with a touch of orange.

Holmes sat down. "So, what do you think of the place?"

"It's beautiful, but it's going to be a lot of work."

"I've already had two offers on it, as is. Both more than I paid for it. I think I can turn a tidy profit on her. It will do me a lot of good not to sit in an office anymore. And I can hire some of the local guys, throw some work their way."

"That's very considerate of you."

Holmes shrugged. "I know their abilities, and most importantly, I know who I can trust."

"Why do I think this is going to be fun for you?"

He grinned. "Because it will be. Brenda McDade has asked me to call her when it's nearing completion. She's been thinking about opening a bed-and-breakfast."

I stopped eating. Wincing, I said, "You might not want to count on her. Rumor has it that she has run through her money."

Holmes burst out laughing. "Are you kidding me? She's the McDade heiress. They own commercial properties up and down the East Coast. Who told you that?"

"Apparently her friends think she's broke."

"The other WAG Ladies?" Holmes stifled a snort. "She could buy and sell them ten times over."

"How do you know that?"

"I'm an architect. Everyone knows about McDade Properties. It's huge."

I took a sip of my drink. "Brenda told me she used to be a teacher."

"Maybe she was. I don't know how involved she is with the day-to-day management of the company. But I'm pretty sure she's loaded."

"But they called her a penny-pincher."

"Now that is helpful to know for when I negotiate with her. I've met that type before. People who have a lot of money often accumulate it because they're tight with it. But it will be a while before the house is ready to sell in any event."

The balsamic sauce for my steak was absolutely delicious. But I was taken aback by Holmes's revelation. Brenda was wealthy, and Joanne had been wiped out. Now I feared Addi might have attempted to murder Louisa, and Brenda could have murdered Seth! I felt like someone had cranked the wheel of reality and everything had changed.

"What do you know about the Barlows?" I asked.

"I know better than to mention the Barlows in front of my parents, and you'd be wise not to as well." Holmes shot me a warning look.

"Family feud of some sort?" I asked.

"You could say that." Holmes put his fork down and took a long sip on his straw. "The Barlows' daughter Bobbie was infatuated with my father."

I couldn't help smiling. "That's kind of cute."

"Not really. She stalked him. You don't often hear about women stalkers, but Bobbie was a nut. They were friends in high school, which isn't all that strange. Wagtail kids often hang out together. But on a school holiday from college, Dad met my mom. Her family had bought a cottage in Wagtail, and Dad claims he was smitten the second he saw her. That didn't go over so well with Bobbie, who showed up at his college and followed him around."

"Bobbie wasn't Addi's mom, was she?"

"Bobbie would have been Addi's aunt. Senior year, Dad proposed to Mom, and Bobbie hit the roof. She kept going to Dad's house and making scenes. She even broke in and hid in my dad's bedroom a few times. Stupid things like that."

"The house where Rose lives now?" I asked.

"The very same. So my granddad had a talk with Judge Barlow. They say it came close to fisticuffs. Grandma Rose even had to ask the Barlows to send Bobbie out of town on the day of the wedding so she wouldn't ruin it."

"That's so sad. If I were crushing on a guy who proposed to someone else, I would be so offended I wouldn't want to see him!"

"Theona took Bobbie to New York City the weekend of the wedding to keep her away."

"That was thoughtful of her."

"Rose and Theona got along. It was the two men who could not come to terms. They say Judge Barlow was furious with everyone for breaking Bobbie's heart, but mostly he was angry with my grandfather."

"Rose's husband." Things started to clear up for me. No wonder Rose didn't want her family to know she was dating her deceased husband's archenemy. What a mess.

"Right. But things got worse. Bobbie overreacted, I guess. Mom said Bobbie married the first man who came along and smiled at her. The judge nearly blew a gasket when Bobbie showed up pregnant. There was a hasty wedding, and they went off to live somewhere else. Bobbie died a few years later, and the judge never forgave my family. Isn't that weird? He was convinced that she would still be alive if she had married my father."

Twenty-Three

❀ ❀ ❀

Given that information, I was surprised that Judge Barlow was interested in Rose. He could have softened with age, or he could be jerking her around. It would be petty, but not inconceivable. Even worse, could he have murdered Seth in Rose's yard to implicate her?

"You're awfully quiet."

I scrambled a little to respond. "It's a wonder they let us play with Addi."

"Oma probably had a lot to do with that. She was friendly with Rose and Theona. And I gather Rose and Theona became closer through their interest in WAG."

We finished our dinner, and Holmes produced a small velvet box. My breath caught in my throat. Was he proposing? It was too soon! I loved him and hoped this would be the path that we took, but I didn't know if I was ready for this yet. I could feel my heart pounding. Slightly terrified, I opened the box to find . . . a tiny high-heeled glass slipper.

My eyes met his. "Am I Cinderella in this scenario?"

Holmes laughed. "I told you I was bidding on something special at the auction. We're taking swing dance classes!"

I hugged him and was so relieved that tears came to my eyes. I dug in my pocket and pulled out the sailboat. Holding it out to him, I said, "We're going sailing, too."

He frowned. "You're the one who bid against me?"

We fell into gales of laughter. I was enormously relieved that we were on the same wavelength. Maybe one day . . .

Holmes magically produced a thermos of decaf coffee and a simple chocolate cake that was chewy and sinfully delicious, like a cross between a cake and a brownie.

"Any word on Louisa?" asked Holmes.

"There's something I need to talk to you about. But you have to promise me that you won't say a word to anyone else yet."

"Sounds serious."

"Could be. I think Addi and Dave are getting romantic."

"But that's great! Who'd have thought it? What's wrong with that?"

"Louisa became ill because she took thyroid pills instead of an antihistamine for allergies. I was down at Addi's room today when it was being cleaned, and her cat was batting around a bottle of the thyroid drug that made Louisa so sick."

In the light of the candles, I could see Holmes's expression change to horror. "Surely you don't think Addi would have poisoned Louisa? That can't be. It's not in Addi's character."

"That's what I think. But the prescription was clear, and it had her name on it."

"It's a coincidence, then."

"I'd like to think so. She was in love with Seth."

"The dead guy?" Holmes stared at me. "You're not saying . . ."

"I don't know what to think. But it has occurred to me

that Addi might be cozying up to Dave for reasons other than that he's a nice guy."

"No. No, that can't be. Anyone in Wagtail at the time could have knocked off Seth."

"That's absolutely true. Of course, some of you were busy fighting the fire at Dovie's house. And someone staying at the inn entered Seth's room, presumably to wipe fingerprints clean."

The corner of his mouth twisted. "What about the other WAG Ladies?"

"Well, if you ask me, Brenda had the most reason to be angry with Seth. Plus, we know she went back to the house, *and* she, her dog, and Seth all had meringue on them. On the other hand, Louisa's husband and Seth framed Brenda's brother as the driver in the car accident that killed Bobbie Barlow. I'm not sure, but it may have set him on the wrong path for life."

"If she knew that, why didn't she tell the authorities?"

"Louisa just found out from her husband. It was a deathbed confession."

"I think we can put Brenda at the top of the list of suspects. I would be enraged about that. Who wouldn't be?"

"Then there's Louisa, who was upset with Seth for not caring more about her husband when he was dying. She thinks he came to visit just to make sure her husband wouldn't spill their secret."

"Which he did."

"Exactly. Seth worked for Oriana at some point. She hasn't said much about him. However, on the day Seth arrived, I saw them out on the green, and she seemed very angry with him. And when Louisa was confused because of the drugs, she said to Oriana, 'I won't tell your secret.'"

"You heard her?" asked Holmes.

"I was standing right there."

"Who is the weakest link?"

"What do you mean?"

"Which one of them is the most likely to talk and spill the beans?"

"I don't know. They seem pretty tight-lipped, like they're protecting someone," I said. "Brenda seems fairly chatty, and, of course, Addi."

"Ahh. I see the problem. If Addi is somehow involved, then we wouldn't want to alert her, nor should we rely on her. On the other hand, she might be very happy to point a finger at someone else. Maybe give up Oriana's secret. Did you leave one out?"

"Joanne. She has serious problems of her own right now. Her husband left her while she was here working on the gala."

"How about I talk with Addi? I can ask her to come over here to see the house. Maybe she'll confess Oriana's secret to me."

"Sounds good. I'll take Brenda. She might open up under the right circumstances."

"Be careful," warned Holmes. "She's my top pick. Is there any reason she would want to kill Louisa?"

"I'll see if I can find out. Maybe Louisa saw Brenda murder Seth?"

"Now there's a thought. Wouldn't she say something, though?"

"They all seem to have secrets, but they're so tight, they don't rat on one another."

"You know the cure for that, don't you?"

I gazed at Holmes. "Turn them against each other?" I wrinkled my nose. "That seems wrong to me."

"Which is why I love you." Holmes scooted his chair closer to mine and leaned over for a kiss.

Trixie barked and jumped into my lap. Twinkletoes wasn't about to be left out. She leaped onto Holmes's lap and pawed at him for attention. Fortunately, Holmes found them as cute as I did, and our romantic dinner quickly turned into laughter, purrs, and a wagging tail.

We enjoyed the night air a little longer before packing up. Holmes was locking the front door when the shrieking wail of an ambulance filled the air.

Holmes and I looked at each other.

"I think we'd better check that out," he said.

I was in full agreement. We loaded the empty food containers onto Holmes's golf cart. Trixie and Twinkletoes were way ahead of us, running down the street.

We hopped into the golf cart and sped along behind them. "It sounded very close," I said.

"There it is, I see the flashing light."

Holmes turned at the corner and, despite the pleasant summer night temperature, chill bumps rose on my arms.

The ambulance had stopped in front of Aunt Birdie's house.

I leaped from the golf cart and ran up her front steps and into the house, barging past an emergency medical technician. I came to an abrupt halt. In the foyer, two EMTs tended to Birdie, whose face was flushed.

Moving in slow motion, she reached out a hand when she saw me. "Holly," she rasped. "I'm dying."

"Aunt Birdie! Don't say that! You're in very good hands, and they'll have you at the hospital in no time."

Dr. Engelknecht arrived at that moment, and I overheard the EMT say Birdie had a temperature of 104.

Ignoring the doctor, she said, "I've left everything to you. Don't sell the family heirlooms. All I ask is that you name your firstborn Birdie."

"Aunt Birdie, I won't have you talking that way." To lighten things up, I asked, "What if it's a boy?"

Her lips barely moved, causing her to slur her words. "It's a perfectly acceptable name for a boy. I can't feel my face."

The EMTs shifted her to a gurney. I stepped aside so

they could carry her out to the ambulance. I followed them, with Holmes right beside me.

Dr. Engelknecht's eyes met mine, and I knew from his grim expression that Birdie was in serious trouble.

"What is it?" I whispered.

"I don't know yet, but I suspect a stroke." His phone pinged, and he glanced at it. He banged the ambulance door. "Looks like we have another one. Take her right now. They're sending a second ambulance."

"Another one? Who?" asked Holmes.

A siren wailed in the distance, the sound mingling with the scream of the ambulance containing Aunt Birdie. Trixie and a few other dogs howled, making the moment even more melancholy.

"It's Dovie," said Dr. Engelknecht.

"No!" I hissed.

Dr. Engelknecht and Holmes gazed at me like I'd lost my mind.

"Holmes, you'd better call Rose and check on her. She might be next. I'll drive."

I called Trixie and Twinkletoes, who gladly hopped on the golf cart.

Holmes stepped in. "Why would Grandma Rose be sick?"

I tensed up. How could I explain without giving away her secret? "She was with Aunt Birdie and Dovie earlier today."

He dialed the number on his phone. "The doctor said he thought Birdie had a stroke. That's not contagious."

"It's unlikely that Dovie had a stroke, too. All I know is that they were together."

"I see. You think she might have been exposed to the same thing."

We followed the doctor to Dovie's house, where the ambulance was already parked outside and neighbors clustered around. When I stepped out of the golf cart, I heard murmurs.

"Poor Dovie. First the fire and now this?"

"What happened to her? Another fire?"

"She's having no luck at all."

I dared to enter the house even though I wasn't a relative. She looked much as Birdie had, flushed and feverish, surrounded by EMTs. She groaned and clutched her abdomen.

"Holly!" she cried. "Rose! It was Rose."

I looked around. Holmes hadn't come inside. He must have been on the phone with Rose. "Rose isn't here, Dovie," I said gently.

"I'm going to die. I can feel it." She reached out for my hand and squeezed it with surprising strength. "It's Rose's fault."

"What? What's Rose's fault?" I asked.

"This is the end," she sighed, closing her eyes.

"No, it's not. You're going to be fine," I said firmly.

Dr. Engelknecht instructed the EMTs to load Dovie in the ambulance. I moved out of their way.

"Does she have the same thing?" I asked Dr. Engelknecht.

"Looks that way. It's interesting that both of them are expressing fear of imminent death."

"Don't people do that all the time?" I asked. "They feel sick and they're scared."

He nodded. "There are some conditions that can cause fear of impending death."

"Like what?" I asked.

Dr. Engelknecht glanced at me sideways, "Like aconite poisoning."

"Wolfsbane again? Why would anyone want to poison two little old ladies?"

"Why is Dovie saying it's Rose's fault?" asked Dr. Engelknecht.

I bristled. "I have no idea. They were together earlier today, but I can assure you that Rose would never poison anyone."

Of course, Seth had died from wolfsbane poisoning in Rose's backyard. Dovie had to be wrong. Maybe the poison was affecting her memory or thought processes.

We walked outside, and I spotted Holmes. "How is Rose?"

"Perfectly fine. I wanted to go by to check on her, but she said she was going to bed."

"I guess she's okay then." I smiled at him.

But Dr. Engelknecht raised his eyebrows and shot me a look. I knew what he was thinking, because the same thought ran through my head. The person doing the poisoning wouldn't be sick because she would not have poisoned herself.

"Would you mind if we swung by her place anyway?" asked Holmes. "It's not far."

Dr. Engelknecht pursed his mouth. "I believe I'll go with you."

Twenty-Four

*   *   *

Every muscle in my mouth wanted to scream, *No!* What if Rose was at Judge Barlow's house? I tried to maintain a casual tone when I suggested, "Maybe we should call to let her know we're coming."

Both of the men scowled at me.

"She might be in her pajamas." Or she might be with Judge Barlow.

Holmes called Rose while the doctor and I looked on.

"Grandma Rose? The doc, Holly, and I would like to swing by." He laughed. "Holly said you might be in your pajamas." He frowned and held the phone out to me. "She wants to speak with you."

"Hi, Rose," I said cheerfully.

"They can't go to my house! I'm not there!" The high pitch of her voice suggested that she was panicked.

I *wanted* to tell her she needed to come clean with her family and Oma and tell them the truth about her relationship with the judge. Wagtail was such a tiny town, it was remarkable that no one had caught on and spread rumors yet. The doctor and Holmes were listening to my side of the conversation. I had to choose my words wisely.

"So you'd rather not have us come to your house."

"They're listening, aren't they?"

"Yes." And then it came to me. Judge Barlow might be sick, too. "You see, Dovie and Aunt Birdie have fallen ill, so we need to check on you and Judge Barlow since all four of you were together earlier today."

"Bless you, Holly! Tell them I'll get dressed and meet you at the judge's place."

"An excellent idea, Rose. See you soon!" I turned to Holmes and the doctor. "She'll meet us at Judge Barlow's home."

We hopped into our respective golf carts and crossed town to Judge Barlow's house. The lights at the front door gleamed, as though the judge and Rose were waiting for us.

I knocked on the door, and Judge Barlow flung it open.

"What in the name of good sense is going on? Why are you bothering me in the middle of the night?"

Rose stood behind him, and I noticed that Fritz was by his side. I had taken care to close the gate behind us, but Fritz wasn't being held back by anyone. He didn't even try to bolt outside. I was a little embarrassed, though, that Trixie and Twinkletoes trotted right inside like they owned the place.

"Well?" demanded the judge.

We filed inside, and Dr. Engelknecht explained, "Dovie and Birdie have been taken ill. I understand they spent part of the day with you?"

"Yes, that's right. What's the nature of their illness?" asked the judge.

"Could we go into your kitchen?" asked Dr. Engelknecht.

"Yes, of course." The judge led the way.

Holmes wrapped an arm around Rose's shoulders.

"Grandma, are you okay? No upset tummy? No fever?" He felt her forehead with his free hand.

"Oh, stop that. I'm fine. What's wrong with Birdie and Dovie?" Rose asked.

The corner of Dr. Engelknecht's mouth twitched as he gazed around the spotless kitchen. He peered in the sink. There wasn't a single dish or glass waiting to be washed. "Did Dovie or Birdie have dinner here?" he asked.

"As a matter of fact, they both did." The judge didn't appear to be concerned. If anything, he was annoyed at being kept up late. "I don't know how we can help you, Doc. I feel quite fine."

"And so do I," said Rose.

After a quick sniff around, the two dogs settled on the floor and watched us. Twinkletoes sat on top of the refrigerator, swishing her tail. I assumed they could tell something was wrong from the tones of our voices.

"Who washed the dishes?" Dr. Engelknecht opened the refrigerator door and looked inside.

"Dovie and I took care of cleaning up the kitchen," said Rose. "What are you looking for?"

"Leftovers."

"Oh, come now," the judge said angrily. "We all ate the same thing. This is preposterous. If you want to see what's in my refrigerator, then you can get a search warrant."

"Grant! You have nothing to hide," Rose scolded. "You go right ahead, doctor. There's a bit of leftover chicken. I think we ate all of the mashed potatoes I brought. There's leftover clafouti that Birdie baked."

Dr. Engelknecht closed the door and gave Rose a harsh look. "Dovie claims that you made them sick."

"Me? Why would I do that? And more importantly, that's obviously nonsense, or Grant and I would be ill, too."

"How do you know they didn't stop for a drink on their way home?" asked the judge.

"Listen to me carefully," said Dr. Engelknecht. "Your friends are desperately ill. They could die. I am required to turn this matter over to Sergeant Quinlan. It will become a police matter, and they will take samples of everything in your refrigerators. This would be the time to come clean and help me save their lives."

"Grant!" Rose cried.

I couldn't help noticing Holmes's reaction when she turned to the judge for help. He watched the two of them carefully.

"Now listen here, young man," said the judge. "I know how these things work far better than you do. Don't you dare lecture me on the law. You have no case. And our good health is proof of that. We all ate the same food from the same serving dishes. If you think someone intentionally poisoned them, then you are looking in the wrong place. Good night!"

We filed out the front door. I could hear Holmes murmuring reassurances to Rose.

The door closed behind us. We stood on the front porch long enough to hear Judge Barlow declare, "We should empty the refrigerators and wash everything."

I took in a harsh breath. That sounded like an admission of guilt!

"Grant, that's ridiculous," said Rose. "We haven't done anything wrong. That would make us look guilty when we're not."

"Rose, I have seen this before. They will paw through everything until they find the most minuscule thing to hang their hats on, especially since the doctor heard Dovie blame you."

"No. I'm not doing that. I haven't poisoned anyone. You always say the truth comes out eventually. I'm for letting that happen because I know one truth, I am not guilty of poisoning anyone."

As if things couldn't get any worse, Officer Dave ran along the sidewalk and up to us on the porch. "What's going on?"

Dr. Engelknecht, whom I usually liked, blurted, "I haven't confirmed it yet, but it's possible that we have two cases of aconite poisoning. Dovie and Birdie are on the way to the hospital in Snowball. I'm sorry to say that Dovie has accused Rose."

"Rose? As in your grandmother, Rose?" Dave looked to Holmes.

"Come on, Dave. You've known Rose since the day you were born. You know she didn't poison anyone."

Dave gazed at me. "How are you involved in this?"

I raised both of my hands, palms out. "I am but an innocent bystander. I was having dinner with Holmes when we heard the ambulance siren."

"Why are we at Judge Barlow's house?" he asked.

Dr. Engelknecht slapped Dave on the back. "This is your problem now. My patients are over at the hospital, and I need to get going. If you find any potential samples, bring them in for testing in case it's not aconite." He loped down the front steps and left as fast as one could in a golf cart.

I wanted to stay with Holmes and Dave. But Aunt Birdie didn't have anyone else. I was her only family in Wagtail. She'd looked so sick. "I'd love to stay here with you two, but I'd better get over to the hospital. Birdie doesn't have any other family here, and she's probably pretty scared right now. Holmes can fill you in on everything that happened.

"Mind if I give Holly a ride home?" asked Holmes.

"You don't have to do that. You'd better stay here with Rose, anyway. We can walk back." I kissed Holmes lightly. "Thanks for a lovely evening." I walked down the stairs. Trixie was right beside me, but I didn't see Twinkletoes. "Twinks?" I called into the night. "Twinkie!"

I heard her soft mew. Trixie did, too, and ran up the

stairs of Mae's house next door. Mae stood on the porch, holding Twinkletoes.

"She's such a beautiful kitty and so sweet. I want to keep her! What's going on over there?" she asked.

I walked over to her and reached for Twinkletoes. "It's a nightmare. Aunt Birdie and Dovie are sick. We were checking to be sure the judge and Rose are okay. I'm sorry to run off, but I have to get over to the hospital. Good night!"

I hurried along the sidewalk. Twinkletoes wasn't in the mood to be carried, but I didn't want to take a chance that she would decide to wander in the night. I held her fast until we reached the inn. When I set her down in the main lobby, she indignantly washed her fur.

Casey was on night duty, and Oma had gone to bed. I told him where I was headed and that Aunt Birdie was in the hospital. After settling Trixie and Twinkletoes in our quarters, I grabbed a light jacket and took a golf cart to the parking lot outside of Wagtail, where I switched to my car and drove down the mountain.

It was dark and lonely at that hour. Even the few houses that I knew were in the distance had no lights on. Thoughts spun through my head while I drove. It had been such a lovely evening with Holmes. But what a way for it to end. I knew in my heart that Rose would never have poisoned anyone. There simply wasn't any question about it. No matter how much she loved the judge, she wouldn't have tried to kill her rivals.

It wasn't until I walked into the emergency room, where Dovie and Birdie were in rooms next to each other, that it dawned on me Dovie didn't have any family. In a way, I guessed the Barlows were her family. Where did she go for holidays? Who comforted her when she was upset? Was she all alone in the world? Maybe she had a brother or sister? I watched her from the doorway for a few moments before I entered her room.

"Dovie," I said softly, "how are you feeling?"

She opened her eyes. "I've stopped throwing up," she slurred. "I'm thingling."

I assumed she meant *tingling*. She wasn't quite as flushed anymore. "Is there anyone you'd like me to call?"

"The judge. Does he know I'm ill?"

I was hesitant to tell her the truth, lest it upset her. "I'll make sure he knows."

She squeezed my hand. "Thank you, Holly."

"I'm going to check on Birdie, but I'll stop back by later."

Dovie closed her eyes.

I slipped out of the room as quietly as I could and peeked in on Aunt Birdie next door. Her color looked better, too. But the monitor to the right of her head indicated a rapid heartbeat. Even I could see that. I tiptoed toward her.

"Aunt Birdie? It's Holly."

"I didn't think you'd come. I've never felt so sick in my life. What does the doctor say? Tell me the truth. I'm going to my maker, aren't I?"

"He said that people with your condition often feel a fear of impending death. So what you're experiencing is natural."

"I'm not dying?"

"I hope not. We need you around." I would probably live to rue those words the next time she fussed at me for something of no importance. But right now she needed to feel loved.

"Have you called your mother?"

"Not yet." I checked my watch. California was three hours ahead. She might not be in bed yet.

"Please call her. Doctors don't know everything. I'd like to see her before I die."

I noticed that she wasn't slurring like Dovie. "Do you feel tingling or numbness?"

"Fingers and toes. Please call your mother."

I pulled out my phone and tapped the contact labeled *Mom*.

She answered with concern in the voice. "You never call at this hour. Is it Oma? Is she sick?"

"It's Aunt Birdie, Mom. She's been poisoned."

After a moment of silence, Mom asked, "What did she do now?"

"I think three women are after the same man."

I covered the speaker on my phone so Aunt Birdie wouldn't hear mom laughing.

"I'm sorry, honey. It's not funny. Will she be okay?"

Aunt Birdie reached an arm toward me.

"Mom, Birdie would like to speak with you." I handed Birdie the phone, which she promptly dropped. I picked it up, wiped it with hand sanitizer, and pressed Speaker.

"Birdie, honey, how do you feel?"

"I'm dying."

Twenty-Five

❀ ❀ ❀ ❀

Mom gasped. "I'll catch the next flight east."

"You'd better hurry. I don't have much longer."

"No! It will take me at least a day to get to Wagtail Mountain. Holly?" said Mom. "Could you step out and find the doctor? I'd like to speak with him."

I walked outside the room and switched the phone off speaker. "I'll look for him and call you back."

"No, honey, wait! I don't need the doctor. Is Birdie really dying?"

"I don't know. I think she's looking better."

"So she's not just being Birdie? Pulling a fast one to get me to leave my family and fly to her?"

At that moment, I felt sorry for Aunt Birdie. She was a pill. In a way, she deserved my mother's reluctance to believe her. I had been highly irritated by her on many occasions since my move back to Wagtail. She was cursed with the demeanor of a haughty schoolteacher who could make a person feel deeply ashamed over a minor transgression.

But I had seen her good sides, too. They didn't often show, but I knew for certain that if our roles were switched, and I was in that hospital bed, Aunt Birdie would be by my side.

"Holly, tell her I'm coming. I'm not, but just tell her that."

"I'm not going to lie to her."

"Then tell her I'm packing. And keep me posted. If the doctor thinks she's dying, then I'll come."

I promised my mom I would text her with updates, and then I went in search of Dr. Engelknecht. I found him comparing results.

He smiled at me. "Definitely aconite again. The difference between Seth and our two ladies is that it was injected in his back, near his heart. Unless that had happened in an emergency room, he had virtually no chance of survival. However, in the cases of Birdie and Dovie, it appears they ingested the aconite, a much more common means of getting it into your system. Each year a few people mistake wolfsbane for something else and put it in a salad or make a tea from it. In fact, in some cultures, it's used medicinally. Not something I would recommend given the high level of toxicity."

"That's why Dovie lost feeling in her mouth?"

"A piece or pieces of it probably touched areas on her mouth when she ingested it. In Birdie's case, it was likely wrapped up in other food, or she might have swallowed it whole with a liquid chaser."

I swallowed hard. "Will they survive?"

"I think so. Aconite poisoning is treatable if you get prompt medical attention. In this case, they were helped by Seth's death. If we hadn't had aconite in mind already, it could have taken longer to figure out what ailed them."

"Thank you, Dr. Engelknecht. Is it safe to leave them alone and get some sleep?"

"The nurses will look after them. I'm heading home shortly, too."

I looked in on Dovie and Aunt Birdie again one more time before I left. They were both asleep. Oma always said sleep heals. I hoped she was correct.

It was four thirty in the morning when I slid into bed.

At six o'clock, I woke to furious rapping on my door. Groaning, I rolled out of bed, threw on a robe, and walked to the door like a Neanderthal. I swung it open to find a small crowd.

Holmes's mom and dad, Grace and Doyle Richardson, walked into my apartment, followed by Oma and Gingersnap.

"I've never been in your apartment before, Holly," exclaimed Grace. "What a gorgeous view of the lake!"

I struggled to get my precaffeine brain in gear.

"Oh, honey! Doesn't your grandmother pay you enough to buy decent nighties?"

I looked down at my bathrobe, which hung open and showed my T-shirt. "Everyone sleeps in T-shirts. Excuse me."

I hurried back to my room to put on decent clothes and at least run a brush through my hair. Wearing a periwinkle shirt and a white skort, I returned to my living room, where Mr. Huckle was pouring coffee for everyone. He had set a tray of breakfast breads on my coffee table, along with napkins. Twinkletoes had settled on a high shelf and observed everyone with feline suspicion. I felt a little wary of this intrusion myself.

Trixie had jumped up into the chair where Oma sat, pleased as punch that we had company.

"Please do join us, Mr. Huckle," said Oma, as if we were having a party.

He handed me a mug of coffee. "I suspect you need this."

Grace smiled at me. "This is such a cute place. It's a pity the apartment won't be big enough when the baby comes."

Oma gasped. "You're pregnant?" I could see the wounded look on her face because I hadn't told her first.

"No!" I said, aghast.

They all spoke at once. Clutching my coffee, I stood in the middle of the room and said, "I am not engaged. I am not married. I am most certainly not pregnant! Now please forgive me, but I had one and a half hours of sleep last night. Why are you here?"

"You have to find out who poisoned Dovie and your aunt Birdie," said Grace.

"We've come to ask for your help," said Holmes's father. "They took Rose to prison this morning."

"What?" It came out louder than I intended.

"Not to prison, actually, but to the police station to be questioned. They might arrest her and take her into custody!" Grace explained. "Your old boyfriend, Ben, was a lawyer. Any chance he would come to Wagtail?"

"No, no, no." Oma waggled her finger. "We are not that desperate. Not the Ben!"

"Where's Holmes?" I asked. If he was at home asleep, I was going to be pretty miffed.

"He and Judge Barlow went with Rose. She's beside herself with fear. You know she didn't hurt anyone."

"I still don't understand why Barlow went with them," grumbled Doyle.

"Honey, that's all in the past. Bobbie has been dead for years. We have to let those old grudges be bygones." Grace clutched her husband's hand. "Especially now."

"My father is flipping in his grave to imagine that my mother is in the same vehicle as Judge Barlow."

"Doyle, calm down. He's doing us a favor, though, for the life of me, I can't imagine why." Grace shook her head.

"As I recall, the judge thought highly of you, Doyle," said Oma.

"That's true. He wanted you as a son-in-law," Grace pointed out.

"He wasn't so pleased with me when Bobbie died. I tell you, I don't like him interfering in our lives. He doesn't have Mom's best interests at heart."

"Holmes is with them," I said softly. "And the judge knows how the system works."

"That's why we're here, dear. We all know that Rose wouldn't harm anyone. You're so good at figuring these things out, Holly. Won't you please help us?"

"Grace, you didn't have to come here and ask me. Rose is like a grandmother to me. I'm very concerned about this situation."

"It is true that neither Rose nor I have been very fond of Birdie and her ridiculous pretenses." Oma stroked Trixie as she spoke. "But this is annoyance, not hatred, and does not lead to attempted murder. And we have nothing against Dovie."

"That's right, Liesel." Doyle spoke firmly. "Rose has no reason to harm those women."

It was going to come out eventually. I hated to be the one who gave up Rose's little secret, but who would have ever expected something like this to happen? I took a deep breath and braced myself. "The judge and Rose have been seeing each other."

"What?" Doyle popped out of his seat like someone had lit it on fire.

"Honey, sit down. I think Holly might be confused." Grace smiled at me.

Oma tsked. "I also believe you are mistaken. Rose would have told me if that were the case."

"Now what would make you think that, Holly?" asked Grace.

"Rose asked me to come over to the judge's house because they thought someone was spying on them. Actually, listening to their conversations."

Mr. Huckle rose to refill coffee cups. "Why, that's appalling!"

"That doesn't mean anything," Doyle protested.

"Did you find the perpetrator?" asked Oma.

I explained about the letters to the three women.

"Can it be that a fourth woman is trying to get rid of them all?" asked Oma.

"That's a distinct possibility. And it's worth pointing out that Seth died from the same poison, and in Rose's backyard."

"It doesn't surprise me that Birdie is chasing the judge," said Grace. "She's been looking for a man as long as I have known her. One has to pity her, really."

Mr. Huckle nodded. "And poor Dovie is like family to the Barlows. Perhaps she mistakenly latched on to the judge in a romantic way. Imagined being his wife now that Theona is gone."

"But why didn't Rose tell us about this?" asked Oma.

"Because she knew you would all object."

"Ach! Nonsense!" Oma sounded miffed. "Although Theona has only been gone for six months. It's far too early to chase her husband." She held up her forefinger. "One year minimum. Even that is too soon."

I smiled at her. "You see?"

Doyle's complexion was worryingly red. "Mom has lost her mind. What's she doing chasing a man anyway? Why can't she just be happy by herself? And to choose Grant? What could she possibly have been thinking? The one man in all of Wagtail who threatened her own husband!"

Grace was the only one who appeared sad. "We let her down. Rose felt she couldn't tell us. What other secrets does she have? I'm horrified that she couldn't come to her own family and be honest with us."

"Well then," said Mr. Huckle, "we must find the fourth woman."

"It's probably someone in our age group," said Oma. "Likely someone we know. I think we can exclude married women, which would narrow the field considerably. Come to my office. We can make a list quite quickly from the Wagtail resident roster. Mr. Huckle, would you please bring breakfast to my office for the Richardsons and me? Holly, keep us posted on what you find out."

The Richardsons were nice people, but I heaved a sigh of relief when they left. I was far too alert to go back to bed, so I hopped in the shower and dressed in a sleeveless blouse and a skort that passed as a proper skirt. I pulled my hair back into a ponytail and flipped it through the elastic holder to dress it up a little bit. Earrings and a necklace completed what I hoped was a competent look. My only concession to total casualness was sneakers. I had a bad feeling it might be the kind of day when I would be on the run.

I was outside, waiting for Trixie to do her morning business, when Aunt Birdie called me.

"I want to go home," she whined. "Can you please come spring me from this torment?"

"I'm delighted that you're feeling better."

"Get. Me. Out. Of. Here."

"Has the doctor released you?"

"Engelknecht? I haven't even seen him this morning," she complained.

"Call me when he comes in. I don't think they'll release you without his permission."

"Come pick me up this minute, or I'll change my will and leave everything to your half siblings."

I laughed. She was feeling much better! "Call me when the doctor comes in. Goodbye, Aunt Birdie!" I clicked off before she could make more threats. I only hoped that Dovie was feeling as well as Birdie.

Dave caught up to us on the sidewalk as we were headed to the dining area. "I thought I would be busy with petty thefts this weekend. Not attempted murder by residents of Wagtail. Is Mercury in retrograde?"

"Not that I've heard. Have you been in touch with Dr. Engelknecht this morning?"

"Not a peep. We have, however, searched Rose's house."

"Did you find anything?"

"I think I'd like to order breakfast first if you don't mind," he said.

That didn't sound promising. The tables were almost empty. I guessed people were sleeping late.

Shelley brought us coffee and tea right away. "Is it true that Rose has been arrested and Dovie and Birdie are in the hospital?"

Dave quickly informed her that Rose hadn't been arrested yet. I didn't like the way he put an emphasis on *yet*. I filled her in on Dovie and Aunt Birdie.

"No offense, Holly, but if your crazy aunt Birdie was being accused of poisoning someone, I would believe it. But Rose? No way."

"No offense taken. I happen to agree with you."

Dave bristled a little. "I have to go by the facts, ladies. I can't allow my personal feelings about a person to influence my perspective."

"You." Shelley shook her forefinger at Dave. "You need to use your heart *and* brain. You are sniffing on the wrong trail. I can assure you of that. However, it won't stop me from bringing you breakfast. Cook's whipping up some breakfast biscuits with ham, southwestern omelets, and berry-and-nut oatmeal."

Trixie yapped at Shelley. "I promise, no cereal for you. How about a turkey omelet?"

They say dogs understand about five hundred words, and I was beginning to suspect that Trixie had quite a vocabulary when it came to food. She wiggled her hind end.

"Twinkletoes has had a lot of fish lately. Maybe turkey for her, too?"

Dave and I opted for the southwestern omelet.

When Shelley left, Dave chewed on his upper lip like he was nervous. "Please don't jump on me." He pulled a plastic bag out of one of his cargo pockets.

It contained a syringe. I looked at it closely. It was empty but had contained something recently. Little globs of moisture clung to the interior walls.

"Do you think this is what killed Seth?"

"I do. We found it early this morning in Rose's backyard."

Twenty-Six

✿ ✿ ✿ ✿

It was the worst possible news. "That doesn't make any sense," I protested. "You searched her yard the day after Seth was killed."

"We must have missed it."

The syringe wasn't all that big. I had to assume that it could have lain in a patch of grass and gone unnoticed.

"We'll be testing for fingerprints right away."

"Why would Rose want to kill Seth? And if she did, why would she kill him during a dinner party at her house? Rose is smarter than that. She would have done it somewhere secluded, where no one would have noticed. Not in her own backyard."

"I wondered about that myself. It's more likely that one of her guests would have tossed it to get rid of it quickly. Although there is always the possibility that she panicked. Maybe someone came around the corner, and she didn't have time to hide it, so she flicked it into the grass."

Shelley brought our food and served Trixie and Twinkletoes first. Trixie's dish was loaded with omelet and lovely chunks of white turkey meat. She took one sniff and ate with gusto. Twinkletoes was more discerning and ate her meal like a dainty feline goddess.

Dave and I dug in, but when Shelley was gone, I asked, "Do you think the use of aconite against Birdie and Dovie was a coincidence? Or did Seth's killer find it handy and make use of it again?"

"That troubles me, too. Wolfsbane is readily available to anyone who takes a hike up the mountain. In fact, I'm told it's in some gardens in Wagtail."

"Is it in Rose's garden?" I asked.

Dave swallowed a bite of his omelet. "No. I had a second look this morning. There's not a spot where she might have ripped it out, either. That garden is pristine. She obviously takes pride in it and spends a lot of time out there."

"All the less reason to murder someone in her garden."

"Look, Holly, I don't want Rose to be the person who killed Seth and attempted to murder Dovie and Birdie. I really don't! But evidence keeps turning up against Rose. She admits to bringing a salad to the judge's house for dinner. That would have been the easiest way to hide wolfsbane. There were only four people present, which narrows the suspect list considerably."

"What about the judge?" I asked. "What if he made up all that stuff about someone listening to them? What if he used the wolfsbane? For all I know, he might be growing it in his conservatory. Have you been in there? It's like a jungle."

"And exactly what would his motive be? Why would he kill Dovie or Birdie?"

"Maybe he was trying to kill Rose, but she ate off the wrong salad plate?"

Dave wiped his mouth with a napkin and tucked it under the edge of his empty plate. "I know about the feud between the Barlows and the Richardsons. But it was so long ago that

I can't believe anyone would care anymore. It's sad that Bobbie ended up with a jerk of a husband, and it's terrible that she died, but the Richardsons didn't choose her husband, nor were they involved in the car crash that killed Bobbie. Even the judge couldn't reasonably blame them for that."

"Since when are murderers reasonable?" I asked.

"Good point. I've got to run."

"Can you give me a minute more, please?"

"Sure." He looked at me, but his body language screamed impatience. He was ready to go.

"I don't know how to bring this up, but Addi is on levothyroxine."

"How do you know that?"

I told him about Inky playing with the prescription bottle.

He sat back in his chair as though the wind had gone out of him. "Are you aware of any animosity between Louisa and Addi?"

"No."

"What about Addi and Seth?" he asked.

"She hasn't told you about her relationship with him?"

He flushed a little and groaned. "I've been so stupid. I never imagined that Addi could possibly be . . . We know Addi. We knew her as a kid. There's not even the slightest chance that what you're implying could be true."

"I don't think I have implied anything. Aren't you the one who said you deal with facts? It's a fact that she's on thyroid meds, and it's a fact that she was once in love with Seth."

Dave winced. "Are there any other facts I should know about concerning Addi?"

"Only that her family didn't approve of Seth. I don't know that for a fact, but that's what she told me."

He nodded, got up, and walked away. All things considered, he had taken the news better than I had expected.

Dave left me sitting there, thinking that no amount of tea would get me through the day without a nap. I watched as Oriana and her husband walked down the grand staircase. He was tall, dark-haired, and handsome enough to star on a TV show. They made a stunning couple.

Inky darted through the lobby, deftly winding between their legs to stop and touch noses with Garbo. Addi, wearing high heels, ran behind her cat and collided with Oriana's husband when he stepped back. He stopped her forward motion, and they all laughed.

I heard him say the word *home* and guessed he was leaving. Addi gave him the two obligatory air kisses, one over each shoulder, then hurried after Inky, who was already scampering down the hallway.

Oriana and her husband were the picture of success. They beamed health and happiness. When her husband departed through the front door, Oriana and Garbo went back up the stairs.

I finished my tea and reluctantly headed for the office to retrieve my clipboard. A few guests were checking out in the reception lobby. The Richardsons and Oma clustered around the coffee table in the office, going over printouts of Wagtail residents.

"Any luck yet?" I asked.

"Only one. Mae Swinesbury," said Grace.

"Of course!" I exclaimed. "The judge's neighbor. How could I have overlooked her?"

"She's a widow, so she might have taken an interest in the judge, but perhaps more importantly, she had access. We need to ask the judge if she was at his house yesterday."

I felt incredibly stupid for encouraging her to keep an eye on the judge. "I can go over and have a chat with her," I offered.

"Liebling, that would be wonderful!"

I seized the clipboard and found Gingersnap, Trixie, and

Twinkletoes receiving pats and attention from departing guests who promised to return.

Familiar with our routine, Gingersnap, Trixie, and Twinkletoes sprang ahead of me up the back stairs to the second floor where most of the WAG Ladies were staying. Seth's room was still marked *Out of Service* on my chart. I would have to check with Dave to see if we could put it back in rotation yet.

Gingersnap stopped at a door and sniffed it. Two seconds later, Brenda's dog, Fagan, emerged with Loki, who was clearly in the mood to play. He ran like a wild man, racing along the hallway to the other end and back again. Gingersnap, Trixie, and Fagan joined in the fun, but Twinkletoes jumped on the stair railing, undoubtedly to get out of the way.

Another door opened, and Garbo bolted out. Oriana watched as she fell in with the other dogs. "So that's what the racket is—dog games! Garbo could hardly wait for me to open our door!"

They charged toward us, Loki in the lead. He swerved and bounded into Oriana's room. Garbo was right behind him. They returned in a matter of seconds, with Loki carrying a stuffed shark.

"Oh no! That's Garbo's favorite toy," said Oriana. "I hope they don't get into a fight over it."

Loki's stocky body led me to believe that he would win a challenge from Garbo but she sidled up to him to grab her toy. And then it was a standoff. Loki on one side and Garbo facing him, they pulled. Fortunately, I didn't hear any growling or see any threatening posture. They were having fun playing tug. Gingersnap lost interest in their game, and at the sound of voices in the reception lobby, she tore down the stairs.

Fagan and Trixie disappeared into Brenda's room, but neither Loki nor Garbo had any intention of giving up their grasp on the poor toy shark. Brenda, Oriana, and I hurried closer to them.

"They're just playing," said Brenda. "Sooner or later one of them will give up."

"Garbo has never acted like this before," said Oriana. "It makes me wonder if I should get her a friend to play with."

Loki suddenly twisted and appeared to have an advantage, but Garbo held on, circling with him, her tail wagging all the way.

It took a full five minutes of play, but when Loki opened his mouth just a hair wider to improve his grip, Garbo won. She pranced along the hallway with the shark in her mouth, proud of her victory. But something was swinging off the toy.

Loki galloped after her and tried desperately to grab the shark again, but Garbo was an expert at lifting and lowering her head and turning to keep her prize.

"What is that?" asked Brenda.

Oriana walked over to the dogs and calmly said, "Give."

Garbo instantly dropped the shark and whatever was on it into Oriana's hand.

"Wow," I said. "She's very well trained."

Oriana winced and nodded. She removed the thing hanging off the toy and handed the shark back to Garbo.

"What is that?" asked Brenda.

"Nothing. Just got caught, that's all." Oriana stuffed it into her pants pocket.

Brenda eyed Garbo as she walked by Oriana's side. "Seth trained her, didn't he?"

Oriana blinked, and I realized that Brenda had caught her off guard. "He was very good with dogs."

Brenda held out her hand as if she expected Oriana to hand over whatever she was hiding.

Oriana stared daggers at her. "I am starving! Isn't it time we all went and had one of those fabulous Wagtail breakfasts? I can tell you my trousers are tighter from enjoying your cuisine. And this lovely mountain air makes me hungry."

By now I was very curious about what she had stashed in her pocket. Oriana might know how to handle her employees and customers, but she'd just flunked with me by trying way too hard to change the subject. "I'd like to see it, too, Oriana."

With great reluctance, she pulled a Sugar Maple Key out of her pocket. "Just my room key."

I didn't think so. She wouldn't have hidden it if that were the case. I held my hand out for it. The room name engraved on the tag was *Hike*. It was for Seth's room.

I didn't say anything, and neither did Brenda. We simply waited for an explanation.

"I was trying to protect Addi. I caught her going into his room, and I didn't want her to get involved with him again." Oriana looked straight at Brenda. "You know how she can't resist him and always ends up brokenhearted."

Brenda's expression softened. "I might have done the same. I'm in for brunch. Holly, are you sure it's not a problem if we stay over?"

"We're delighted to have you. I'm sure you wouldn't be comfortable leaving Louisa here alone."

"Perish the thought!" said Oriana. "Give Addi and Joanne a call, will you? We ought to go check on Louisa after we eat."

Oriana gazed at my hand as though she wanted the key back. I couldn't think of a single good reason for that. I fastened it to my clipboard and forced a smile at her.

I continued on my way. At the end of the hallway, I took back stairs down to the cat wing.

Addi was just coming out of her room, this time with Inky wearing a pink ladybug halter and matching leash.

"I see you caught your little escapee."

"Joanne still hasn't found Hershey. She's so upset. You can imagine! I don't want to be in her shoes. Inky is going to be on leash from now on whenever we leave the room."

"Did you take her with you when you went to Seth's room?"

I'm no shrink, but the surprised look on her face was real.

"Seth's room?"

"I thought you went up to see him that day before he died."

"I never had a chance. I ran into you and tripped on the stairs, remember? And then Joanne was being so demanding, and I felt guilty for running late. After that, we had dinner at Rose's house, and then Seth died. When would I have gone to his room?"

I believed her. She could have carved some time out of the schedule, but it seemed as though she was telling the truth. That was the day I had found her sitting on the stairs. "I'm sorry, Addi. I must have been confused."

"No problem."

She didn't even seem perturbed.

"I'm on my way to brunch. Want to join us?" she asked.

"Thanks, but I have some things to take care of."

"Of course, you do. You're not on vacation!" She ambled down the hallway talking to Inky. "Try to be a good kitty, and don't hiss at anyone."

I spied Garbo gazing down the cat wing from the library.

As soon as Addi had reached the main lobby, I scurried forward to the library. Oriana sat on the window seat with her cell phone to her ear. "Daddy will be home this afternoon. And I'll be back as soon as Aunty Louisa is out of the hospital. I promise."

I waited at a discreet distance, which wasn't saying much because the library wasn't very large.

Oriana made some kissing noises and said, "I love you," before hanging up. She smiled at me. "My children don't understand why I'm not coming home with their dad."

I nodded. "How many children do you have?"

"Three. They'll be fine. Their grandmother is staying with them."

I inched closer as I spoke. "On the day that Louisa was so ill, she said she would keep your secret."

Oriana licked her lips. "Those drugs really messed up her mind. She was delirious!"

"I don't think so. She might not have said that out loud for anyone to hear if she hadn't taken the drugs, but she didn't say anything like that to me. Only to you."

Twenty-Seven

❀ ❀ ❀

Oriana's neck muscles became taut.

"I did something terrible," said Oriana. "It could ruin my life if it got out. I confided in Louisa. That's all."

"You didn't get Seth's room key from Addi, did you?"

"No."

"Did you swipe it from him, or did he give it to you?" I asked.

"He gave it to me. I had an affair with Seth. It was a mistake. Such a huge mistake. I love my husband. I have a wonderful family. I don't know what I was thinking. And I certainly didn't want Addi to know. She wasn't seeing him anymore, but it still smacks of betrayal, going behind her back and having a relationship with her former boyfriend. It was wrong on so many levels. I didn't know he would be here. And then, of all the crazy things, he was staying here at the inn, and his room was just across the hall from mine, and, as if that wasn't bad enough, my husband was arriving the next day!"

She massaged her forehead. "When we returned to the inn to change for dinner, I went to his room. He tried to seduce me, but I was very firm. We were through. I couldn't do it anymore. I didn't want to do it anymore."

I wasn't sure I believed her. "Then why did you have his key?"

"He must have dropped his room key into my purse, because I found it there that night. I had told him my husband was coming the next day, and he made some veiled threats about outing our relationship. I suspected he put his key in my bag in the hope that my husband would discover it. It would serve to back up any story he told my husband. But then he died! And I realized how it would look. So that night, I took the little bottle of hand sanitizer that I travel with and I wiped down his room. I had to lock the door when I left, but what was I going to do with the key? I mean, Seth was dead. It wasn't like the key could turn up anywhere or suddenly be turned in or discovered at the reception desk. So I buried it in a bag of Garbo's toys and stashed it in the closet until my husband left and I could figure out what to do with it."

She closed her eyes and pressed her lips together. "Please, Holly. I beg of you, please don't tell anyone. I will lose everything. Everyone I love will turn against me. Please."

"I have no reason to tell your husband or any of your friends. But I have to tell Sergeant Quinlan. And I have to say that it doesn't bode well for you. I'm sorry, Oriana."

I left her crying silently with Garbo's head nestled in her lap. I felt terrible for her. But the truth was that I could very easily imagine a slightly different scenario than what she had told me, and I suspected that Dave would see it, too.

Oriana might have gone to Seth's room as she said. And Seth might have threatened to tell her husband about their affair. Oriana realized her mistake and that she would, as she had said, lose everything and everyone. That was certainly motive for murder. She had to silence him before he could blab. And she was the one who took his room key. I could imagine her filching it when she was leaving his room. She planned to return to wipe it clean of her fingerprints, exactly as she had done.

Nevertheless, a few questions remained in my mind. When had she collected wolfsbane? If she hadn't known he was coming, which could have been a lie, when would she have had time to get a syringe? And why did Seth go to Rose's house? Did he go on his own? To upset Oriana? She couldn't have set the fire because she was with Oma, Rose, and the WAG Ladies. They would have noticed if she had left the dinner.

Maybe she was telling the truth after all.

I brought my clipboard back to the office. Oma and the Richardsons were gone. In case she needed me, I told Zelda that I was headed for Mae Swinesbury's house and left the inn thinking about the WAG Ladies and Seth.

He'd seemed so nice on the surface. Who wouldn't like a guy who found missing dogs and cats and brought them back home? And if Garbo was any example, he was a good dog trainer, too. But underneath that good-guy image lurked someone who manipulated people to his advantage. Addi had said her family didn't approve of him. I wondered what they knew. Or were her parents better judges of character than I was?

Judge Barlow's house appeared quiet and calm. I couldn't tell if he was home or not. I passed his gate and walked up the sidewalk to the house next door.

From the street, it didn't look as large as the Barlow home. Italianate in style, I thought, given the detailed brackets and small third floor with three arched windows. The porch was Wagtail chic at its finest. Giant ferns hung between the columns, and in true southern fashion, the ceiling had been painted sky blue. There were forest green rocking chairs with white cushions that didn't seem like props. They were pleasantly worn, as though Mae spent evenings out on her porch observing the world. Tall, trendy lanterns flanked the front door along with no less than a dozen sculptures of cats in a variety of poses.

I knocked on the varnished-brown front door and could hear Mae walking toward it. She opened the door wearing a floral shirtdress with a Carolina blue apron. "Holly! I was just planning to take a little break from my housework. Could I offer you a glass of iced tea?"

"That would be lovely."

She paused and frowned at Trixie. "Maybe I should bring the tea out here. I don't think my kitties would appreciate a dog in their home." She leaned over to Trixie. "Nothing personal, dear. I think you're darling." To me she said, "Go around to the side and I'll bring it right out."

We followed the porch around the corner to more rocking chairs and ferns. Mae emerged from a side door that I suspected led to her kitchen. We sat down, and I realized that she had a perfect view of the Barlow house. Granted, there were bushes and a few trees in between their houses, but if anyone could spy on the judge, it was Mae.

I thanked her for the tea and sipped the icy brew. How to draw her out? "This is a lovely home."

"Thank you. I take a lot of pride in it. I'm always going through magazines looking for decorating ideas."

"You're a cat person?"

"Oh my, yes! I don't know what I would do without them. They bring me such joy. Dogs are fine for some people, but there's nothing like the love of a cat."

"I understand your husband passed away?"

"That's what I tell people," she whispered. "More like ran away, the louse. Ran off with a woman ten years younger than me. Good riddance. She can take care of the lazy bum in his old age."

Ouch. Not much love lost there. "I'm sure Judge Barlow can give you a hand if you need it."

"Theona was more likely to do that. She was the practical one. I do miss her. She used to come over here and sit with me sometimes. We'd gossip and carry on. She was a fine person."

"I imagine the judge must be very lonely without her."

"Hah! There's been a steady stream of women going into his house. I thought I'd take him some dinner when Theona died, but Dovie shooed me away. Said they had so many casseroles that they were stacked up in the refrigerator. But they keep bringing them. They're not all women his age, either. A pretty redhead about your age showed up to visit with him just the other day. She was in there for a good long while, too!" Mae raised her eyebrows as though a visit from a pretty redhead was quite the scandal.

"What day was that?" I asked.

"Let's see. I believe it was the day the WAG Ladies arrived in town. Or maybe the day after."

"Did she have a dog with her?" I asked, wondering if it could have been Louisa.

"I don't believe so." She lowered her voice as though she was speaking confidentially. "I've been over a few times when Dovie wasn't there. I wait until I see her leave and then I drop in to visit the judge."

"I'm sure he appreciates that." In truth, I seriously questioned whether he welcomed her visits.

"He does! I've been waiting for a year to pass since Theona died, but women in this town are not playing fair. One of whom, I might add, is your very own aunt Birdie. She comes around here like a cat that smells tuna. And her, with all her proper airs. I can't imagine why she doesn't think rules of polite society apply to her as well as everyone else."

"Aunt Birdie can be a bit of a pill."

"It's no wonder that your mother went so far away. But

Birdie isn't the only one slinking around the judge. Still, I have an advantage living right next door."

I was getting a little concerned and set the tea down. How stupid of me to drink it! Had this sweet lady poisoned Dovie and Birdie to get rid of them? But wouldn't she have poisoned Rose, too, if her goal was to keep the judge all for herself? Or had her plan gone awry somehow?

I went along with what she was saying. "You certainly are in the best position to see who comes and goes."

"During daylight hours that's very true. But after dark, I can't see a thing over there. And my bedroom looks out at the backyard on the other side of the house, so I don't hear anyone coming or going at night, either. I have considered moving into the bedroom that's on this side of the house, but it's just not big enough for me and my kitties. They'd be very upset if there wasn't room for them."

She was starting to worry me. Did she really have nothing better to do, or was she hoping the judge would be the new man in her life? Maybe she had been lonely since her husband departed. I played along.

"You're a good neighbor to keep such a close eye on the judge."

"Addi has been coming around more lately since she's been in town. I did wonder why she stayed at the inn instead of with her grandfather. That seemed odd to me. I think I might be offended if my granddaughter didn't stay here in the family home with me when she came to Wagtail. And that young man who was murdered. Wasn't that something! I saw him go into the house. They claim it was about finding Fritz. Do you think Rose killed him, like they're saying?"

Seth's death in Rose's garden was probably a hot topic of conversation in town. "No. I'm fairly sure we can exclude her."

"But I heard they took her over to the police station in Snowball for an interrogation!"

"That doesn't mean she's guilty. Rose didn't even know Seth. Why on earth would she kill him?"

"I'm sure I don't know why. Rumor has it that she gathered wolfsbane from her own garden and killed him with it. It's a pretty plant with those purple flowers."

"Do you grow it?" I asked.

"Not anymore, really. I used to, but my husband yanked most of it out. He was afraid of it! A few still come up and make me think of him. Do you know why it's called wolfsbane?"

"I have no idea."

"A long time ago, when people had problems with wolves, like maybe they were attacking chickens or cattle, they'd mix wolfsbane in a tasty dish of food and leave it out for the wolves. Killed 'em dead." She glanced at her watch. "Oh my. Will you look at the time? That nice Wylie Landon is coming over to build me a catio. Have you seen them? They're outdoor enclosures for cats so they can go outside without wandering away. He's a widower, you know."

"I'd better get going then. I was wondering, did you have dinner with the judge, Dovie, Birdie, and Rose the other night?"

"Wasn't that something? I brought them some fresh basil from my garden just to be friendly."

I knew exactly what she meant—to snoop!

"You'd think the polite thing would have been to invite me to join them, but Birdie took the basil and shooed me right out the door!"

"I apologize for Birdie. Thank you for the tea."

"Drop around again, dear. I'm always glad to have company."

When Trixie and I left, I felt terribly sorry for Mae. She struck me as infatuated with the idea of having a gentleman friend. If one of the other widowers or single gentlemen in town had been her neighbor, she would very likely have zeroed in on him instead of the judge. She did admit to having wolfsbane in her garden, which was a strike against her. Dave had said Rose did not have wolfsbane growing in her garden. Still, I felt that I ought to check for myself. Maybe Dave had missed it.

I headed for Rose's house. But as Trixie and I entered the green, I spotted Joanne sitting on a bench under a tree.

"Joanne?"

"Holly! I'm still looking for Hershey. This is the last place he was seen. It's as though he vanished after this point. I hope nothing bad happened to him."

"It has only been one day. Maybe he's getting hungry right about now and he'll come out of hiding."

She rubbed the back of her neck. "I've been looking up in the trees. He could be sitting among the leaves watching us."

"That would be just like a cat."

"Losing him would be worse than being broke. He's my baby!"

I knew exactly how she felt. "Let's not give up on Hershey yet. Do you garden?"

"The full extent of my gardening is buying cat grass for Hershey to nibble on. Why do you ask?"

"I was just talking with someone about wolfsbane, the poisonous plant that killed Seth."

"Brenda's the one who lives to garden. If you have any questions about the most esoteric plant in the world, Brenda will know all about it."

I smiled at her exaggeration. "I take it she has bored you with plant talk before?"

"Once or twice. It's her thing. I'm sure she tires of my chitchat about my business. Is she under suspicion for the murder of Seth?"

"I presume so. What do you think?"

"I have learned that I am not as observant as I thought.

I didn't notice where anyone was that night. I have reviewed it in my head like an old movie, but I still can't see who was where and when. That's the crucial part, and I am no help at all. I can see moments clearly, but mostly what I recall is the fire. Watching it and thinking that my life was going up in flames without any blaze. Poor Dovie. She was lucky, though, because she didn't lose her home. I just couldn't help thinking that everything can be gone in an instant. You don't even need a real blaze. We're all so fragile. We think we're not. We soldier through the days, feeling accomplished, but in the end, everything can be lost. I spent the first part of my life coveting everything. And the second part of my life acquiring what I had coveted. And now it's gone. I'd have been better off if my house had burned down. At least it would have been insured. Sadly, no one issues insurance for the way people treat you. It's bad enough when they're strangers, but all the ills of my life have been visited upon me by family."

I was horrified and had no idea what to say. I thought the subject had been Brenda, but somehow, Joanne had brought it all back to her and her problems.

"Maybe a good lawyer can help," I uttered weakly.

"I don't need a lawyer. I need a private investigator to find out where the slimy weasel is and what he did with my money." She shot me a sad smile. "Too bad Seth didn't run into me that night at Rose's. I'd have kept him alive because I think he knew where my husband went."

Twenty-Eight

❀ ❀ ❀ ❀

"Why would Seth know that?" I asked.

"I've been obsessing about how my husband managed to pull this off. They played golf together about a month ago. It seemed so unimportant then. I remember wondering, *Why Seth?* But now I know. Seth has done a lot of back-packing through the gritty underbelly of Central America. Mind you, I don't mean the beautiful beaches and lovely resorts. I mean the places people go when they want to disappear. I'd have gone to Seth if I had been in need of that sort of advice. My best source of information on that sub-ject is now deceased."

"I wish I could do more than tell you how sorry I am. Joanne, if there's anything I can do to help, I hope you'll let me know."

"Know a good PI?" she jested.

I left her sitting there, steeped in her problems, and headed for Rose's garden. Her beautiful home with the gor-geous rose arbor at the gate looked peaceful and gracious.

Anyone new to Wagtail would never imagine the horror that had transpired there. I walked along the bushes and flower beds, looking for wolfsbane. I kept checking the photos on my phone, but I didn't see any plants that resembled wolfsbane.

At the rear, bushes, trees, and vines covered most of the fence. The gate was open, as it had been the night Seth died. I wandered through it, tracing the path Fritz had used. A thick layer of discarded pine needles provided a cushion underfoot. It wasn't like the city, where one could often see all the neighbors' houses. I caught a glimpse of a couple of homes as I walked. The trees were old and large and had clearly been there for decades, providing privacy for the residents of the street. I knew when I reached Dovie's house because the odor of the fire lingered in the air.

I turned to the right and sneaked into her lot. Trixie led the way. A burned-out heap that used to be her shed was emotionally wrenching to see. But her bungalow appeared to be fine. Smoke had left it filthy. She would have to put on a fresh coat of paint.

I studied the black heap. Could Birdie have set the fire? She was brash, opinionated, and self-centered, but I had never thought her stupid. In fact, she had always struck me as highly intelligent. She didn't mince words and didn't suffer fools at all, but was she capable of doing anything so foolish as setting a fire? I didn't think so.

Nor did I believe that Rose was so desperate for the judge's affections that she would have poisoned her rivals. This wasn't 1500s Italy, when people allegedly offered their rivals tainted wine to kill them. This was Rose, who was sweet and helpful to everyone.

I could see why it would be easy to blame Rose for poisoning the salads. And it would be equally easy to blame Seth's death on Brenda. The town gossips might even wish they could blame the fire on Aunt Birdie. But none of that seemed right to me. There were holes in all the theories.

It did seem reasonable that the person who killed Seth was the same person who'd poisoned the salads. Unless there was a copycat in town. Could it be the same person who had been snooping on the judge?

My phone rang. In response to my cheerful hello, Aunt Birdie cackled, "Get me out of this place!"

Uh oh. I could just imagine how eager the nurses were for her to leave. She was back to her usual cranky self.

"Has the doctor discharged you?"

"I don't care what he says, I'm leaving. Come and get me right now."

"It will take me a while to—"

She hung up the phone.

I called Dr. Engelknecht's office to ask if Birdie was ready to go home and was told she would be discharged in an hour or so. Trixie and I returned to the inn. We found Oma and Gingersnap enjoying the beautiful weather on the private patio outside the office.

"Rose is coming home," she said. "I can't believe they put her through an interrogation."

"I'm sure she's glad it's over."

"I still don't understand why she didn't tell me about her relationship with the judge," said Oma.

I sat down in a chair, and Trixie observed the lake from the lawn. "Because not enough time had passed since Theona's death, and she knew it."

"Yes, this is a problem. What was she thinking? It is true, I would have told her it was not the right time for such a thing yet. Am I so critical that my best friend finds it necessary to keep secrets from me?"

I sighed. There was no tactful way of answering that question. "Yes."

Oma gazed at me in shock.

"You are very outspoken. That's not a bad thing. People know what you think."

"You are painting it with a fine brush. It is a problem when a friend cannot confide in you for fear of being struck down. I must let Rose know that I support her no matter what."

"I'm sure she'll appreciate that. May I leave Trixie with you and Gingersnap while I drive to the hospital to bring Dovie and Aunt Birdie home?"

"Of course."

"Trixie, you're going to stay here with Oma because you can't go into the hospital. But I'll be back soon. I promise."

I gave her a hug and a smooch, which reminded me of the lipstick on Fritz's head.

"I'll be back in a couple of hours."

"Ja, ja. Take your time."

I probably should have stopped for lunch, but I knew how anxious Birdie was to go home. I would feel the same way.

But I took the time to check on Louisa first. A nurse directed me to her room, and as I approached, a man exited. He was attractive, with chestnut brown hair and tortoiseshell glasses. I felt as though I had seen him before. I didn't think he was medical staff, because he wore jeans and a hunter green golf shirt. I didn't see a name tag like the staff wore.

"Louisa?" I said from her doorway.

"Holly!" A flush of red flashed up the sides of her face.

"How are you feeling?"

"Much better, thanks. I'm sorry everyone has had to make such a fuss over me."

"Have they told you when you might be discharged?"

"Soon. Maybe tomorrow. It's all so embarrassing."

"Embarrassing? You're a victim. It's not like you took the wrong pills on purpose."

"That's true. And they do look so much alike. I was flabbergasted when Dr. Engelknecht showed them to me side by side." She wilted a little. "Why would someone have done that? Why try to hurt me? I've been lying here thinking of almost nothing else. I don't know who to trust."

"Do you think it could have been one of your WAG friends?"

She stiffened. "They've all been here to visit, and every time I want to shout, 'Which one of you did this to me?'"

"Which one do you think did it?" I asked.

She squirmed uneasily. "I can't believe any of them would harm me this way. I thought they were my friends! But now . . ." She paused, trying to collect herself. "It seems that one of them wants me dead!"

"What about Oriana? Maybe she was afraid you would spill her secret."

The flush drained from her face. "That's just silly. What secret?"

I was impressed by her loyalty to Oriana, even in the face of the possibility that she had tried to kill Louisa. "About her seeing Seth."

"You know about that?" Louisa asked.

I nodded. "Oriana told me."

"I wish we had never come here. Everything is falling apart."

"Not everything. All your friends are staying until you can go home with them."

"Really? I didn't know that. I've been so self-absorbed that I didn't even consider them. You're right. They're good friends."

They were very good friends, with the exception of the person who had switched the pills on her.

"Louisa, did you go to visit Judge Barlow?"

She studied my face. "I don't see why that would be any of your business, but yes, I did."

"May I ask why?"

She let out a long sigh. "To pay my respects."

"Oh. I'm sorry. I didn't realize that you knew Judge Barlow."

"I didn't. But I knew Theona. And she was a wonderful person. When Tom died, a couple of people I had never met took the time to visit me and tell me things about him that I didn't know. I appreciated that they bothered to come by and share little parts of his life with me. I wanted to do that for Theona. To let her husband know how much she would be missed."

I felt deeply ashamed. Here I was, nosing around, when Louisa had done something noble.

"Did you talk about Wallace and Seth?" I asked.

"He didn't bring it up, and neither did I. I decided that it might be better for the letter to speak for itself. It came from Tom's heart, and I didn't want to diminish that by adding my two cents."

"I hope you're back on your feet soon."

I said goodbye and went to spring Dovie and Aunt Birdie. They fussed with the nurses in the hospital. And they fussed with each other on the drive back to Wagtail. I understood how moms felt when they drove arguing children around.

Dovie refused my offers to make her a cup of tea and help her get settled, saying, "All I want is a nap. Those crazy people never let a person sleep. Always coming in to poke me."

Aunt Birdie, on the other hand, informed me that I would make her a cup of tea while she showered and got rid of the hospital malodor clinging to her. I gladly put the kettle on and found some nice cookies with chocolate icing in the cupboard that I thought she might like. I set them on a table by the chair I presumed she probably preferred. Her house was decorated with flair, but as an antiques expert, she had more than her fair share of ancient and uncomfortable furniture.

She emerged from her shower in an elegant bathrobe with her hair wound in a turban. "Is Rose in prison?"

"I certainly hope not."

Aunt Birdie gasped. "Your lack of concern for your sole living relative overwhelms me. Which team are you on, Holly?" She peered into her teacup. "I hope this isn't wolfsbane tea."

"Aunt Birdie! Now stop that. You know Rose didn't poison you."

"You'd feel differently if your stomach had twisted and churned until you thought you were dying."

She had a point. "How do you know it wasn't the judge?"

She choked on her cookie and hacked. "He is one of the most respected men in this town. How dare you even jest about such a thing?"

I hadn't meant it seriously, but now that I thought about it, maybe the judge was behind the poisoning. In fact, what if he was behind all those silly things that had happened to him? The window, the oatmeal, the floral mix-up, even the letters. He was in a perfect position to have done all those things. For attention, perhaps? Was he too lonely without the lovely Theona? Was it a cry for help of some kind? He could even have murdered Seth. He walked all over town. No one would have thought a thing about it if they had seen him out on a walk. Aunt Birdie wasn't with him that night, nor was Dovie or Rose! In fact, until Holmes and I returned Fritz to him, he was most likely all alone.

Aunt Birdie was blathering on about something. I leaned over and kissed her cheek. "I have to run now. Call me if you need anything."

I was already walking out the door when she cried out, "Will you answer if I call?"

I went straight back to the inn and found Mr. Huckle having a cup of tea. "I thought you were off today."

"You were tied up with your aunt and Dovie, and your grandmother very much wanted to visit with Rose, so she called me to fill in while you two were out. It's been very quiet here."

"Where's Trixie?"

"She took the dogs to Judge Barlow's house with her. I think Fritz likes their company."

"Barlow? Rose didn't go home?"

He smiled coyly. "My dear Miss Holly, you are the one who informed us that there is an affaire d'amour between the judge and Rose."

"Thank you, Mr. Huckle." I left in a hurry.

As I ran along the corridor to the registration lobby, Twinkletoes sprang out of nowhere, probably thinking I was up to something fun. I grabbed a golf cart key and beat a hasty exit. Twinkletoes readily jumped on the passenger side of the front bench.

We sped to the judge's house as fast as the golf cart could go. Oma's golf cart was parked in front of the house, which was a relief. At least she hadn't left Rose alone.

I knocked on the door, and Holmes opened it. Twinkletoes sped past him into the house.

"Holly!" Holmes grabbed me in a bearhug. "I'm so glad you came," he whispered. "It's been the worst day." He let go of me, took my hand in his, and smiled at me. Trixie bounded to me, acting like she hadn't seen me in a month.

I closed the door and swept her up into my arms. "How did it go?"

"It was a nightmare. Grandma Rose had nothing to tell them. She doesn't grow wolfsbane. She knows about it, the way we all do. It's a plant that grows on its own in the mountains. She has no ill will toward Birdie or Dovie. The cops over on Snowball don't know her like we do. Dave says the best thing is to get Oma and the WAG Ladies together to see if we can account for her whereabouts the night Seth was killed."

"Poor Rose. How's she doing?"

"The judge is out in the conservatory with my dad and the dogs. Have you seen it?"

"I have. Where are Rose and Oma?"

"Upstairs. Rose wanted to rest. She's wiped out."

"Great. Don't leave anyone alone with the judge."

"What?"

"Just trust me. I'll explain later."

Twenty-Nine

* * *

I shot up the stairs and listened for voices. It was quiet, though, and I didn't hear a peep. Doors were open to most of the bedrooms. But the door to the last one on the east side of the house was ajar. I peeked inside.

Oma sat in a chair by the bed. Rose was stretched out with her eyes closed. When Oma saw me, she signaled not to make any noise.

I entered the room. Rose didn't look any worse for her interrogation. But she was clearly wiped out.

I drifted over to the window that looked out toward Mae's property. A cat sat in the upstairs window. It must have been the small room she had spoken of. The cat stood on his hind legs and scratched against the window as if he wanted to get out.

My eyes narrowed for a better look. That ruddy fur looked an awful lot like Hershey's. In fact, the more I studied the cat, the more I thought it was Hershey! It was definitely a Somali.

Moving as quietly as I could, I left the room and hurried down the stairs and into the conservatory, where Holmes kept the judge company. Trixie jumped to her feet as though she knew something was up.

"I think Mae Swinesbury has a cat that belongs to one of our guests," I blurted.

"How can you tell?" asked the judge. "She has so many."

"It's a Somali. They're quite distinctive, with long fur and fluffy tails. I'm going over there."

The judge and Holmes stayed put, but Trixie and Twinkletoes accompanied me to Mae's house. I knocked on the front door.

Mae opened the door a crack. "You're back."

"I noticed a cat in your upstairs window. It looks just like one that went missing. He belongs to a guest at the inn. I'm sure you must have seen the texts I sent out about Hershey."

"Mmm. I may have seen a text. But I haven't seen the cat. Sorry."

Mae began to close the door. I stuck the toe of my shoe in the crack to stop her. "Are you certain? Maybe I could have a look?"

"Really, Holly. I'm busy right now. I don't have the cat."

"Why don't you step outside and I'll point him out to you?"

"That's not necessary. All the cats in my house belong to me."

At that precise moment, Twinkletoes dashed over my foot and squeezed into Mae's house.

"Twinkletoes!" I cried.

Trixie didn't help the situation by barking.

"Now you've done it," Mae grumbled. "Let me shut this door so I can fetch Twinkletoes."

"I don't think so. Why are you so eager to close the door?"

"So my cats don't get out!"

"Then I'll have to come in."

"No!" Mae appeared a little taken aback by my response. "It's a mess. I don't want anyone seeing it this way."

"I won't look."

"Then you'll fall over things. No. I'm sorry, I just don't like people in my house."

"Twinkletoes!" I called. "Twinkie!"

Half a dozen cats ran to my foot and mewed. None of them were Twinkletoes or Hershey.

"What's going on here?"

I heard footsteps on the porch behind me.

"Hi, Trixie," a male voice said.

I glanced over my shoulder to see Dave.

"Now look what you've done," Mae hissed. "The law is here!"

"Twinkletoes is in Mae's house, and I think she might also have Hershey, the cat who went missing."

"I see. Hiya, Mae." Dave smiled at her sweetly.

"Hi, honey. If she would let me close the door, I would get her cat for her."

Dave gazed down at my foot. "Why don't you let us in to help you? You know how elusive cats can be. Twinkletoes might not let you catch her."

"No. She can go home when she wants to. Maybe Twinkletoes would rather be here with me. I didn't drag her inside. She left Holly and came in of her own free will."

"Mae," said Dave kindly, "I'm not going to fight with you over this. We all know Twinkletoes belongs to Holly. Now open the door."

I felt the door squeeze against my foot. "She's trying to close it," I muttered to Dave through gritted teeth.

"Mae Swinesbury, you open that door right now," Dave ordered in a stern tone.

"Holly!" I recognized Holmes's voice. "Is everything okay?" He jogged over and up onto Mac's porch.

I explained the situation to him.

"Mae," said Dave, "this is utterly ridiculous. Now open the door so Holly can get her cat."

She backed away and let the three of us in. Trixie managed to squeeze in underfoot without being noticed.

"Could I offer you boys some iced tea?" asked Mae.

I had a feeling they were too stunned to answer. I had never seen so many cats in my life. To Mae's credit, the house wasn't a mess at all. But cats of every color lounged happily on cat trees, sofas, and tables.

"Um, Mae? Just how many cats do you have?" asked Dave.

Trixie romped up the stairs, and I followed her quickly in the hope that she could smell her buddy Twinkletoes.

Trixie trotted into the room at the top of the stairs, where I thought I had seen Hershey. Sure enough, Twinkletoes and Hershey sat together on a bed, looking at us.

I picked both of them up. Thankfully, Twinkletoes was amazingly light. Neither of them squirmed when I carried them down the stairs. Holmes reached out for Hershey and took him into his arms.

"No, no, no." Mae shook her head and waggled her forefinger. "You can have Twinkletoes, but you don't get to come into my house and help yourself to my cats."

"Mae, I'm pretty sure this is Hershey."

"No, he isn't."

"What's his name, then?" I prodded.

She hesitated, just long enough for it to be obvious she had to make up a name and fast. "Harvey."

"Mae," said Dave, like he was a disappointed parent speaking to a child.

"He's wearing a collar," said Holmes, picking up a tag. "It says *Hershey*."

Dave frowned. "Isn't that white Persian one Rita Jones's cat?"

"The one that went missing a year ago!" I exclaimed. "And that Siamese, that's Judy Nelson's cat."

"Oy," said Dave. "You're a cat seducer, Mae."

Holmes and I looked at him.

"This is becoming a problem all over the place. People assume they can keep cats that wander into their homes. Meanwhile, the true owners are out of their minds with worry and they have no idea that the cat is living next door or down the block. It's a big problem in England. We haven't seen much of it in Wagtail yet, but it can be difficult to detect. Mae has clearly been seducing cats for over a year."

"I have not. They all came here on their own. It's not like I stole them from anyone. It was voluntary on their part. They want to live with me."

"Take those two," Dave said to Holmes and me. "I'll call Rita and Judy and do a check of all the cats reported missing over the last couple of years."

As we walked out the door, I heard Mae saying, "You can't take my cats away from me."

Dave replied with a curt, "You took them from their rightful owners. Now you have to give them back. It's theft, Mae. Plain and simple."

I drove the golf cart back to the inn while Holmes hung on to Hershey. "Poor guy," he said. "She shut him in her house, and he couldn't get away."

"Do you think she does that because she's lonely?" I asked.

"Maybe she's lonely because she has fifteen hundred cats in her house."

I laughed even though there might have been some truth to that.

When we walked into the inn, the WAG Ladies happened to be gathered in the main lobby. Joanne shrieked at the sight of Hershey and swept him into her arms. I could hear him purring.

She thanked Holmes and me over and over before she whisked him to their room to spend some time with him.

"Have you had lunch?" I asked Holmes.

"Not a bite since breakfast. I'm starved."

"Follow me." It was late for lunch, but being part owner of an inn had its perks. I peeked into the commercial kitchen. "Any leftovers for Holmes and me?"

"You caught me just in time. How about burgers with a big basket of home fries?" asked our cook.

"Perfect!" I grabbed tall glasses and filled them with ice cubes and traditional freshly brewed tea.

The terrace was empty, so we selected a table with a large umbrella and settled in. Trixie roamed around, and Twinkletoes curled up in a chair. A few minutes later, the cook's assistant arrived with a huge tray.

"Coleslaw on the side, trout for Twinkletoes, and where's Trixie?"

At the sound of her name, she came running. He set a bowl in front of her. "Here you go, sweetheart, a burger and green beans!"

We thanked him and reached for the fries at the same time. They were still warm.

"What's the problem with the judge?" asked Holmes. "I thought it was just my family that has issues with him."

"The judge!" I gasped and reached for my phone.

"It's okay, Oma and my mom are there with them. My dad is still bristling about Rose being involved with the judge. It might take some time for them to get over that hurdle. I guess you can't erase thirty years of animosity and blame in one day."

"I'm glad your mom is there. I don't have the same issues with the judge as your family. But it occurred to me that he could very easily have set up all those weird occurrences himself. What if there isn't anyone listening to their conversations? It would have been so easy for him to open the window on the sly. To buy a box of oatmeal and leave it on the counter. To order the wrong color of roses intentionally. He could have actually sent those emails to Aunt Birdie, Rose, and Dovie."

"But why? What would possess him to do that?"

"Maybe he just wanted attention. Rose and Dovie were there a lot. Maybe he wanted excitement. Or to have them fussing over him."

"Why would he poison them? That's not so harmless."

"I don't know. But one other thing has been bothering me. Dovie allegedly let Fritz out when the gate was open, and he ran off. But he didn't seem to want to run away when we brought him home. And while Trixie and Twinkletoes jumped up and went to Mae's house with me, Fritz was content to stay home with the judge."

"Absolutely true. Not a sign of him wanting to abscond," said Holmes in between bites.

"Which makes me wonder if he was really missing."

Thirty

❀ ❀ ❀ ❀ ❀

Holmes set his burger down. "What are you saying?"

"I'm not sure. It seems like it fits in with the other things the judge may have invented. *They put the wrong flowers on my wife's grave and now my dog is gone, too. Oh, woe is me.*"

"I see what you're getting at. All cries for help?"

"Someone said to me that the hardest time after a death is when everyone goes back to their normal lives, except for the spouse, who goes home to an empty house, and every single thing he or she touches and sees reminds the spouse of the person that's gone. That it's painfully quiet, and suddenly they're completely alone."

"I can see that. There's the big funeral. The whole family comes, everyone is concerned about the bereaved spouse, and, whoosh, it's over and you're all alone. The judge could have been overwhelmed and then felt that loneliness when everyone went home."

"Maybe. It doesn't solve Seth's murder, but have you noticed that not a soul has suspected the judge? He could have been anywhere that night. He could have even set the fire at Dovie's as a diversion."

"You think he's gone completely looney. But why murder Seth when he had been hired to find Fritz?"

I raised my eyebrows at Holmes.

"I see. You're suggesting that Fritz wasn't really missing. It was a ruse to bring Seth to Wagtail. Besides, he would have had to plan the murder well in advance to have the aconite ready in a syringe."

"No question about that," I said. "No matter who killed Seth, that person came prepared. There wasn't any time to find and pick aconite and prepare that syringe. And he or she certainly didn't get into a squabble and kill him in the heat of the moment. All that was carefully planned. The judge would know exactly what to do and how to get away with it."

"You think the judge murdered Seth to avenge Bobbie's death," said Holmes.

I sat back in my chair and munched on a French fry.

"I spent quite a while with Dave this morning. He says the WAG women are sticking together. He thinks they know more than they're saying to protect one of their own." Holmes picked up a pickle slice that had fallen off his burger onto his plate and popped it in his mouth.

"They think one of them murdered Seth. They must suspect Brenda," I said. "She's the one who went back to the house. She, her dog, Fagan, and Seth all had meringue on them. I know that's not proof that she murdered him, but she must have been close to him to get the meringue on him. That would be hard to dispute. Plus, she has a whopper of a motive."

"Do you think she killed Seth?" asked Holmes.

"I like all of the WAG Ladies. They're an eclectic group, but they're all nice. In a weird way, I even admire their loyalty to one another. I don't know about Brenda. She's afraid of her own brother. Maybe she was afraid of Seth, too."

"Do you think there's any chance that Brenda's brother, Wallace, is in town?" asked Holmes.

"It's interesting that you ask about Wallace. When I stopped by to see Louisa this morning, a man came out of her room as I was arriving."

"That doesn't mean anything. He could be Louisa's brother."

"Absolutely. But she flushed red when I walked in, which made me wonder if it was an awkward moment for her. Maybe she didn't want anyone to see him? I wouldn't know what Wallace looks like in any event."

After our late lunch, Holmes went home for a nap, and I retreated to my own quarters to sleep. I should have been thinking about the murder, but I was beat. Trixie and Twinkletoes accompanied me, and I noticed that neither of them was scampering ahead. We were all pooped.

I woke a couple of hours later, much refreshed. It was close to dinnertime. When I walked down the grand staircase, the lobby was empty. The dining area was closed, and the inn was quiet. Trixie and Twinkletoes seemed to have a little more spring in their steps. We strolled through the hallway to the reception lobby. The office door was open, and I peeked inside.

Oma sat on her little patio, looking out at the lake.

Trixie sped to her and wiggled with excitement. Gingersnap greeted me by leaning against me and wagging her tail.

"How is Rose?" I asked.

"She'll recover. She is very upset that the police could even imagine that she tried to harm anyone."

"Mae brought them basil," I said.

Oma snorted. "Basil looks nothing like wolfsbane."

"How does Rose think the wolfsbane got into the salad?"

"There were only three other people present that evening. It has to be one of them," said Oma.

"Since only two of them got sick, it would have been added to the plates shortly before they ate. Right?"

"That seems logical to me."

"Is there any possibility that they left the salad for a moment? Maybe it was in the kitchen and they went into the conservatory or stepped outside?" I asked.

"Clearly they must have. But it's most likely one of the people present did it. The judge and Rose told us about the person who is listening to them," said Oma. "Do you think such a thing is possible?"

"Unfortunately, it's all too easy. There are wireless transmitters that aren't much bigger than a credit card. There are also listening devices that look like surge protectors, computer cords, remote controls, and even a computer mouse."

"Someone could be listening to us right now."

"They could be. Did the judge or Rose have any suspicions that connected the person listening to the wolfsbane?"

"They discussed that possibility. Aunt Birdie?" Oma shook her head. "Is it possible that she is not right in the head?"

"That would be awful! What would we do?" My mind reeled with possibilities. Would I have to take care of her? Place her in a retirement home?

Oma smiled in a mischievous way. "She is not *my* relative."

That wasn't funny! "Well, we could say the same thing about Dovie, I suppose."

"It could be either one of them."

"I don't know, Oma. You didn't realize that it's possible to listen in on someone using new technology. I don't know if either of them could figure out how to do it."

"Perhaps you are correct. Can you watch the inn for an

hour? I would like to go over to check on Rose. She went home, but I am worried that she is not safe there by herself. Maybe I can convince her to stay with us until this matter has been resolved."

"Good luck with that." Rose would want to stay home. Not that I could blame her.

Oma and Gingersnap left to see Rose. I cleaned up Oma's teacup and was locking the office when Oriana showed up at the registration desk.

"I want to let you know that there's a possibility we'll be leaving tomorrow. Louisa may be released from the hospital in the morning."

"I'm glad to hear that." I tried to sound casual. "Did someone from home drive up to visit her? A brother maybe?"

"Not that I know of. Why do you ask?"

I tried to brush it off by saying lightly, "Nothing. I must have been mistaken." I changed the subject quickly. "Is Brenda allowed to leave Wagtail?"

"Apparently so. Her family attorney referred her to a lawyer in Virginia, who said they can't force her to stay here. If they don't charge her with a crime, then she's free to leave."

That was interesting. If Brenda had murdered Seth, wouldn't she have left immediately? It would have meant breaking the circle of the sisterhood, but they would have understood if she needed to get out of town. "Good for her. I guess they can't make a case against her in spite of all that meringue."

I took some paperwork and settled in the back of the dining area where I could keep an eye on the main lobby. The WAG Ladies met to go to dinner with the complete entourage of their pets. Brenda was still taking care of Loki, who, true to form, bounded out the door with Brenda trailing him.

Oma convinced Rose to come back to the inn with her,

probably by scaring her half to death. Or maybe Rose felt better about being around people and having an alibi if anything else happened. I booked her into Stay, a popular and spacious room with a view of Wagtail. It also happened to be close to Oma's apartment.

The three of us raided the magic refrigerator and shared a feast of rare roast beef, buttery mashed potatoes, fresh caprese salad, and peach cake. Gingersnap and Trixie snarfed chicken dinners, while Twinkletoes dined on baked trout.

Our mood was still somber. I could tell that Oma tried to steer the conversation away from Seth and murder, so I followed her lead. After dinner, I sent the two of them off with Gingersnap to relax while I cleaned up the private kitchen.

When I finished, Twinkletoes had completed her after-dinner cat bath and curled up in a cushy chair. Trixie and I crossed the lobby and stepped out on the front porch.

Lights twinkled in restaurants along the sides of the green. I sat quietly in a rocking chair at the far end of the porch. Trixie jumped up on my lap. The heat and humidity had abated. The night air was gentle, and as I looked out at the people strolling along the sidewalks, it was hard to imagine that a killer lurked among us.

The front door creaked ever so slightly as it opened. Joanne stepped out, clad in her black running outfit. I didn't think she noticed me. Trixie and I watched as she walked down the front steps. She turned her head from side to side like a periscope checking the waters. But she forgot to look behind her.

I waited until she had darted across the plaza before I dared to stand up. I flew into the inn to grab a flashlight. Glad I was wearing sneakers, I headed into the green after her. The occasional streetlamp helped light our path. Trixie ran ahead of me but not far enough to catch up to Joanne.

For a while, I caught a glimpse of her every now and then as she passed under a light. I began to feel silly for following her. She was jogging just like anyone else.

But then I lost her. She must have turned off somewhere. I ran ahead but didn't see her.

We were nearing the far end of the green. I turned east and walked along the sidewalk, catching my breath by window shopping. We were only a couple of blocks from Judge Barlow's house.

Rose was safely at the inn with Oma. I wondered where Aunt Birdie and Dovie were. At their own homes, I hoped. But since we were so close, I strolled toward the judge's house to see if one of them was lurking near his place.

Not a soul stirred on his street. I paused at his front door and took a good look around. Mae's lights were on, and I could see her moving inside her house. No one seemed to be spying from behind trees.

Judge Barlow's inside lights were on, too. I dared to knock on his door.

He opened it with Fritz by his side.

"Good evening, Judge Barlow. I was in the neighborhood and thought I'd stop by to see how you're doing."

"Are you armed?" he asked.

Panic swept over me. I hadn't expected to find him in trouble. "No. Are you in danger?"

"Not if you're not armed."

Very funny. "Any more unwelcome guests trying to get inside?"

"Not today. But then I had company for a good part of the day. I wasn't alone."

"Would you like to stay at the inn where there are more people? We'd gladly put you up for free."

"That's very kind of you." He smiled at me. "You remind me of your grandmother. I think I'm brave enough to stay at home now that I have my Fritz back."

"Where exactly did the person try to break in?" I asked.

"Around back, down the stairs to the basement. It wasn't so much breaking in as making awful sounds. Terrifying!"

"I'll just take a look around there if that's okay with you. If anything happens, please call Dave right away. And me second."

He nodded, looking worried. "Good night." He closed the door, and I waited to hear the deadbolt click.

Armed with my flashlight, I walked around the side of the house to the backyard. Trixie ran in a frenzy, undoubtedly thrilled to be sniffing Fritz's territory.

She picked something up and brought it to me, her tail wagging happily.

"What did you find?" I asked. "One of Fritz's toys?" I gently took it from her mouth to see what it was. When I shone the flashlight on it, chills ran down my spine.

It was a fabric cartoon mouse with little legs sticking out like it was surprised. My mouth went dry. The company that manufactured them must have made thousands, if not hundreds of thousands. I tried to tell myself it didn't mean anything. But I knew it belonged to Hershey and stuck it into my pocket.

Mae Swinesbury might have encouraged Hershey to enter her house, she might even have carried him inside, but it wasn't a coincidence that Hershey had been in this neighborhood. He had gone missing the day Aunt Birdie, Rose, and Dovie received the strange emails and the day the judge said someone had been making frightening noises at the basement door.

I walked over to look at it, shining my flashlight to see better in the dark. Old-fashioned concrete walls and steep steps led down to a small landing with a door and a round drainage-grate cover. I guessed they had been installed decades ago. I walked down for a closer look. Trixie sprang ahead of me. There really wasn't much to see. I tried a shiny new door handle. It was securely locked. Just above the handle was a brand-new bolt lock. Shadow had done a good job.

Trixie stopped sniffing and looked up the stairs. She zoomed up them and barked. Little barks, then silence, as if she was listening.

I followed her up the stairs and shone my flashlight around the yard. It was fenced in. An old swing set and slide remained. I imagined the Barlow children running around the spacious yard playing with dogs.

Trixie must have been barking at a squirrel or a possum wandering about. Her nose twitched, and she stared at something. She started yipping, her nose in the air like she was sending a signal for all to hear.

I aimed the flashlight in that direction.

Thirty-One

❀ ❀ ❀ ❀

Footsteps crunched on fallen twigs and branches under the trees. I directed my flashlight toward the sound but didn't see anyone.

Trixie chased the person, yipping as she darted after them. I followed more slowly. I didn't want to be blind-sided. I pulled out my phone and dialed Dave's number.

"This better be important," he grumbled. "I'm about to hit the sack."

"Someone is in the judge's backyard. They're running from me."

"Holly! Don't give chase!"

"Then how are we supposed to catch this creep?"

I could hear Dave sigh. "Okay. I'm coming. Don't do anything stupid." As he hung up, I heard him say, "As if . . ."

Following Trixie's barks, I dodged through the trees at a trot.

And then I heard someone cry out, like they had fallen.

I slowed down, and in a matter of minutes, I reached the fence, where a piece of black fabric clung to a wire on top.

Trixie pranced restlessly at the fence. I flashed the light around but didn't see a gate. The fence was chain link and five feet high. I had climbed chain link as a child. Surely I could do it again. Trixie would pose a problem, though.

"Trixie, no squirming. Got it? I don't want to drop you." I scooped her up and held her tight in one arm while using the other to pull myself up the fence. The diamond openings between the links seemed a lot smaller than they had been when I was a kid. I could barely get the toes of my sneakers in them. But five feet wasn't that high, I reasoned.

I had managed to get off the ground and up to the top before Trixie twisted in a desperate move to get away. I clung fast to her. "Just a couple more minutes."

I swung one leg over the top, then the other one. Halfway down, I dared to jump and landed on my backside. The concrete sidewalk offered no cushioning whatsoever. Trixie took that moment to leap out of my grip and run down the sidewalk faster than the speed of light.

There was nothing to do but follow in the direction she had gone.

I called her as I jogged along but didn't see her anywhere. When I emerged from the green, the front lights of the inn gleamed on her white fur. She spied me at the same time and ran toward me like I had been away for a month.

She put her front paws on my legs, begging to be held. I picked her up. "You abandoned me."

She licked my nose.

I accepted her apology, crossed the plaza, and walked up the front steps and into the inn.

The WAG Ladies sat in the Dogwood Room with Oma and Rose, who were serving them after-dinner drinks.

Oma called me over. "Look who is here!"

Louisa sat with her friends. Loki lay at her feet as if he didn't plan to let her take a single step without him.

"You're out of the hospital! Congratulations!" I said.

"They decided to spring me a little early. I have to say, it feels great to be back to normal."

"I'm so relieved." But I wondered how she felt sitting with the person who most likely had poisoned her. Was she watching her drink to be certain no one added anything to it? I would be.

Hershey mewed and circled around my legs. Then he sat in front of me and stared at me, as though he wanted something.

"If I weren't adopting one of those kittens I would definitely be looking for a Somali cat," said Brenda. "He's trying to tell you something."

I gazed around for Joanne. "Where's his mom?" I asked.

"She fell and scraped her knee when she was out running," said Brenda.

"I don't know how she can run after dinner," said Oriana. "Do any of you do that?"

"Not me," said Louisa. "Dogs aren't supposed to go for walks or run after they eat. I figure that probably goes for people, too."

I knelt to pet Hershey, and my phone rang.

Dave sounded like a grumpy old man. "Where *are* you?"

"I'm back at the inn. But I think I know who it was. Meet me here?"

He agreed and hung up.

Hershey, however, pawed at me.

"I hope that wasn't as sinister as it sounded," said Addi.

They all stared at me in silence. But Hershey didn't care. He continued pawing at me. His claws were retracted, so he was gentle, but I was clueless until he tried to stick a paw in my pocket.

"You are one smart kitty." I pulled out his mouse toy that Trixie had found in the judge's backyard.

Everyone laughed when he grabbed it and threw it up into the air. When it landed, he pounced on it as if it were a live mouse.

"So what's going on?" asked Addi.

"I think I'd better wait for Joanne."

"And here she comes!" exclaimed Rose. "Are you all right? Your knee looked pretty nasty."

I stood up and turned around to face her.

She looked me straight in the eyes, without remorse or fear. For a long uncomfortable moment, neither of us said a word.

Dave noisily tromped into the Dogwood Room, saying, "This had better be good, Holly."

As calmly as I could, I said to Joanne, "I think the jig is up."

Thirty-Two

✽ ✽ ✽ ✽

"Holly!" cried Oma. "What is happening here?"

Dave was paying attention, but I couldn't help noticing that he stood by Addi, who gazed at him with adoring eyes.

"I think Joanne should explain," I said.

"I have no idea what you're talking about. What are we drinking? Is that the Sugar Maple Inn after-dinner drink that I've heard so much about?"

"It is!" Rose poured one and handed it to her.

But I was getting impatient with Joanne's act. I withdrew the swatch of fabric from my pocket and held it in the air.

"What is that?" asked Dave.

"I believe you'll find that this is a perfect match for Joanne's torn running pants," I explained. "Would you care to fetch them for us?"

Dave walked over to me, pulled out an evidence bag, and placed the fabric inside it. "How did you come to have this?"

"It was caught on the chain-link fence Joanne climbed over to get away from Trixie and me."

Joanne sipped her drink. "This is delicious."

"Joanne, I would like to have a word with you privately," said Dave. "I presume I can use the inn office?"

"Of course," said Oma.

Brenda frowned at us. "I don't understand. What has she done? Is this about Seth?"

Joanne stiffened. "Oh, for heaven's sake. I haven't done anything wrong." She took a seat but didn't look comfortable. "Honestly, I didn't expect this to become such a big deal. In the beginning, I'll admit that I wanted to harm the judge."

Rose and Addi gasped.

"I never meant to kill anyone, but I was angry. Thoughts of hurting him ran through my head, but that's not a crime. You can't imagine how long this has been building in me. I was four when my mother was killed by Brenda's brother."

Suddenly, Brenda appeared more uncomfortable than Joanne.

"All I had left was my dad and vague memories of women I called Mommy and Grandmum. I didn't know any real names."

Addi's eyes grew large. She was fixated on Joanne.

"I remembered a big man everyone called Pops and a huge house with lots of dogs and the scent of cinnamon. My most vivid recollection was the sound of church bells ringing. But that could have been anywhere. Sometimes I wondered if I had dreamed the bells."

"That's why you asked about them in the churchyard," I said.

Joanne nodded. "I didn't understand where those people had gone. I didn't even know if they were real. If they were, why did they let my father take me? Why didn't they look for me? Why didn't they realize that I needed their help? Were they glad to be rid of me? I used to lie in bed at night and wish Grandmum and Pops would come and take me away. I dreamed of a life where unicorns were real, and where I lived in a house that smelled of cinnamon instead of a succession of run-down one-room shacks that reeked of sweat and beer. It wasn't until I moved my dad into an Alzheimer's care facility two months ago and cleaned up his mess that I found a document with the name Mary Roberta Barlow on it."

"Is that your real name?" asked Oriana.

"No. I think she was my mother. Naturally, I began to search for her. The only Barlow I knew of was Theona. Her obituary says she was predeceased by her beloved daughter Mary Roberta Barlow."

"I'm your cousin!" shrieked Addi.

"I don't understand," I said. "Why did you listen in on Judge Barlow's house?"

"Because I was hurt. Because they were my family, but they put more effort into finding Fritz than me. I wanted him to know what it's like to not have any control. To be alone, all alone. Every holiday, when most people were surrounded by loving families with cozy fires in their fireplaces and turkeys on their tables, I wondered what that would be like. Holidays were miserable for me. If there was a bar in town that was open, my dad would be there, and I would be home alone. There were no toys or new clothes. Forget holidays, Dad never considered that I might need basics like shoes or a coat. Neighbors who pitied me would bring me garments their kids had outgrown. I was the only child who never wanted school to end because it meant days of being alone while my dad drank himself stupid."

In a small, calm voice, Addi said, "You're Joy."

Joanne blinked at her and looked at me in confusion. "Joanne. My name is Joanne."

Addi shook her head. "That's why you couldn't find yourself anywhere. Your name is Joy Marie."

"How do you know that?"

"Because every holiday, my mother and Grandmum

Theona made me set an extra place at the table in case little Joy Marie found her way home. Grandmum Theona spent a small fortune looking for you. She hired private investigators and psychics. I remember everyone howling and teasing her about the psychics." Addi's lips pulled taut. "You just missed her."

Oriana cleared her throat. "Exactly what is it that you're accusing Joanne—Joy—of doing?"

"She broke into Judge Barlow's house and set up listening devices," said Dave. "Based on conversations she overheard, she took actions to upset him."

"I did not break in," protested Joanne.

"Then how did you get into the house?" asked Dave.

"I had a key."

"Where did you obtain the key?"

"I made a copy of the one under the mat by the front door."

"Under the law, that is breaking and entering." Dave gave her a stern look.

Rose had listened silently. "You're the one who bought the oatmeal and opened the window and switched the flower arrangement on Theona's grave. You even banged on his basement door and made scary sounds. You meant to drive your own grandfather mad."

"Not to mention the emails you sent," I added, "pretending to be the judge and telling people he didn't want to see them anymore, and one to Dovie, firing her."

"I see," said Oriana. "Well, I'm the one who sent the emails."

Everyone stared at her.

Addi chimed in. "I changed the floral arrangement and opened the window. Louisa, I suppose you bought the oatmeal?"

"It's hardly a crime," said Louisa. "Everyone should eat their oatmeal."

Dave groaned aloud. "No, no, no. I see what you're doing. It's not that easy to make this go away. You can't just claim responsibility for what Joanne did." He looked at Joanne straight on with a grim expression. "Were you responsible for poisoning Rose and Birdie?"

"Absolutely not! I told you I wouldn't harm anyone. And I wouldn't know wolfsbane if you handed it to me," said Joanne.

I could see from his face that Dave was not convinced.

"If any of you were planning on leaving Wagtail tomorrow, your plans have just changed," said Dave.

Brenda said quietly, "You do know now that it was Seth who was driving the night your mother died. My brother, for all his many, many faults, was not the one who killed your mom. And please know how very sorry my family and I are about that."

Joanne squinted at her. "Sure. Blame the dead guy."

"No, it's true," Louisa protested. She dug in her purse. "I sent a letter to Judge Barlow. My husband dictated it to me on his deathbed. Where is that thing?" She pulled a piece of paper out of her purse and unfolded it. "Judge Barlow has the original." She handed it to Dave.

"This is dated two months ago," he said.

Louisa nodded. "I mailed it to Judge Barlow. And when I arrived in Wagtail, I went to see him."

Dave read it aloud.

Dear Judge Barlow,

Please accept my sympathy on the loss of your wife. I did not have the pleasure of knowing her, but my wife always spoke of her in the highest regard.

I have reached the end of my own road in this life. I want you to know that my single deepest regret is my role in the death of your daughter Bobbie. I was merely a passenger that night, but as I look back, I find it hard to believe that we were so young and careless that we could not foresee the terrible consequences of our actions. I have carried the tragedy of her death every day of my life since it happened and can only hope that I will find forgiveness when I arrive at Saint Peter's gate.

I'm sure you remember my statement that Wallace McDade was driving the car at the time of the accident. That was a lie. Seth Bertenshaw was at the wheel when your daughter lost her life.

I understand that clearing my conscience by telling you this may leave me feeling better as a person but may bring you deep pain. I hope that is not the case.

With sincerest regret,
Thomas J. Twomey

"How do I know you didn't make that up?" asked Joanne.

"I didn't!" cried Louisa. "Wallace is the only one of the three still living. I suppose he can confirm it."

"He told us," said Brenda in a dull voice. "I was only six when it happened. He was ten years older than me. I remember him insisting that he was in the passenger seat, but when Tom sided with Seth and claimed my brother was driving, no one believed Wallace. It ruined your life, Joanne, because you lost your mother. I have no doubt things would have been different for you if she had lived. But it ruined our lives, too. Wallace was never the same after that. He got off light, but that accident followed him like an albatross his entire life. I always thought it was because he had killed someone, but now I know he learned far too early that you can't trust even your best friends or your family. We all failed him and made him what he is today."

"On that note, I'm going to take statements from each of you about your participation in Joanne's crime," said Dave. "I suggest you take into consideration how lying about it could impact your lives as Brenda has just so eloquently explained. Holly, if you could unlock the office for me, please?"

I escorted him to the office and unlocked the door. Dave began to interrogate the WAG Ladies and took their statements one at a time while the rest of us waited in the Dogwood Room.

Rose said to Addi, "Don't you have an uncle who is still living? What was his name?"

"Tanner. Elliott died as an infant."

"Where is Tanner these days? What's he doing?" asked Rose.

"We don't see much of him. He's a seismologist in California. He and Pops had a falling out over his gambling problem. It's very sad. My mom says Pops insisted it was tough love to get him to stop, but I feel like there must have been another way."

While they chatted, I wondered if Dave was uncovering any new information about Seth's death. I had considered the judge as a suspect, and now that it was apparent Louisa had sent her husband's deathbed confession to the judge, I had to wonder if it impacted him enough to avenge his daughter's death.

I watched Brenda, who fussed over Fagan. Would she have killed Seth for lying about her brother's involvement in the death of Joanne's mother? If Holmes was right and she was extraordinarily wealthy, then why did she pinch pennies? I wondered if, in some way, her clothing indicated a desire to live in a time before the accident. Before her brother attacked her father. A time in her life when everything seemed possible, and, as Joanne had said, unicorns might have been real.

Or had Oriana tried to save her own way of life? Her husband seemed like a decent sort. Would the truth about her relationship with Seth have sent her on a downward spiral where she lost everything and everyone that was dear to her, as she claimed? It wasn't outside the realm of possibilities.

Loki was so happy to be back with Louisa that he didn't leave her side. He must have been terribly confused while she was in the hospital. She had recovered but still looked delicate, with her fair skin and freckles. Had someone tried to kill her because she had murdered Seth? Had she made a deathbed promise to her husband to knock off Seth? Surely not. But maybe she knew who killed him. What if she had seen something the night of the fire and she knew who was guilty? Had one of his lovers felt the need to take revenge? Oriana or Addi?

It always came back to the fact that Addi took the exact type of pill that had nearly killed Louisa. Was it remotely possible that one of her friends had removed the pills from her room and put them in Louisa's pill bottle? But why? So far, I hadn't noticed any reason. Unless . . . Oriana! She might have done it to keep Louisa from spilling the news that she was having an affair with Seth.

I observed her, over elegant, stroking Garbo. Oriana could have murdered Seth to keep him from exposing their affair to her husband. And she might have switched the pills so Louisa wouldn't tell her secret, either.

It was midnight before Dave came up to the Dogwood Room and said he was through. "I'd like to be present when you introduce yourself to the judge, Joanne. And it might be wise to ask Dr. Engelknecht to be there as well. It will be a wonderful surprise, I'm sure, but at his age, the shock might be overwhelming."

The WAG Ladies drifted off to their rooms, and Oma whispered, "Any luck?"

Dave mashed his lips together and shook his head. "Did you see what they did for Joanne? Each of them claiming to have pulled one of the pranks on the judge? They're doing the same sort of thing about Seth. They're protecting one of them. I think it's Brenda. Everyone knows she went back to Rose's house by herself. She was close enough to him to get meringue on him, and she's got to be angry with him for what he did to her brother."

I liked Brenda and her independent ways. I wished she would tip better, of course, but in general, I liked her. "Do you have enough to press charges?" I asked.

"Maybe. I'll be talking to the prosecutor tomorrow."

After Dave left, Oma and I cleaned up. I was collecting empty glasses when Joanne returned. I heard her ask Rose, "Did you know my mother?"

Joanne couldn't have picked a worse person to ask.

But Rose smiled at her. "Bobbie was the fun Barlow. I think that's why her death hit everyone so hard. She was beautiful and smart. And if Bobbie was there, everyone knew it would be a good time. She, um, she had a crush on my son. But then he met someone else and Bobbie was very frustrated. Unrequited love, you know. She was a cheerleader in high school, and she sang with a band! I have no doubt that she would have been a great mother."

Tears ran down Joanne's cheeks. "Thank you," she whispered.

Thirty-Three

❈ ❈ ❈ ❈

At six in the morning, Brenda was the only WAG Lady up. She wore a sleeveless green A-line dress, which I suspected was vintage. She sat at a dining table with Mr. Huckle.

"May I join you?" I asked.

"I'm glad you're here, Holly. I was just about to confess."

I wondered if I should call Dave.

Shelley arrived with coffee, tea, a basket of breakfast breads, and a small platter of bacon.

We ordered eggs Benedict for the humans, roast chicken and fried eggs for the dogs, and roast chicken for Twinkletoes.

"Brenda has been telling me about the excitement last night," said Mr. Huckle. "Joanne must be in a state of shock."

"It's going to be an interesting meeting with the judge this morning. That's for sure," said Brenda.

"How has Wallace taken the news that you now know he

wasn't the driver the night Bobbie was killed?" asked Mr. Huckle.

"He said, and I quote, 'Too little, too late.' And then he hung up on me." Brenda sipped her coffee. "I never dreamed that my brother's reckless ways would land *me* in trouble. When I was growing up, I knew that some people didn't want me around because of my brother. They thought I was like him, I guess. I always acted like I didn't care. You get a thick skin after a while and learn to pretend. I resented Wallace for that. I used to hear my mother and grandmother talking about the way people looked at them. The whispers they heard on the street and in the beauty salon. It was like a curse on our family that we couldn't escape. Even worse, it was as though *we* were guilty. We weren't the bereaved family. We were the guilty family. And that guilt oozes right over onto you like a slime you can't wash off."

It wasn't until our eggs arrived that Brenda finally said, "I did see Seth in Rose's yard. I went back because I didn't see Fagan anywhere on the street. The pretty overhead lights were still on, and I saw Seth clear as day." She closed her eyes as though she was seeing him once more.

She opened them again. "Louisa had told me the truth. I knew that Seth had lied. I was furious. You can't begin to imagine the anger in me. Not just for Wallace, but for my entire family. It welled up in me. He looked sick, was lurching a little bit. Seth said, 'I need help. Can you call an ambulance?'"

She paused, and her hand clenched into a fist. "But I didn't call anyone. I slapped him. I've never done that before to anyone. I slapped him so hard my hand stung from the impact. I can still hear the sound of my hand hitting his face. He didn't quite fall down. He leaned against the table and flailed his arms in an effort to stand. I think that was when he knocked the berry meringue pie off the table. He grasped the light cord. When he pulled on it, the lights went out, but I could see him, a shadowy figure staggering backward. I left. And in every waking hour since then, I have pondered whether he would have survived if I had called an ambulance like he asked. And the stupid thing is that not only do I get to live with that thought hammering at me, I may end up in jail. It all began with three boys driving drunk, and all these years later, *I'm* the one who will go to jail."

My eyes met Mr. Huckle's. I didn't know what to say to her. Was she lying? Or had she deftly slid the syringe needle into his back and watched him die?

"Have you told this to Dave?" I asked.

"No. I told Dave I didn't see him. No one else was there. If someone had just poisoned him, I would have seen his killer. Wouldn't I?"

"Brenda," I whispered, "I believe you. Did you see anything at all? Any tiny little thing? The easiest way to defend you is to find Seth's real killer."

"All I know is that it wasn't me." She sliced into her egg and ate.

"I saw you returning to the street to watch the fire," I blurted.

Brenda nodded. "That was when I went back to wash the meringue off Fagan's whiskers. He must have gotten into the pie, and then, when I picked him up, it rubbed off on me. Meringue is some sticky stuff! I didn't go in the backyard again to check on Seth. I killed him by not calling for help. I knew he was back there, and something was very wrong with him."

If what she said was true, then someone else had been prepared to kill Seth and had injected the poison. I watched as the WAG Ladies arrived for breakfast and wondered which one of them had done it.

When I saw Louisa take Loki out, I excused myself and called Trixie as an excuse to follow Louisa to the doggie facilities.

"Good morning, Louisa. Are you feeling better?" I asked.

"Almost back to normal. I have to admit that it was scary for a while. The worst part now is that I'm afraid of everything I put in my mouth. I hate that someone did this to me and that I don't know why." She frowned and rubbed her face. "I can't believe that one of my friends would hurt me. Okay, so I did tell Addi that Oriana was seeing Seth. That's hardly reason to knock me off."

"You suspect Oriana of switching the pills?"

"They're my friends. They're the people I go to with my troubles. You should have seen how wonderful they were to me when Tom was sick. They thought of everything. When I needed someone, one of them was there, even if it was to sit quietly and just listen. I can't fathom that one of them would kill me."

Louisa ducked her head and shielded her face with her hand. "Oh no."

"Who are you hiding from?" I whispered.

The man I had seen exiting her hospital room strode in our direction from the green. He wore a Walley World T-shirt, exactly like the one the dogs had fought over.

"Is it Wallace? Brenda's brother?"

"No. I don't think so. I've never met Wallace. I wouldn't know him if I saw him. He's a friend of Tom's. Unlike Seth, he was so kind and helpful. He was always there for Tom, right to the end. But after Tom died, he—" she waved her hand "—indicated that he would like to date me. I'm not ready for anything like that! He's so persistent. And it's hard to be angry with him because he's been so kind. But he doesn't get it. I made the mistake of telling him I was coming to Wagtail, and he came here looking for me."

She stopped whispering as he neared, smiled politely at him, and introduced us.

"You look beautiful, Louisa," he said.

She flushed, and I could tell she was struggling to be nice. "I feel better, thanks."

"I rented a pontoon boat. It's such a beautiful day. I thought we could take a picnic lunch and enjoy the lake."

"I'm really sorry, but I'm busy today."

"The gala is over. You would have been home already if you hadn't gotten sick." He seemed almost angry.

"We have a meeting at the judge's house due to unexpected developments," I said.

Louisa shot me a grateful look. "It's true. We were all interrogated by the police last night."

"Interrogated? Why?"

"Because of Seth's murder."

"You're a suspect?" He took a step back in horror.

"Yes." Louisa said it with her head held high, which surprised me.

It amused me and worried me at the same time. She obviously had more moxie than I'd thought.

Her friend backed up. His expression revealed his fear of her. "I'll see you around, Louisa." He turned his back and power walked, then broke into a full-fledged run.

Louisa tried not to laugh. "Thank heaven there weren't any rooms at the inn for him," she whispered. "He's staying at a bed-and-breakfast. I told him I was busy, but he showed up at the gala in jeans, acting like he was my date. I was mortified. I don't want to date anyone. Especially not him! And he was bidding on romantic getaways for two. Ick! That's all I need. I just want him to leave me alone."

"I think you may have accomplished that." The two of us giggled all the way back to the dining area.

Louisa joined her friends for breakfast, and I went off to call Dave privately from the inn office.

When he answered, I told him about Brenda slapping Seth. To be honest, I felt like I was ratting on her, but Dave had to know. "She feels like she killed him because she didn't get him help when he begged her."

There was a long silence on Dave's end. "It's really hard

to get fingerprints off skin. They've tried a number of ways but without much success. The medical examiner reported the slap mark on his face, but we didn't think we'd be able to nail the person. What Brenda said sounds about right. If he was begging for help, that means she came upon him after someone injected the poison. She slapped him, and then he must have crawled toward Fritz and collapsed."

"Does that mean we can eliminate Brenda as a suspect?" I asked.

"Good grief, no. But I do think she may have been telling you the truth. We know now that the judge didn't make up the story about someone listening in on him. But that doesn't mean he didn't murder Seth. I've been trying to track down information about his whereabouts that night."

"And?"

"No luck at all. Mae spies on his house, but she's angry with me for removing the cats that belonged to other people, so she refuses to cooperate. Either he's brilliant at sneaking around, or he was home like he claims."

"Something has been bothering me all along, Dave. When I've gone to the Barlow house, Fritz seems entirely content to stay at home. He never darts out the door like some dogs. I wonder if the judge dropped him off somewhere as an excuse to call Seth and get him to come to Wagtail."

"They say Dovie wasn't paying attention and let him out by mistake."

"That just doesn't fly with me." I inhaled sharply. "The judge knows exactly what kinds of mistakes murderers make. What if he told Dovie to call Seth? That way he wouldn't be implicated."

"I'll see if I can get phone records."

"Do you want to be there when we break the news about Joanne being his granddaughter?"

"Yes, most definitely. How's three o'clock this afternoon?"

"Works for me." When I hung up, I coordinated with Rose because I knew she would want to be present, then headed for the dining area to inform the WAG Ladies.

The next few hours dragged by. I forced myself to pay attention to inn business, but I was relieved when two thirty rolled around. Twinkletoes snoozed in the office and didn't even lift her head when I left to meet the WAG Ladies in the lobby. "Where's Addi?" I asked. "Running late again?"

"She went to see a house that's being renovated," said Oriana.

"With your boyfriend," added Brenda in a snide tone.

I wasn't worried. I knew Holmes was pumping Addi for information on her friends. "I trust she'll meet us there."

We set off for Judge Barlow's house with a full entourage of dogs. Louisa kept Loki on a leash, but the others behaved well enough to run freely on the green.

"I think I'm as nervous as you are," I said to Joanne.

"That's not possible. I've heard people talk about butterflies in their stomachs, but until today I've never experienced them."

Rose opened the door on our arrival. The first thing I noticed were framed photos of a young woman on the table in the foyer.

"What's this?" I whispered to Rose.

She shrugged. "They're all of Bobbie. Grant says Dovie put them up."

"Does she know about Joanne?"

"I don't know how she could. I haven't uttered a word. However, I suspect they're there to throw a burr in my relationship with Grant. She's trying to dredge up old hostilities." She pointed at one of the photos. "Can you see the resemblance?"

I definitely could. Joanne didn't look a lot like her mother, but I could see a connection. "Is Dovie here?"

"Grant said she made his breakfast, left his lunch in the fridge, and promised to be back in time to make his dinner."

"Maybe that's just as well."

We filed into the grand living room. Rose had set it up for tea. I helped her bring tea and goodies to everyone, including cookies for the dogs. True to form, Fritz lay quietly by Judge Barlow's feet.

Dr. Engelknecht said to Judge Barlow in a gentle tone, "We're here today because we have some wonderful news. I don't want you to get worked up about it. If at any time you feel light-headed or woozy, I want you to tell me. Okay?"

"Young buck, I've seen things your little mind couldn't even imagine. Bring it on!"

We all looked at Joanne, who said, "Judge Barlow, I grew up without much family. Recently, I was going through some papers and discovered the name Mary Roberta Barlow in them. I think she might be my mother."

Judge Barlow promptly spilled his tea.

Rose assisted him and patted him dry until he said, "Enough already, Rose." He peered at Joanne. "How old are you?"

Joanne wasn't offended by his skepticism. "I'm thirty. I lost my mother when I was four. I recognize this house." She waved her hand gently. "It's foggy, but I think the Christmas tree went in front of that bay window."

"I never thought I'd live to see this. What's your name?" asked the judge.

"Joanne Williams, but I'm not sure that's my birth name. My dad moved us around a lot, and I think he may have changed our names."

"That certainly fits. Bobbie married poorly. I'm sorry if I'm offending you, but we never did approve of that man." He rose from his seat and located a photograph on a bookshelf. "What did your dad look like?"

"Round face, a little pudgy. Medium brown hair that was straight and receded as he aged. Blue eyes. He was nice looking."

The judge scowled, "That could describe half the men in

Wagtail. "Where is he now? Is he going to walk into this room?"

"I'm afraid not. He's in an Alzheimer's facility."

"I'm sorry to hear that," muttered the judge.

"Sir," said Dave, "I'm afraid Joanne is the perpetrator of the pranks."

He sat down and glared at her. "What would possess you to do that?"

"Anger. I had a terrible life with my father. But I knew there was someone else. Someone whom I hoped would come to find me and take me away from my misery. When I researched Bobbie's background, I suspected she was my mom. And when I came to Wagtail, I knew my memories of Grandmum and Pops and the church bells were real. I was furious. You had money, prestige, respect. Everything you ever wanted or needed. You sat in your house like a fat cat in the sunshine while your own granddaughter suffered. I wanted you to know how it felt to be scared and alone."

"Mmpff. Well, you were right about one thing. I find oatmeal very frightening."

The mood lifted when he said that. I didn't know about anyone else, but I realized I had been holding my breath.

The judge regaled us with stories about Bobbie, who, by all accounts, had been every bit as fun as Rose had described.

"My dear," he said, "I only wish Theona could be here to meet you. She spent her life looking for you. Your father knew we would want custody and get it if we could find you. We had no idea that your life was so miserable. I'm terribly sorry for that, and I hope you'll let the remaining Barlows make it up to you."

"Thank you. If it makes you more comfortable, I'm willing to have a DNA test done so you'll know I'm your granddaughter."

The judge nodded. "It's kind of you to offer. But it won't do us any good. Bobbie was adopted."

Thirty-Four

❋ ❋ ❋

Teacups around the room clattered into their saucers. I thought Joanne might burst into tears.

"You're not my grandfather?"

"Of course I am. But not genetically. Theona and I said we would treat Bobbie as one of our own, and we did. She was a Barlow through and through."

"So Bobbie and my dad were my real parents, but you and Theona are not my grandparents." Joanne's expression revealed what a blow she had received.

"Correct. But had we been able to locate you, we would have brought you back here and raised you as a Barlow, too. Bobbie was our daughter, no matter whether she came from our genes or not."

"Do you have adoption information?" asked Rose. "Maybe Joanne could track down her genetic grandparents."

Judge Barlow laced and unlaced his fingers. He didn't say a word. It was painfully quiet in the room. "It was a different time, you know. Thirty years ago, it wasn't as common to have babies out of wedlock. Bobbie's mother was desperate. She didn't have the backing of her family and certainly didn't have the money to raise a child on her own. I'm afraid the father left the picture quite quickly."

"So you know who she was!" exclaimed Rose.

"I do. She worked for Theona and me, helping care for our children. It seemed like the best of both worlds. She could be with her daughter every day and no one would be the wiser."

Rose shrieked, "Dovie?"

My eyes met Dave's. Dovie had let Fritz out. Dovie had called Seth to come to Wagtail. But she had been with me during the fire. She couldn't have killed Seth, could she?

Dave looked at his phone. "If you'll excuse me, I have an emergency to tend to." He nodded at me.

Dr. Engelknecht unwittingly covered for our departure by asking the judge how he felt.

Dave, Trixie, and I flew out the door. He scanned the street before he said, "I can't believe this. We've been thinking that Seth killed Judge Barlow's daughter, which he did, but she was also Dovie's daughter! Do you know where Dovie is?"

"No."

"Let's hope she's at home." We hopped into his police golf cart and cruised over to Rose's.

"What are we doing *here*?" I asked.

"I don't want Dovie to realize what we're doing. Maybe she'll think we're checking on Rose."

I followed him through the rose arbor and into Rose's backyard. We traced back along Seth's presumed steps through the trees.

"At what stage was the fire when Holmes brought Dovie to you?" asked Dave.

"It was getting big. I first saw the smoke from Rose's backyard."

"So Seth was following Fritz, but why would Fritz be here?"

"He was carrying the kittens over to the judge's house."

"But why here? He could have run down any street. You know dogs, they follow their noses."

"If Dovie was the one who let him out, maybe Dovie was feeding him. He doesn't look like he missed any meals."

Dave's eyes widened. "Oh, excellent. Dovie was luring Seth here. She could have readied the poison, and when Fritz came through, and Seth was behind him, it would have been so easy for her to be friendly to Seth, maybe even hug him and then, whammo, she jams the needle in his back."

"Ugh."

"Dovie wasn't stupid. She knew she needed an alibi, so she set her own shed on fire as a distraction, and you were her convenient alibi, but the deed had already been done. Seth stumbled along and reached Rose's backyard, but it had been vacated because everyone was out on the street, worried about the fire."

"Dovie kissed Fritz and shooed him away because she had to start the fire."

"I believe I need to talk to Dovie," said Dave. "Maybe she's home."

Trixie and I followed him around the house to the front door. Dave knocked and shouted, "Dovie?"

No one answered. He tried again.

I peered into a window. "No sight of her."

"She's probably out shopping or running errands."

We walked back the way we had come, keeping our eyes on the pine needles in case the killer had dropped something.

"I hope we're wrong about Dovie," said Dave. "I don't want to arrest her, especially now that she has a granddaughter. What a crummy thing that would be. Maybe the judge is the killer. We don't have anything on Dovie that definitely ties her to Seth's death. The judge has the disposition and knows how to murder someone. He might also be the one who set Dovie's shed on fire."

We had just reached Rose's house when I thought I saw a movement through her kitchen window. I grabbed Dave and ducked. "There's someone in there."

"Maybe the party at the judge's house broke up and she came home."

I texted Rose. Are you home yet?

She wrote back promptly. No. Is something wrong?

"It's not Rose," I whispered.

"I'm going to check it out. You stay here. I mean it, Holly. Don't creep up in back of me or anything. And keep Trixie here with you."

Dave crouched and darted toward Rose's window. He slowly raised up to see inside, then promptly squatted again. He scuttled sideways and tried the back door. I watched as he opened it and scooted inside.

Thirty-Five

❧ ❧ ❧ ❧

The wait seemed interminable. Worse than wait-
ing for a flight at the airport. Had he found Dovie? I checked
my watch, only five minutes had passed.

Trixie whined at me and pulled as if she was desperate
to run to the house.

"Okay. We'll go see what's happening, but you might give
my presence away, so I'll have to carry you." She squirmed
in my arms as though she thought being carried was a terrible idea.

I scooted to the same window that Dave had looked in.
I didn't see anyone, so I dared to stand up.

Dave lay on the floor on his side. I didn't see anyone
with him. Still holding Trixie, I tried the back door. It
opened easily. I closed it behind me.

"Dave?" I hissed.

He didn't move. I could see his chest rise as he breathed,
and I sighed with relief that he wasn't dead. I dialed 911 and
blurted, "Officer down! Officer down!"

The dispatcher spoke calmly. "Am I speaking with Holly Miller?"

"Yes. Sergeant Dave Quinlan is on the floor. He hasn't opened his eyes or responded, but he's breathing. And there's something on his face."

"Like an animal?"

"No, like leaves."

"Stay on the line with me until the emergency crew arrives."

I hung up immediately and dialed Dr. Engelknecht. "It's Dave. We're at Rose's house. He's on the floor and not responding. I've called 911 but you're closer."

"I'll be right there."

It seemed an eternity. I wasn't sure what had happened to Dave, and, worse, I had no idea whether someone else was still in the house. I clung to Trixie and dared to squat next to Dave.

I jiggled his shoulder. "Dave? Dave, it's me, Holly!"

He moaned but still didn't open his eyes.

I kept trying. "Dave, come on, wake up!" I hustled to the sink and wet a paper towel. I returned to him and placed it on his forehead.

A sound at the back door scared me. I had never been so glad to see Dr. Engelknecht.

Clutching Trixie, I moved away so the doctor could tend to Dave.

"What happened?" he asked.

"I have absolutely no idea. Someone was in the house, but he made me promise to stay outside."

"What's this on his face?"

"I don't know. I can tell you that he didn't have those leaves on his face before he entered the house."

"I think it's wolfsbane, and it looks like something whacked him on the head. He has a significant hematoma. Probably has a concussion as well."

I eyed the cast-iron skillet on the counter. "Could some-one have hit him with a cast-iron frying pan?"

He nodded. "Where is it?"

I pointed at it. "I haven't touched it. Maybe they can get fingerprints."

The doorbell rang. Now that Dr. Engelknecht was in the house, I wasn't as worried that someone might jump me. I walked to the front door and opened it for the emergency crew from Snowball. I pointed to the kitchen. "Right through there."

I wanted to snoop, but I knew better than to touch any-thing lest I mar fingerprints.

The EMTs loaded Dave on a gurney and rolled him past me.

I leaned over. "Dave, are you okay?"

He looked straight at me and said two words, "It's Dovie."

Dr. Engelknecht stood beside me while we watched them load Dave into the ambulance. "I see something that looks suspiciously like wolfsbane in the refrigerator. I'll call the police and let them know. Can you inform Rose that her house is a crime scene?"

"Will do." I locked the doors and left. I assumed Dave had the keys to the police golf cart, and I probably wasn't supposed to drive it anyway. Trixie and I walked over to the judge's house.

Rose opened the door before we were on the porch. "What happened?"

I told her the whole story.

After asking about Dave's condition, she said, "That wicked woman put wolfsbane in my refrigerator to frame me!"

If Dovie hadn't smeared wolfsbane on Dave's face, I might have been skeptical about that. But Dovie had left her mark.

Rose agreed to continue staying at the inn until Dovie was located. She couldn't go home anyway, but the fact that

Dovie had been in Rose's house worried me. Maybe the judge should come stay at the inn as well. Just until we found Dovie.

Trixie and I walked home, found Oma in the office, and told her the entire story.

"Dovie is Bobbie's birth mother?" Oma shook her head. "It doesn't seem possible. I remember when Theona lost her little boy to crib death. We thought she would never get over it, and then, about a year later, she had Bobbie, and we were all so happy for her. This is incredible. I never even suspected."

"Maybe you could call the judge and offer to let him stay here overnight? I imagine they'll send a policeman, but Dovie could be anywhere."

"She must feel very desperate to have treated Dave so badly. You should be careful, too, Holly."

"Don't worry about me, Oma." The sad truth was that Dovie scared me. She had managed to fell Seth swiftly. I wasn't sure he even knew what had happened to him. And who was to say that she didn't have another syringe or two of wolfsbane in her pocket at the ready?

I spent the early evening contacting various people around town. The guys at the parking lot outside town, where Dovie probably had a car, were on the lookout for her.

At eight o'clock, I was sitting in the Dogwood Room with Oma, Rose, and the judge, debating where Dovie might go, when the WAG Ladies returned from dinner.

Louisa hurried to me. "Has anyone seen Addi? She never showed for dinner."

A wave of fear rolled over me. "When is the last time you saw her?"

"After lunch. She was going somewhere with your boyfriend and was supposed to come to Judge Barlow's house later on."

I phoned Holmes. Maybe he knew where Addi had gone after she left him. His phone rolled over to voice mail. I stood up. "Oma, call Shadow. Ask him to round up some of the local guys and come to the Victorian house Holmes is renovating. I'll call the police on my way there."

"You can't go by yourself," Rose protested.

"I'll wait for Shadow and his buddies. But I need you to keep Trixie and Twinkletoes here. Their presence would give me away."

"I should go with you," said the judge.

"That could be helpful. Dovie might listen to you."

I excused myself and ran to the office to grab a golf cart key and a strong flashlight.

When I returned, the judge rose to his feet and Fritz jumped up, his tail wagging as if he was ready to go. "Sorry, old pal," said the judge. "Not this time."

Oma and Rose held on to Fritz and Trixie while the judge and I exited the front door. I phoned the police and explained the situation to them.

The judge walked steadily but slowly, and I realized that it might have been a mistake to bring him along. He was in no shape to run for his life if need be. Hopefully Shadow and his friends would be at Holmes's house and he wouldn't even need to get out of the golf cart unless he felt like it. I crossed my fingers.

We made it as far as the golf carts when a brown-haired woman stepped out of the bushes and flung her forearm around the judge's neck.

The judge bellowed, and I screamed.

"Another sound and he gets a wolfsbane shot in the back." I recognized Dovie's voice.

"I think we all know how that turns out," she said.

"Dovie, we only want to help you." I tried to sound calm and nonjudgmental. "You know the judge loves you. He wants what's best for you."

The judge managed a "Gah."

"Please. Give me the syringe." I held out my hand.

"I don't think so. This is mighty powerful stuff."

I desperately tried to remember the silent button to push on my phone in emergencies. The side button five times? I tried that. I had to keep her talking. "Why did you wait so long? Why now? Bobbie was killed twenty-six years ago."

"Because of Theona. I spoke of finding Wallace and taking revenge many times. But Theona always reasoned with me. What if we find Joy Marie? She used to say, 'I'm not bringing her to prison to visit you. There's nothing more we can do for Bobbie. Put your energy where we can do good. Let's find Joy Marie.'"

"Good advice, if you ask me. What changed?"

"Theona took her own advice to look for her beloved granddaughter but died without ever finding Joy Marie. I knew it was hopeless. I don't know how long I have. I couldn't sit by any longer without avenging the death of my daughter. Wallace was out of prison and living the good life in a house his sister bought him. And then I saw the letter from Louisa's husband. She sent it to the judge, but I intercepted it and never gave it to him. I couldn't believe it when I read it. Wallace had taken the punishment, albeit light in my opinion, for Seth's crime."

The judge's arms flailed to no avail. He choked out, "Stole my mail?"

"So you claimed Fritz was lost, but he wasn't really, was he?"

"You think you're so clever. You can't hire a pet detective unless you lose a pet."

"But Fritz gave you a hard time because he wanted to go home."

The judge gurgled, "Dovie, loosen your grip!"

"Did you poison the salads?"

She smiled.

"Did you accidentally mix up the plates?"

"I'm not that stupid. I put some of the wolfsbane in mine to frame Rose. And it worked, too. No one suspected me!"

It wasn't cold outside, but chill bumps rose on my arms. She was insane. "Where are Holmes and Addi?"

"The grandchildren." Dovie smiled. "Addi told me about her cousin. Is it true? Is she Bobbie's child?"

"It seems that way." I tried to sound friendly. "She's hoping you'll donate some DNA so we can all be sure that you're her grandma."

Dovie's voice changed. "I never thought I'd see Joy Marie again."

At that exact moment, the sliding glass doors to the reception lobby opened. Trixie, Gingersnap, Loki, Garbo, Fritz, and Fagan stormed out like bulls. They were upon us in seconds.

Fritz leaped at the judge, knocking him and Dovie to the ground. Loki joined the fun. Not a single dog snarled.

Dovie's brown wig fell off, and Loki claimed it as his prize.

I reached out to the judge and heaved him to his feet. "Are you okay? Did she inject you?"

"I don't think so." He dusted off his sleeves.

I shined my flashlight at Dovie, who lay on the ground. She sat up and looked at her leg. A syringe jutted out of it.

Thirty-Six

❀ ❀ ❀ ❀

"I'm dying," she whispered.

She reached a hand up to me. "I want to meet my grand-daughter. Please don't deny me that. It's my dying wish. Please!"

I didn't know how safe any of us were. She'd managed a pretty strong grip on the judge. I glanced over at him. He looked like he might keel over. I hoped he wouldn't have a heart attack. "Sit down in one of the golf carts," I said.

He nodded and climbed in. Undoubtedly hoping for a ride, all the dogs except for Fagan piled in with him.

I took out my phone and called 911 again. The dispatcher said someone was on the way. I told her we would need an ambulance, too.

Then I phoned Dr. Engelknecht. I had no idea what to do for Dovie. I suspected that taking the syringe out of her leg might be appropriate, but I had no intention of getting that close to her.

Fagan trotted to me, carrying a black bag. Leaves and twigs stuck to it. I assumed it belonged to Dovie.

She screamed. "The plunger went all the way down. You miserable curs! You've killed me! Holly, do something! Don't just stand there. Help me!"

For all I knew, she had another syringe in her pocket. I wasn't taking any chances.

Lights appeared on the road and came toward us. Golf carts loaded with residents of Wagtail pulled into the parking lot. Shadow stepped out of one, along with Holmes and Addi.

Holmes ran to me and grabbed me in a hug. "Thank heaven you're all right."

"How about you and Addi?" I asked.

"Dovie was lurking in the house. She jumped at me and whacked me with a steel pipe. Addi almost got her, but Dovie was like a madwoman and wielded that pipe like a saber. Have you called an ambulance? She knocked Addi out cold."

"They're on the way. Did she use wolfsbane on you?" I asked.

"Dovie tied us up and threatened to inject us with wolfsbane, but she never did."

Dovie's eyes seemed to glow. Her expression was positively wicked. "I would have liked to. But I was reserving my last two syringes for Rose and our own nosy parker, Holly Miller."

Shadow shined his flashlight on Dovie. "Maybe we should remove the syringe?"

"Don't go any closer to her. She has another one in her pocket," I warned.

"Why did she come after you?" I asked Holmes.

"I think it was a mistake," he whispered. "She thought the house was empty and that she could hide there until dark. If Addi hadn't told her about Joanne, she might not have come here."

Dr. Engelknecht walked up and assessed the situation. "Shadow, do you think you could approach Dovie from behind and grip her arms?"

"Sure." Shadow walked behind Dovie.

At the same time, two men grabbed her hands. She was effectively incapacitated.

Dr. Engelknecht felt the pockets of her garment and pulled out another syringe. "Oh, Dovie," he sighed.

Lights flashed as an ambulance arrived.

"Wait, please. Won't you let me see my granddaughter? I'm going to die. Won't you please let me see her?"

Joanne stepped out of the crowd. "I'm Joanne Williams. And I think I'm Bobbie's daughter, Joy Marie."

Tears sprang to Dovie's eyes and rolled down her cheeks. "You're so beautiful," she whispered. "Just like my Bobbie."

"Can we test your DNA to know for sure?" asked Joanne.

"You may if you like, but I know in my heart that you're mine." Her eyes closed, and she lay back.

She didn't regain consciousness while they loaded her into the ambulance.

Thirty-Seven

✽ ✽ ✽

When the ambulance left, everyone piled into the inn. Holmes, Oma, and I busied ourselves making drinks and serving snacks. I was in the commercial kitchen, slicing a strawberry torte, when Holmes wrapped his arms around me. "I wasn't sure I'd see you again."

"Same here." I turned around and kissed him.

Oma barged through the door. "There are fifty people out there waiting for food, and the two of you are in here smooching?"

We laughed and got right back to work.

People mingled like we had planned a party. Dr. Engelknecht had insisted that Judge Barlow be checked out at the hospital, but other than the two of them, everyone was there.

I brought out Pupsie Cupsies, our homemade doggie ice cream, for all the pups. They settled down in the Dogwood Room to lick them. Twinkletoes, Hershey, and Inky crunched on dried salmon treats.

The WAG Ladies collected in the Dogwood Room as well.

"If you wouldn't mind," said Louisa, "I would like to know who switched my pills."

The WAG Ladies didn't say a thing.

"That's really not fair to me. One of you hates me enough to have made me terribly ill. I could have died!"

One after the other, each of them denied it.

"Maybe we could reconstruct what happened the night Seth died?" I suggested.

Addi licked her lips. "He came to my room. I was so stupid. Why did I fall for him every time? He said he wanted to see me again. Pick up where we left off. He was so sweet and told me how much he had missed me. For all of ten minutes, I really wanted to believe him. Then he slipped up. Such a small thing actually. He said Oriana's husband was coming to the gala and asked if I would be his date. That was when I thought of what Louisa had told me."

Oriana's eyes grew large. "Louisa!" she huffed. "Why did you tell her about Seth and me?"

Louisa's fair skin flushed red. "She had to know, Oriana. Did you want him to get involved with Addi again? He was no good! Neither of you should ever have been involved with him."

"When he left," said Addi, "I followed him. The back stairs that come up from the registration lobby land at a balcony that curves around. It's the perfect spot to spy on the hallway where Oriana's room is."

Oriana appeared horrified. "You watched me?"

"Not you," said Addi. "Seth."

"That was when I saw you on the stairs," I said.

"Exactly. What you didn't know was that Seth was in—"

Oriana interrupted her. "He was *not* in my room!"

"No, he wasn't." Addi sounded very calm. "He was in Louisa's room."

"It was nothing improper," said Louisa. "He came to tell me how sorry he was about Tom's death and ask me out to lunch. I thought maybe he wanted to reminisce about Tom and our college days, but I turned him down."

I could see suspicion in her friends' eyes, but I felt as though one mystery might be solved. "Did he use the bathroom?"

All of them gazed at me like I had lost my mind.

"As a matter of fact, he did," said Louisa.

"So that would have been when he swapped Addi's thyroid pills for your allergy pills," I suggested.

Louisa's hands trembled. "And I took one right after he left."

"Did you possibly take another pill later that night?"

"I think I may have. I was already feeling sick, and I thought it was probably allergies. But why? Why would he do that?"

"Didn't you say that his real purpose in visiting Tom was to be sure Tom didn't confess to lying about who was driving the car the night of the accident?"

Louisa inhaled sharply. "Of course! I was the only person left, besides Wallace, who knew the truth. Tom did exactly what Seth was afraid he might do. He wrote a letter of confession to the judge. But Seth didn't know that." She shook her finger at Oriana. "What did I tell you? Seth was evil. He almost murdered me."

"Louisa," I said, "Seth had the key to your room."

Her horror appeared genuine. "He must have picked it up off the dresser. That worm! He was determined to kill me. I bet he intended to sneak into my room at night and knock me off if the medicine didn't do it." She leaned against Oriana for support.

"Where did he go next, Addi?" asked Brenda.

"When Seth left Louisa's room, he crossed the hall to his own room, Hike."

Oriana breathed deeply and closed her eyes as though in relief.

But she opened them wide when Addi said, "And that was when Oriana paid him a visit."

Joanne winced. "Please tell me you weren't still carrying on with him."

"I was terrified that he would reveal our relationship to my husband. I'd spoken to him earlier in the day. Yelled at him, actually. I thought he had come here because of me, and I asked him what he wanted from me. You can imagine what he said. He laughed and said he was in control now and that if I wanted him to keep our little secret, there were a few things I could do for him. He suggested I visit him later that evening to discuss it further. I was furious and stalked away."

All eyes were on Oriana. She had omitted a few things when she previously told me about going to his room. I hadn't realized exactly how desperate she was.

"A few days ago, I heard Oriana whisper to Brenda, 'You don't think she would actually hurt him?' Who were you talking about?" I asked.

Brenda's face turned as red as tomato juice. "Addi. We knew she would be terribly upset if she found out about Oriana and Seth."

"I'm sorry, Addi. I never meant to hurt you," said Oriana.

Addi stared at her. "I think dating Seth was punishment enough. You should have learned from my relationship with him. And for your information, I would never have harmed Seth. He wasn't worth going to prison for."

One month later, as promised, Dave rewarded Trixie with a steak dinner at Chowhound, her favorite restaurant. She sat on a bench next to me and politely ate sliced steak and baked French fries off a plate. Next to her,

Twinkletoes ate steak, too, but she turned her nose up at the potatoes.

"How do you feel?" I picked up a French fry from my plate.

"Like an idiot. I underestimated Dovie. I won't be doing that again. From now on, I will be much more cautious around little ladies of a certain age."

"She was surprisingly powerful," I said. "And heartier than anyone expected."

"Maybe the knowledge that she had a granddaughter helped her pull through. Have the DNA tests come in yet?" Dave sipped iced tea.

"It's a match. Joanne is changing her name to Joy Marie Barlow. She's been to visit Dovie in jail a few times. She stays at Dovie's house and might even run her business from here."

"Did she ever find her rotten husband?"

"She thinks he's hiding in Mexico. But if anyone can find him, it will be Joy."

"Any word from the others?"

"Brenda adopted the mom cat that Fritz found and one of her kittens. Oriana took the other three. One for each of her children. I guess you know better than I how Addi is doing."

"She's at a gallery in Pittsburgh this week. We're still getting along pretty well. She found a new housekeeper for the judge, and so far, it's working out. How about you, Holly? I heard Holmes bid on a surprise for you at the gala."

"It's dance classes. We're going to learn to swing dance!"

After an ice cream dessert, Trixie, Twinkletoes, and I leisurely walked home to the inn. I thought about Addi, Joy, and maybe even Brenda moving to Wagtail. Trixie and Twinkletoes scampered along toward the front porch. Lights glowed in the windows as twilight descended on the town. I couldn't blame them for moving. There was no place on earth that I would rather be.

Recipes

One of my dogs suffered from severe food allergies that did not allow him to eat commercial dog food. Consequently, I learned to cook for my dogs and have done so for many years. Consult your veterinarian if you want to switch your dog to home-cooked food. It's not as difficult as one might think. Keep in mind that, like children, dogs need a balanced diet, not just a hamburger. Any changes to your dog's diet should be made gradually so your dog's stomach can adjust.

Chocolate, alcohol, caffeine, fatty foods, grapes, raisins, macadamia nuts, onions and garlic, xylitol, and unbaked dough can be toxic (and even deadly) to dogs. For more information about foods your dog can and cannot eat, consult the American Kennel Club website at akc.org/expert-advice/nutrition/human-foods-dogs-can-and-cant-eat.

If you have any reason to suspect your pet has ingested something toxic, please contact your veterinarian or the

Animal Poison Control Center's twenty-four-hour hotline at 1-888-426-4435.

❧

Mandarin Salty Dog Cocktail

For people only. NOT for dogs.

Kosher salt
Lime
2 ounces mandarin vodka
6 ounces grapefruit juice

Pour the salt into a small dish or shallow bowl. Rub the rim of a tall glass with lime and dip it in the salt. Pour the vodka into the glass and follow with the grapefruit juice. This is a tart cocktail.

❧

Tomato, Corn, and Quinoa Salad

For people only.

⅓ cup olive oil
2 tablespoons and 1 teaspoon white wine
   vinegar
2 tablespoons fresh minced parsley
1 teaspoon garlic powder
1 tablespoon sugar

1 teaspoon salt
¼ teaspoon black pepper
2 cups thawed frozen corn
2 cups cooked quinoa
1 cup cherry tomatoes, sliced in half

In a jar with a tight-fitting lid, mix together the olive oil, vinegar, minced parsley, garlic powder, sugar, salt, and pepper and shake very well.

Place the corn, quinoa, and tomatoes in a serving bowl and mix well. Top with the dressing.

Steak with Balsamic Dijon Sauce

Serves 2.

Dogs may eat small pieces of sliced steak without fat. The sauce should NOT be served to dogs.

Salt and freshly ground pepper, to taste
1–2 teaspoons high-heat oil, like sunflower or
*   canola*
2 New York strip steaks
2 tablespoons balsamic vinegar*
¼ teaspoon salt
1 tablespoon Dijon mustard
2 tablespoons heavy cream

Salt and pepper the steaks. Pour the oil into a cast-iron pan. When a drop of water sizzles in the oil, add the steaks. Sear both sides. Use a meat thermometer to determine when they are done. Medium rare: 130–135°F; medium: 135–140°F.

Remove the steaks from the pan and let stand for at least 10 minutes. Meanwhile, deglaze the pan by adding the balsamic vinegar and salt and scraping up the bits that remain in the pan. Allow to cook about two minutes. Remove the pan from the heat and stir in the mustard and the cream.

Drizzle the sauce over the steaks.

* Balsamic vinegar can be quite strong. If you are sensitive to vinegar, reduce this amount.

❀

Firefly Sparklers

NOT for dogs!

Serves 2.

1 cup cold ginger ale
1 cup cold mango juice
2 ounces vodka
2 ounces Grand Marnier
Crushed ice
Fresh strawberries, for garnish

Mix together the ginger ale, mango juice, vodka, and Grand Marnier. Fill old-fashioned glasses with crushed ice, add the drink, and garnish with a fresh strawberry.

Mixed Berry Meringue Pie

For people.

1 sheet puff pastry
Flour, for sprinkling
1 6-ounce package fresh blueberries
1 6-ounce package fresh raspberries
1 6-ounce package fresh blackberries
12 medium strawberries, cut in half lengthwise
¼–½ cup sugar (depending on how sour the
*   berries are)*
¼ cup tapioca
¼ cup water
1 tablespoon unsalted butter
4 large egg whites, at room temperature
¼ teaspoon cream of tartar
6 tablespoons sugar

Preheat the oven to 400°F. Thaw the frozen puff pastry at room temperature for 40 minutes or according to the directions on the package. Note: There is a short window of opportunity between being frozen and getting sticky. Be sure to roll out the puff pastry at 35–40 minutes. On a lightly floured surface, roll the pastry out large enough to fit a 9-inch pie pan. Move the pastry to the pan and prick the bottom with a fork. Cut off excess corners. Cover with aluminum foil and bake for 25 minutes. Remove from the oven and turn the oven temperature down to 350°F. Save the aluminum foil in case you need it to cover the edges later.

While the crust is baking, prepare the berries in a large bowl. Toss together the berries, sugar, tapioca, and water, turning gently a few times to spread the tapioca evenly. Fill the baked pie crust with the berry mixture, dot the top with butter, and bake for 20 minutes. If the crust begins to get too brown, cover only the crust edge with aluminum foil. Dots of tapioca may still be visible.

While the pie bakes, make the meringue. In a mixer, beat together the egg whites and cream of tartar until the eggs are foamy and begin to take shape. Slowly beat in the 6 tablespoons of sugar. Beat until the mixture holds a firm peak, at least 6–8 minutes.

Swirl the meringue over the hot pie. Return it to the oven for about 15 minutes or until the meringue is lightly browned. If the edges are getting too dark, cover with aluminum foil. When cool, refrigerate overnight. The tapioca will have blended in by the next day.

❧

Salted Brownie Picnic Cake

NOT for dogs!

⅓ cup all-purpose flour, plus extra for sprinkling
10 tablespoons unsalted butter
3 ounces unsweetened chocolate
3 large eggs
1⅓ cup granulated sugar
1 teaspoon vanilla extract
¼ teaspoon salt
Flaked salt, like Maldon
Sweetened Whipped Cream (optional; see recipe below)
Summer berries (optional)

Preheat the oven to 350°F. Grease and flour a 9-inch cake pan. Line the bottom of the pan with parchment paper.

In a microwave-safe bowl, melt the butter and chocolate in the microwave at half power in 30-second increments, stirring when the mixture begins to melt. Stir until smooth. Set aside to cool.

Beat the eggs and sugar until thick and light yellow. Add the vanilla and continue beating. Add the ⅓ cup flour and ¼ teaspoon salt and mix. Add the chocolate mixture and mix until combined.

Pour into the pan, sprinkle with 2 generous pinches of flaked salt, and bake 20–25 minutes, or until the center is just set.

Cool completely in the pan before turning onto a serving plate and peeling off the parchment paper.

Serve plain or with Sweetened Whipped Cream and summer berries.

❧

Sugar Maple Inn After-Dinner Drink

NOT for dogs!

½ ounce Godiva chocolate liqueur
½ ounce Kahlúa
1 tablespoon maple syrup
1 cup decaffeinated coffee
Sweetened Whipped Cream (see recipe below)

Pour the chocolate liqueur, Kahlúa, and maple syrup into a mug. Add the decaffeinated coffee and stir. Top with Sweetened Whipped Cream.

🐾

Sweetened Whipped Cream

1 cup heavy cream
⅓ cup powdered sugar
1 teaspoon vanilla

Beat the cream until it begins to take a shape. Add the powdered sugar and vanilla. Beat until it holds a peak.

🐾

Florentine Havarti Scramble

For people. Dogs may have a bite.

¼ cup baby spinach
1–1½ tablespoons unsalted butter
8 large eggs
½ teaspoon dried thyme
1 tablespoon heavy cream
¼ cup Havarti cheese, shredded
Salt and pepper, to taste

Wash and dry the spinach and chop it into small pieces. Heat a frying pan on medium-low and add the butter.

In a large bowl, whisk together the eggs until frothy, then whisk in the spinach, thyme, and cream. Pour the mixture into the pan and continually scrape the eggs inward until just set. Sprinkle the cheese over the eggs and mix to melt. Season with salt and pepper to taste. Serve immediately.

Note: If your dog will be eating some, take his or her share out before adding salt and pepper. This should not serve as a meal for a dog. Think of it as a small treat.

Pupsie Cupsies

Homemade Frozen Treats for Dogs

Please read the label of your peanut butter to be absolutely certain it DOES NOT CONTAIN XYLITOL, which is extremely toxic and deadly to dogs. Take your dogs to a veterinarian immediately if they have ingested xylitol.

You will need small cups or bowls that are freezer- and dog-safe, preferably paper Dixie Cup–style. (Small Dixie Cup–style containers can be purchased at Amazon.com.) DO NOT REMOVE the Pupsie Cupsie ice cream from the cups or bowls. Your dog should lick this, NOT SWALLOW IT WHOLE. You may need to hold the cup for your dog if he or she tries to eat the ice cream whole. Please watch your dog while he or she enjoys this treat.

 2 tablespoons peanut butter (see warning above)
 ¼ cup hot water
 1 teaspoon honey
 1 cup 0% fat FAGE Greek yogurt

Scoop the peanut butter into a small mixing bowl and
pour the hot water over it. Mix to soften the peanut butter into a liquid form and add the honey. Add the Greek
yogurt and stir well. Pour about ½ cup of the mixture
into each cup or bowl. Freeze. Serve to your pup frozen.

🐾

Steak Feast

For dogs.

Makes enough for two Gingersnap-size servings and
one Trixie-size serving.

 1 teaspoon olive oil
 1 sirloin steak
 1 cup water
 ¾ cup frozen corn, thawed
 1 medium zucchini, cooked
 1 cup cooked quinoa
 2 cups cooked barley

Heat the olive oil in a pan. When a drop of water sizzles, add the steak. Brown on one side, then flip and
brown the other side. Cook until a meat thermometer
registers 130°F. Allow to cool for 10 minutes.

Meanwhile, pour the water in the pan and deglaze it by scratching up any bits clinging to the pan. Set aside. Combine the corn, zucchini, quinoa, and barley in a large bowl. Cut the steak into thin ½-inch pieces. Add the steak to the bowl of veggies and grains. Pour the sauce from the pan over the ingredients and mix well.

Acknowledgments

As I write this, two dogs and two cats are spying on me. Oh, they may look away, even pretend to snooze, but they're paying attention to my every move. *Did she stand up to go outside? Is she going to the kitchen? Oh, boy! Is she near the treat jar? Ho hum, she's just making another cup of tea.* Those of you with pets know exactly what I mean. They are the perfect spies with those innocent faces. They watch our every move and know all of our secrets. So I have to thank my cats and dogs for their cleverness and their antics that gave me ideas for this book.

In this time of COVID-19, our furry companions are even more important than ever. And so are our dear friends who stay in touch daily. I am so grateful for my writing pals: Ginger Bolton, Allison Brook, Laurie Cass, Kaye George, Daryl Wood Gerber, and Margaret Loudon. They are always just an email away, ready to discuss some grammatical oddity or just chat about life during the pandemic.

My editor, Michelle Vega, is always a joy. I am ever so thankful for her eagle eyes that catch what I have overlooked. And last but never least, I do not know what I would do without my agent, Jessica Faust, whose advice has always steered me in the correct direction.

Ready to find
your next great read?

Let us help.

Visit prh.com/nextread